International Praise for
Liz J. Andersen's First Novel,
Some of My Best Friends Are Human

"Excellent!"

—Andre Norton, Science Fiction Writers of
America Grand Master

"I finished your book last night. I settled down with it in front of a cozy fire and wound up staying up until 3:00 to finish it. I couldn't put it down! I had to find out what happened to these interesting characters."

—Jerry Oltion, Nebula winner, and twice nominated
for the Hugo

"Teens and adults will enjoy this fast-paced sci-fi adventure!
The book is written in journal-style entries of an orphan teen girl named Tajen. The occasional slang words used by her and all of her classmates are really unique. One can imagine that teens coming together from diverse planetary civilizations would absolutely have their own short-hand language to communicate with each other. The descriptions of the isolated world where they learn to survive, their medical technology, diversity of main characters and animals kept the story fast paced and held my interest. I enjoyed reading about the astonishing discovery they made towards the end. Very likeable characters and a satisfying read!"

—Patricia M. Prisbrey, Ret. YA Librarian

"This is a coming of age story set within a distinct and well crafted SF universe which I thoroughly enjoyed.

"The story starts off with a set of orphaned teenagers living in an underground orphanage on an alien world. Life and civilization outside the orphanage is sprawling and contains many varied species; of which the orphans comprise of. The main character is a girl called Taje who struggles to fit into day to day life within the orphanage. Her one love in life which sustains her is her love of animals which shows itself with her many pets and her desire to one day work within a related field. This love is the cause of the main plot point mentioned in the synopsis; namely being the opportunity to go on an ecological field trip. Her route to get there is interesting which is where I'll leave it with plot.

"The most impressive feature of this book to me was the sense of optimism and hope running throughout. The characters are all young and inexperienced but want more out of life than their birth afforded them. They are trying to achieve more of themselves which lends itself to this optimism and forward thinking. It was a genuinely nice experience reading this as it's rare to read a book where the hope of the characters is based on their wanting more from themselves and will not abuse others to achieve this; it's all on themselves and their strengths and many weaknesses."
—Joseph McLoughlin, U.K. Book Reviewer

"I love your book!..Sitting in my 'space lounger' it's a very good reading matter!"
—Caroline Michal, a German fan

My New Best Friend
Is an Alien

Labbwerk Publishing, Eugene 97404
©2024 by Liz J. Andersen
All rights reserved. Published 2024.

Library of Congress Control Number: 2023943579
Paperback ISBN #978-0-9988448-4-8
ebook ISBN #978-0-9988448-5-5

Labbwerk Publishing gratefully acknowledges
the generous support of:
Editors: Jackie Melvin & Brian J. Boudler
Cover Design: Cricket Harper
Cover Background Artist: Anders Andersen
Cover Silhouettes: TJ
Cover Photos: from Liz J. Andersen's Collection

Names: Liz J., Andersen, author
Titles: My New Best Friend is an Alien

Summary: Freshman interplanetary vet students Taje and Giem desire a
fun offworld summer externship with plenty of adventure, excitement, and
romance. But their assignment forces them to face dangerous, monstrous
animals. Kind people help, but nefarious characters also appear. When the
students discover a break in planetary disease protection, they split up to
find the truth. Taje and Giem encounter challenges they never expected. Will
they survive long enough to advance to sophomore year?

Science Fiction. | Action and Adventure fiction. | Crime—Fiction. | Romance
Science Fiction. | Extraterrestrial beings—Fiction. | Survival—Fiction. |
Friendship—Fiction.| Veterinary Students—Fiction.| Bildungsromans.
OCLC Record: 1381685423

My New Best Friend Is an Alien

Liz J. Andersen

Labbwerk Publishing
Eugene

This Book is Dedicated To:

George,
Moonrock,
Stonewall,
&
Rocket.

I will always love you and miss you.

CHAPTER 1

"Gel-sea quartians—in the last lecture." I sighed. "How many credits did they waste shipping that guest prof's environment tank down here? No biped air-breather will ever be asked to work on a quart', and to cram this intricate obscurity into our pulmonary physio final next week—"

Jekkan, Sakken, and Jan gave me sympathetic looks as we all stood up, ready to leave our last freshman lecture of a long Olecranon year (one and a half standard years), but not Giem of course. No sympathy there.

"At least FIL Law ended last week," she said next to me. "And worry is a completely wasted emotion." Giem irritably sealed her cloak and stuffed her mass of brown hair in her hood. "Life is too short for worry. Better to look on the Bright Side." She thrust her golden human hands into her gloves. "You never know—we could die tomorrow," she said, one of her usual mottos.

"But Giem," I said, using the nickname I'd given her.

She managed to march on through the wicked wind that shoved us to our interplanetary veterinary classes each day. I remembered our welcome by the dean, and her reminder that we were simply lucky, because there just wasn't room for all the qualified applicants. You can imagine how that made us feel. And our teachers drove us mercilessly down a grav well, justifiably afraid that if we didn't learn our lessons well, we might maim or kill our patients instead of healing them.

Now after our long year on this desolate planet, I wondered if I really qualified for this dream career, for which I'd left all my smooth ecology friends aboard *Onnarius*. If I'd known where and what Dr. Hako was sending us for our summer externship, I might have refused. But somehow I never seemed to be able to avoid painful paths.

We entered the toasty Olecranon Interplanetary Vet Med Admin building. Giem unsealed her cloak, released her thick brown hair from her hood, and yanked off her gloves.

"Giem, do you really think Gel-sea quartians are worth studying for pulmonary physiology?"

"Hush. There's Dr. Hako's door, and it's open."

The Dean of Olecranon Interplanetary Veterinary Student Welfare looked up from his cluttered desk and motioned us into his claustrophobic office with two of his pale blue fingers. Giem and I stepped inside and looked in vain, as usual, for an empty chair to sit on.

"Giemsan Fane and Tajen Jesmuhr, you received my message, I see," Dr. Hako said. "I'm sorry to keep you waiting so long."

"Rather strange, considering we must have been among the first to submit our names together," I said. I ignored Giem's almond-eyed glare at me as I moved a teetering stack of intricate equipment onto an even more precarious tower in one corner and dropped down into the chair I'd uncovered. Apparently it was made for a Telmid. My knees came nearly to my bust. Giem grunted under a heavier heap of instruments she shunted to the floor to empty a larger chair next to mine. Taller, she towered over me in her seat.

"We will receive a joint assignment, won't we?" I said.

"I wouldn't dream, as you humans say, of trying to separate the only two freshman roommates who haven't threatened mayhem, Taje."

Golden-faced Giem laughed along with blue-faced Dr. Hako, while I wondered how much of my checkered past Hako had access to. I hadn't caused any major problems here. Yet. "What's our summer assignment?"

"A parasitology survey on a small FIL R&R station on Big Maxson's Planet, at the request of the station biologist." Were the corners of Dr. Hako's blue lips twitching, or was I just imagining it?

"Will we study working animals or farmed animals?" I said. Maybe machine technology was limited on Big Maxson's Planet.

"Both," Dr. Hako said.

That probably meant a colony too new or primitive to have meat cell culture vats. Yuck.

Hako eyed my all-too-human expression. "That's part of a Federation of Intelligent Life interplanetary veterinarian's job."

A fact I'd tried to conveniently forget, although work on a FIL SEAR Ship had rubbed my nose in farm animal visits, and our classes didn't ignore the subject. I wanted to specialize in pets and mounts, although I didn't know how I'd manage that on a FIL Survey, Education, Assistance, and Research Ship.

"Will we work under a local veterinarian?" Giem said doubtfully.

"No, you'll work for the station biologist, Dr. Kiernan Bioh," Dr. Hako said. "He's all they can afford currently, which is why you're needed. He's very good. I can personally vouch for him."

"That's the R&R station that's becoming famous for its cuisine, right?" Giem said. Giem knew just about everything, and what she didn't know, she learned quickly. My roomie was a real black hole. I just made it into a famous FIL interplanetary vet school by working very, very hard.

"You've heard of it." Dr. Hako seemed pleased and surprised.

"Why parasites?" I said, to cover my ignorance. "I hate parasites!"

"This must be your fault." Giem turned on me.

"All those mind-boggling life cycles, and such countless, despicable creatures. Does this have anything to do with the C I got in parasit?" I ended lamely. I hadn't earned such a vac-brained grade since I'd fallen behind in my Orphan Center pre-ecology class. And the profs here never forgot to emphasize our failings for one micro.

"And no spy jobs either?" Giem smirked, probably to cover up her own hopes for our summer. She'd agreed first to the extra training—an honor Hako had shrewdly offered us together—somehow without mentioning all the tedious evening FIL law classes, or the early morning hours of self-defense lessons we'd have to stuff into our overburdened schedules.

I gently rubbed my sore nose. Today I'd earned the dubious distinction of being the first in our self-defense class to lose any circulatory fluid. One misfired blow from my sparring partner, and abruptly my classmates were subjected to the shocking display of bright red human blood on the practice mat. I hated extra work; nevertheless I also hated being left behind. When Giem had said "Yes" to Dr. Hako, what could I say?

"Remember, you've just begun your special ed, and you shouldn't even be talking about it." Hako shook his fingers at Giem.

"As a matter of fact, we don't seem to be ready for anything," I said.

"And you won't become 'spies,'" Dr. Hako impatiently reminded us, ignoring my irreverent interruption. "You'll graduate, along with various other professional students, as registered Federation of Intelligent Life Undercover Observation Agents. FIL-trained, we hope, to simply detect and report trouble, not create it. Do please try to stay out of hot oil."

The skin around Dr. Hako's browless electric blue eyes crinkled suspiciously. Was there really more to this assignment than he wanted to admit? Or was this simply revenge for poor performance on my parasit exams? And how come my wristcom translator never gave me a clue with this person?

"Sounds exciting," Giem said, in a completely unconvincing tone. "This must be all your fault, Taje."

"My fault?"

"I earned a respectable B in parasitology."

"Rather a bad sign in your run of A's."

"Check your baggage requirements and limits carefully," Dr. Hako said sternly. "I've sent prep reports to your room coms, along with your trip itinerary and travel passes. You're expected to know as much general background material as possible before you land."

"And we have to ship out right after we finish our finals next week, right?" I slapped my knees. "That leaves us a whole lot of time."

"What's the matter, Taje?" Hako said, with wicked relish. "Haven't you kept up in your classes all quarter long, as we strongly recommended during orientation, your first day here?"

He knew I was a crammer. Somehow he knew. "Why, you blue-eyed—"

"Come on." Giem stood up and abruptly hauled me out of my chair by my coat collar. "Thank you, Dr. Hako, for teaming us up together—"

"Parasites—why—" I tried once more to vent my outrage, as I failed in my struggle against Giem's powerful Ballophonian grip. (Her homeworld had higher gravity.)

"—although I'm not quite sure why we requested it," Giem finished her line as she yanked me out the doorway. We both thought we heard a translated snicker as I broke her hold. We spun around, but the door had slid shut behind us.

"What in the Universe is wrong with you today? Going down the Dim Side?" Giem swiftly turned on me outside Dr. Hako's door. Nearly a head taller than me and a much heftier human, Giem was easily an imposing figure when she wanted to be.

"Nothing."

"Great Galaxy, Taje, you're the worst liar I've ever met. What were you going to call him, a blue-eyed BEM? Do you realize Dr. Hako is kindly sending us to an R&R station for our first externship? Do you think maybe he realized we both need a vacation so badly we can taste it?"

I stared sullenly at my dusty boots.

"I like Dr. Hako. I can talk to him. Why can't you talk to me?" Giem demanded. I still had no answer. She snorted, turned her back on me, and stomped off towards the front doors. I had to sprint to catch up with her.

"Finals get us all down, yet you've complained nonstop all day," she said, as we plunged into the bone-chilling wind which shoved us to class each day. "What happened this morning? Did you get up on the Dim Side of your bed? Let me guess—that Istrannian vet student knew nothing about your old roommate, or you never got up the courage to ask him."

Obviously it's a huge coincidence if two people from the same world know each other. But he had heard of Shandy. "Wrong!" I cried out.

"Why am I wrong?" Giem said, obviously irritated.

"We talked in the cafeteria at breakfast."

"What did he tell you that ruined your whole day?" Giem said vengefully, clearly annoyed I'd given her no details, and I have this unfortunate habit of making friends too shrewd for me to outwit for very long.

"They deported him," I said angrily.

"Who deported whom?"

"The Istrannians convened something called a Great Circle and decided Shanden Fehrokc must go." My first roommate, a dear friend who had saved my life. Why had he never sent me any messages when he left for Istrann and after he left?

"Why did they deport him?" Giem always wanted to know why.

"Their best teachers failed to teach Shandy empath control. They couldn't stand him any longer." The Istrannian student had spoken quite rudely about human transmutes, not knowing I had more than one transmute friend.

"Why couldn't they block his emotions? He's mostly human," Giem said.

"How should I know?" I said.

When at last we returned to our closet-sized dorm room, we found Giem's golden-furred geepers literally racing around our walls on six suckered feet each, and squealing for dinner. While Giem tried to snag them, I found an end-of-year congrat holo message on my deskcom. Wild-haired Aerrem swished her furry tail, while she petted my krel, Dizzy. (After I'd reviewed student accommodations at the FIL University on Olecranon, even with chilly, windy walks outside, I knew a krel would have gone nova here. I was going nova here.)

I also found a kind message from handsome orange-eyed Krorn, and, as usual, I had nothing from Shandy or Branem.

Thank the Universe, Giem closed her geepers in their crate with full dishes, so I could think. We scanned Dr. Hako's collection of background reports on Big Maxson's Planet—an excellent excuse for putting off studying for finals.

"This should prove interesting—it's a planet with no native warm-blooded animals," Giem said from her Bright Side. "But blast it all, when you add up personal items necessary for more than several months and required school equipment, our shipping limit doesn't allow backpacking equipment. What will we do with our two weeks off at the end?"

Our measly end-of-the-school-year break, after mucking with parasites on a planet with life no more exotic than Earth's past. I threw myself down on my lower bunk to sulk. We'd probably matched as roommates because we both loved backpacking. "Where in the Galaxy has Shandy gone?" I said. "How will I ever find him?"

"Why do you even care?" Giem said. "Shandy's never sent you one com message. At least you get messages from Aerrem with holos of Dizzy, and from Krorn playing his flute," Giem grinned.

"Oh, your geepers make up for leaving your horse Swiftsure at home, as do your parents' messages with holos of him?" I said, evilly.

"Aren't we in a great mood."

"At least you have parents, Giem."

"Feeling sorry for yourself, Taje?"

"Where will I go if I flunk out of here?"

"You're not going to flunk!"

I hoped not. Now I could at least guess why Shandy had never sent me any messages after we said goodbye on *Onnarius*. While I'd gotten into one of the best interplanetary vet schools on full scholarship, maybe he'd simply felt too humiliated by failure. Why didn't he come to me for sympathy? He was my first roommate and saved my life! I hid my tears in my pillow.

CHAPTER 2

I cradled my space-lagged head in my hands and moaned. Somehow a com error had squeezed me between two little Telmid food tourists who talked nonstop together over my lap, mainly about the merits of different Big Maxson cheeses. I had to work hard at not vomiting in either of their laps.

At last I thought to turn off my wristcom translator, which shows just how well my brain was functioning post-tanking. Unfortunately I'd been among the last to have my entire micro-biome replaced aboard our paraship. I let out a putrid burp, startling my shuttle seatmates into silence and shriveling their antennae as we landed.

I punched my harness release, pushed my way to the front luggage racks and the open hatchway, and I leapt onto the ramp as it finished extending to the ground.

Fresh air, at last! I dropped my bags on the ground and sucked in lungfuls of moist, alien air. I knew the smell would become an undetectable background noise before long. For the moment, I just drank it in.

Blurrily visible through sheets of rain, a simple perimeter fence (no force field!) barely held in check more towering greenery than I'd scanned since I'd graduated from prevet duty aboard *Onnarius,* which took its crew to multiple worlds, none as desolate as Olecranon. The whole feel of a new world under my hiking boots, thank the Universe, began to stir my blood again, and my stomach decided to come in for at least an amphibious landing.

"What are you waiting for?" Giem shouted from the small crowd surging past me. The amplitude of the rain smacking the tarmac increased violently, and startled passengers began to run across the unprotected landing field towards the small rock-walled port building.

I calmly shouldered my bags. I'd never been willing to squander my savings on anti-grav luggage, and many of my prevet experiences had taken place on such primitive worlds that even wheeled suitcases would have proven useless. I sweated as I loped heavily across the landing field to catch up with Giem.

I met up with her at the double set of back doors which locked us all inside, the first real evidence of any dirtside security. Back traveling in space, we'd learned a fleet of low orbit Big Maxson satellites patrolled to detect, report, and prevent private planetary landings. All ships and ship shuttles must dock at the Big Maxson Orbital Station, and passengers had to take the Big Maxson shuttle down—standard low-cost protection for a small, unimportant port. I sighed as I watched fellow passengers crowd the front doors with their wristcoms set on ID. I could see through the clear doors a clot of relatives, friends, and associates waiting for them in the front parking lot.

"Have you asked them to go out with us?" I nodded jealously at the backs of Giem's seatmates, two handsome human traders, who, I had to admit, would have been wasted on me. Not that I needed to be strapped in the middle of a cuisine debate instead.

"What? You expect me to ask for both of us?" Giem flashed a mocking grin at me, even as she tried to push ahead. "Well, I suppose one of us has to be strong." Another Giem motto. "And I can't say I'm not hoping—"

We both sighed as we watched the two traders reach the front doors well ahead of us. Their wristcoms allowed them to pass on through, and they fell into the passionate embrace of two more male friends outside.

"Well, maybe not."

We watched the mad scramble everyone made for private and rental aircars parked outside in the rain. We saw no sign of the diminutive furry biped depicted in our prep notes, and the port building fell silent.

"Where's our welcoming committee?" I dropped my dripping bags on the floor.

Giem parked her anti-grav luggage—a getting-into-vet-school gift from her generous parents—at the foot of a large comscreen, where she asked for the big picture of our location.

My waist-high Telmid seatmates, the only two other people left in here, they couldn't resist the first available food dispenser. They twitched their antennae at the screen next to Giem's, and munched excitedly from aromatic little cheese packets. I slipped around to Giem's other side.

"WELCOME TO BIG MAXSON'S PLANET" our screen announced as a holo map rotated the planet's largest continent, South Maxson, into view. A red dot near the eastern coast located the only FIL establishment on Big Maxson, the R&R station to which this port belonged.

Giem stuck a finger through the dot, and a detailed map of the station blew up, with the spaceport in the far left lower corner. Giem scanned the directory, while I checked for messages. Immediately the lower screen switched from extolling the commercial virtues of "BEAUTIFUL, RELAXING BIG MAXSON'S PLANET" to a privately logged communication for us:

"Welcome to Big Maxson's Planet, Giemsan Fane and Tajen Jesmuhr. I am very sorry my work keeps me from meeting you properly, in person, at our spaceport. Instead, may I please invite you to dinner, 18:00 local time tonight in my home, adjoining the Big Maxson Biological Laboratory. Please refer to the station map for the location of my lab and the Big Maxson Hotel, where I've reserved free room and board for you. I know you'll need time to unpack and adjust, so I won't plan on seeing you before dinner.

"Sincerely, Dr. Kiernan Bioh, FIL Station Biologist, Big Maxson's Planet."

"Appropriate last name for a biologist," Giem said, and we chuckled. I asked the comscreen to download the station map into our wristcoms, and set them for local time.

"It's Big Maxson who ought to feel embarrassed about names," I said, as I discovered hours were somewhat shorter here, and that it was morning, even though ship time had me thinking afternoon. "What an ego. Suppose that's the FIL explorer who discovered this planet? We could ask the com—"

"Probably a pre-FIL explorer. Let's look into it some other time," Giem pleaded. "I'm starving, even if you aren't. Let's go find our hotel. If there's room and board, it must have a restaurant."

We gathered up our luggage and vectored for the front doors, a few steps behind the nibbling Telmids. I lagged, to escape the odor of their repast, and Giem waited impatiently for me to catch up. That's when I frowned at the debit reading on my wristcom.

"What's the matter, my Dim Side friend?"

"For two maps, two time sets, and a local message retrieval? What a server racket! You get to pay for a car into town," I told Giem.

"Too late," Giem said, as we stepped back out into the rain, and watched the last rental aircar whoosh off with the two cheese-lovers. "And it's just as well. Look at those rates."

She pointed at the holo ad, ordered her luggage to follow her, and set off at a rapid pace down the only road in sight. "Besides, we can use the exercise, and get a closer look at the scenery along the way. Look at all this greenery. Sure beats Olecranon all to micro fragments—I think Dr. Hako was truly trying to be nice to us!"

CHAPTER 3

That was my new friend Giem, always looking at the Bright Side of the planet. Thick-leaved giant plants and trees promptly formed a green tunnel over the dirt road and protected us from most of the rain. A mild breeze rustled and shimmered thousands of elaborately veined and serrated leaves on interwoven branches and coiling vines.

Life! Some of the smaller local fauna even showed up, after the passing disturbance of rushing aircars gradually wore off. little four and six-legged reptiles scurried along the edges of the road. Jewel-like insects hovered over pale, intricate blossoms. Camouflaged amphibians stared at us balefully from their perches on rocks and branches. Miniature dragons screeched across our path, and we could hear more croaks, whistles, and hisses in the vegetation all around us. Giem and I matched grins. We'd found ourselves in vet student heaven.

Next we stumbled across some clawed tracks which easily matched the size of our boot prints in the mud. We both gulped, remembering prep reports of native lifeforms large enough to make a meal out of us. I was out of breath after over a standard year of sitting in classes. I doubted I was in any shape to outrun a serious predator. Too bad I hadn't gotten to keep my ecology class stunner.

"They say," Giem began, hesitated, cleared her throat, and began again. "Our prep data claims the larger and more aggressive animals don't tend to roam anywhere near station territory, or anywhere close to the more populated areas of this continent." But she moved on at once, and her stride quickened noticeably.

"Those tracks could be one of the domestics, or even one of the intelligent natives," I said, between breaths, as I puffed alongside her.

"True." Giem's smile returned to her face, although I don't think she felt as much excitement as I did over meeting more aliens. Life in a FIL University demolished the novelty of that experience for most, while minor glitches in even the best translators put a daily strain on everyone.

Since I spent too much of my youth cooped up in a FIL Orphan Center, I loved travel, and scanning new kinds of people was part of the spice of it for me. I perked up and tried to pick up my pace. I was too spacelagged and loaded down with baggage to keep up with Giem's long strides that first day. And I almost didn't notice when I did catch up with her, because I'd scanned something big—and I mean big—swimming along in a roadside creek. At last I found myself standing beside Giem, waiting for me under the last dark green arch of trees and vines at the perimeter of the station town.

Ahead of us the profuse native foliage was under precarious control, barely making room for a motley collection of synthetic prefab, wood, and stone buildings, lined up along more or less straight, crisscrossing dirt and gravel streets. The slackening rain left large puddles everywhere. How far across the galaxy had Dr. Hako sent us?

We'd had plenty of time on our long trip to finish reading his prep notes, although paraspace "distances" could be very deceptive. This was like many of the young colony worlds I'd visited on fringe patrols as a prevet. Big patches of blue sky broke through cloud cover that would have persisted for months on bleak Olecranon, and I squinted through sunlight prisming off of wet surfaces and fluttering insects.

"Giem, Hako's sent us to a real backwater," I said— with delight and excitement, mind you. I loved out-of-the-way places. I turned and pointed with even more enthusiasm at the vigorous swirling in a wider part of the creek.

"Do you see it?"

"Taje—what?"

"Right there, under the surface—"

An explosive hiss, followed by my overactive imagination, led me to whirl back around on the muddy bank. I slipped, toppled backwards, and landed butt first with a loud splash in the cold pool.

The source of the hiss, a pony-sized reptile, ridden by a tall human as unusually dark as I am pale, and accompanied by a tri-colored dog, came to a halt on the cross-street before us.

Laughter exploded from the woman's smooth face. "A backwater hole, eh? Rather rude coming from a green newcomer. Our world has just given you a proper retort. Welcome to 'Beautiful, Relaxing Big Maxson's Planet.' Ha ha!"

Giem laughed with her while I sputtered and swiped wet hair out of my eyes. I thrust my hands down into the squishy creek bottom and groped for purchase. My luggage dragged me on down, and a sparkling cloud of tiny rainbow bugs swirled festively around my face.

"This is how you treat newcomers?" I snapped, my recent good mood vanishing into the mud as it sucked me farther down. I snorted a bug out of my left nostril. "Talk about rude—"

"I'd quit talking at all, if I were you, and extract my butt from there before it gets bitten." And with that, the slender rider leaned forward in her worn saddle and urged her mount into a fast trot into town.

I came flying out, dripping, muddy baggage and all—I'm not quite sure how I did it—while Giem choked so hard on her laughter that she could barely breathe. I stared anxiously back over my shoulder at the murky water. I eyed Giem, who was making a final effort to suppress some of her mirth. "Think she was making up a big fish story?"

"Maybe," Giem said. "I don't know."

Now that I was too soaked to appreciate it, the light drizzle died entirely. Soon we scanned more people out on the boardwalks. I shivered, and my face still burned as I turned once more toward Giem. "Okay, let's look at our station maps."

"What for?" Giem laughed again. "The hotel is right over there." She pointed at the one story, rambling stone building, just down the cross-street. Large red tiles spelled out "BIG MAXSON HOTEL" over the clear front doors. "Come on, let's go check in."

CHAPTER 4

The real person at the check-in desk gave my drowned-rat appearance a smirk as he downloaded our room number access code into our wristcoms. He called a cart for my bags, before I could sully the carpet. I loaded the cart, he ordered it to clean my luggage, and it got busy as it followed us to our room.

About four times the size of our dorm room, not to mention our tiny shipboard cabin, the hotel room felt like a glorious luxury. We even had a real window looking out on the thick foliage surrounding the town. Giem took a turn in the shower after I got out—recycled ship and orbital station air leaves a stale smell on everyone. I'd tossed my travel clothes in the cleanser before my shower. I dressed in clean clothes, nabbed the bed next to the window, and watched small reptiles climb and flit around the trees.

"Are you at least ready for a light meal? Or should I go without you?" Giem said as she dressed.

"I guess I should try."

"Let's go."

"Suppose we should dress up?" I stalled, as I scanned our casual student clothes doubtfully. "This hotel is a little fancier than I was expecting." Like having a real person at the front desk.

"We'll be spending three and a half standard months here. I don't intend to start a bad habit like that right away. Come on, I can't wait any longer, and it might help make your stomach feel better if you get something into it."

"You're probably right."

"Unless it's nerves," Giem added as she led us back out into the quiet hallway. "Your new set of custom-tailored super-microbes is supposed to keep you and everyone else here from getting sick, not make you feel sick."

In fact, most people seemed to pop out of the shipboard microfloral exchange tanks feeling better than when they went in—all hidden infections wiped out, and prime examples of symbiosis at its fullest potential.

As a former ecology and current vet student, I understood we're all just giant mobile environments for vast zoos of microscopic inhabitants. Some we needed, some seemed harmless, and some threatened our health or others. FIL's latest interplanetary disease prevention scheme completely slaughtered this mess, and replaced it with a physical shield of synthetic microbes engineered to be too dependent on their hosts to survive anywhere else, totally benign and useful, tough enough to block any invaders. Hence "rebugging" was born, to put it crudely.

So why did I feel like my body and my new microfloral barrier engaged in a battle which ended, at best, in an uneasy truce?

"Well, a few of us get side-effects from the microfloral exchange tanks," I said, "and an upset stomach is the worst. Poor Shandy ended up chronically nauseated from a plague this process might have prevented, and I thought I understood how bad that was. I'd rather be in straightforward pain. Anyway, what makes you think it's nerves?" As if ranting on again about Shandy hadn't given me away.

"Oh, you also got nauseated the mornings before your parasit exams for no particular reason, huh?"

"This is a sick Dim Side conversation. Let's switch to another topic, okay?"

"Fine by me. I'd rather not hear another word about veterinary medicine, whenever I have to." Giem stopped us in front of the desk again. "Can we eat anything on the menu?"

It was a good question, if I'd cared the slightest about the answer. The desk clerk gave my dried, brushed red hair and complete change of clothes an amused scan. "Stick to the human budget items in blue, if you don't want alien food, or FIL charging you for luxury items."

"Thanks." Giem led us into the dining room. "It's a nice touch, having a real person at the front desk," she said, as we chose a table next to another enticing window. There weren't any windows at the U of O. There was little to look at, even if we'd had time. "Wonder why they bother, though?"

"This is an R&R station, remember—"

"And if it's good food you're after, this is the planet to land on," the male partner of a Kralvin pair interrupted me. They'd stood up, apparently finished devouring some sort of late breakfast or early lunch. They had emptied their platters except for piles of bones, an unhappy sight my multi-species life experience had prepared me for. "But if you're serious traders," he lashed his dark furry tail, "my best advice is to leave now."

"It was your vacful idea to try this filthy, prehistoric world in the first place," his female partner, hackles up and claws extended, snapped back at him. "Better have that cheese deal settled by tomorrow's shuttle, because that's when I'm leaving."

"Hey, I know when to quit." He sneezed explosively. "I told you that deal fell through—and I found out connoisseurs don't want sterilized stuff anyway. We'd be better off running packaged tours—"

"If you think I'll ever return here, I have a planet to sell you—"

Giem and I felt oddly flattered to be considered potentially serious traders. However, we couldn't insert one word into the embarrassingly public dispute before the two Kralvins stormed out.

"I wonder what that was all about?" I eyed my wristcom translator settings dubiously. I desperately selected a favorite imported citrus drink I'd have to pay for, and forced myself to add two fried quelsh eggs to my order. I was tempted by what I guessed was a Telmid child-sized plate—one quarter of an egg—and decided I'd have to try to do better than that.

"It sounds like doing a parasitology survey might not be the worst job here." Giem grinned evilly at me, and ordered a hot cereal and a brilliant magenta native fruit juice.

"I thought you didn't want to talk anymore about vet med—hey!" A micro after my pink juice popped up, a dismaying, huge platter slid out of the table for me. On it laid my two fried eggs, in a steaming orange stack like two giant pancakes. "What is this?"

"I believe the description is 'prehistoric.'" Giem laughed again, and I finally joined her.

CHAPTER 5

We both felt better after the meal, and we wandered out into the streets afterwards to peer in shops and do some people-watching. I wanted to scan some real natives, and I was surprised how long it took me.

I did wonder how FIL got away with a foreign name for the planet, when I finally spotted a Pio. The lizard-like biped, about one hundred sixty centimeters in height, walked past me in the street while I tried not to stare too openly.

The Pio's gait wasn't any less fluid than a human's. Different joints led to unfamiliar movements. I couldn't see much beyond that because the dark green native wore a decidedly nonnative cloak, similar to Giem's, except with lots more pockets. A tail poked awkwardly out the bottom, and unshod feet left familiar claw marks and scale prints in the drying mud.

Giem, I noticed, concentrated on human pedestrians, some of whom I at least found interesting. Nearly everyone, human or otherwise, dressed casually. I had fun trying to guess locals from tourists. Some nonnative vacationers gave themselves away by their own native dress, others by absurdly overdone attempts at the Adventure Look. All in all, though, it did seem like a calm, pleasant day on beautiful, relaxing Big Maxson's Planet—

"This isn't what I ordered!"—a human voice came through the open door of a shop. The ruckus drew our attention to the display window, showing off a heartbreaking display of top-of-the-line backpacking gear.

"No, no, I asked for a Mark VII with all the options."

While I drooled over multimodal stoves, Giem peered beyond. She shook my shoulder. "Look."

"Hey, I know, I couldn't even bring my old trimode—"

"No, Taje—"

"How can I defend myself with this—this stick?" The angry voice drew my eyes past the display, to the human standing inside.

"Sir, 'this stick,' which I had to special order for you, is the finest wooden longbow made in this sector of the galaxy. Furthermore, it's at the FIL tech limit for privately owned offworld weapons on Big Maxson." The Lorratian salesperson's coppery shoulder spikes erected defensively.

"Come on, let's go in for a better scan." Giem towed me inside, ignoring my embarrassment. She docked us in an aisle close to the sales counter, where we could ostensibly study an enticing selection of gourmet camping meals.

I couldn't see the customer's face so I ogled a nicely muscled, stocky body, outfitted in rugged clothes, with the right number of pockets on vest, shirt, and pants, and a belt carrying just enough gear to appear ready for action, without overdoing it. An unrepaired scar slashed across the back of a golden hand, adding a ridiculous dash of roguishness. Giem sighed beside me. No one like this was available in vet school, not even to merely admire from a light year or two away. Everyone was simply too overworked to stand a chance. Although I received some very friendly holos from Krorn, that just wasn't enough.

"Alright, just sell me some power cartridges," the customer said. "I'll also need a new knife, and some of your fishing bait."

"What about the bow—"

"I'll shop elsewhere. What bait do you carry?"

"Delucian crabs, Kesselfarm minnows, krazzles, crakkies, and Sclorroscian worms, all put into stasis within micros of kill and sterilization—"

"Nothing native? Okay, I'll take some of the worms."

"Well, he's not perfect," I whispered. "I've never seen those worms catch much of anything for anybody, on any—"

"Shhh," Giem hissed, still entranced with the view. The stranger downloaded credits from his wristcom to the Lorratian's, signaling the end of the show. The two of us tried a little harder to study self-heating biodegradable food packets laid out in colorful rows before us.

"That junk won't put any meat on your bones." The twenty-something golden-skinned human nearly startled me out of my skin as he passed us. "Try the store down the street." Only slightly taller than Giem, he grinned wickedly at her, and she got a good look into his gleaming almond eyes, peering out from under black bangs. He departed, leaving the dealer cursing quietly.

Giem smiled happily, but my surprise turned to chagrin when I happened to glance upwards. "Look." I pointed at the monitor above and behind the counter. My pale, red-haired hologram pointed back at us accusingly.

"No." Giem's smile faded, on the screen and beside me.

"Come on, let's get out of here. I've endured more than enough embarrassment for one day. I think I'm ready for some rest back in our room."

"That sounds good to me too," Giem said, as we stepped back outside. We both glanced surreptitiously up and down the boardwalk, for a figure that had vanished. It commed. Wasn't there some way we could just lock up any troublesome hormones until we graduated, eons from today? What good did they do?

CHAPTER 6

"I'm drugged, Giem. By Evil Spies. I've already blown my cover somehow. You'll just have to carry on without me." Woozy and stuporous from simultaneous changes in light cycle, atmosphere, gravity, and time, I was barely able to shut our alarm off.

"Over your necrotic body." Giem groaned as she sat up in her bed. "What did you slip in my juice this morning? Betrayed—by my own partner."

"Hey, I thought we were in this together."

"I'll say."

We crashed down a gravity well from there. I must admit being allowed more than one shower in twenty-four hours was one huge advantage of living dirtside again. We still weren't prepared for an evening town grown festive and crowded with FIL ship crews on planetary R&R. We bumped our way down the streets, and I may have even scanned a Big Orange Cube before it slipped away down a side-street. It was hard to care. My stomach had decided to return to high orbit by the time we found Dr. Bioh's wooden door.

We stood vac-headedly before it for several minutes, before we realized it lacked any sensor or buzzer. Finding no other alternative, I tried banging a dented metal disk, set into the middle of the door, with a small wooden mallet lying on the doorstep. Abruptly the door swung outward, forcing us to jump back out of the way.

"Welcome," the diminutive biologist greeted us as he held the door open for us. He wasn't wearing anything besides a wristcom, and his very fine, long, agouti hair looked too warm for this climate. "I am Dr. Kiernan Bioh. Please come in."

I dropped the mallet by his door and we ducked inside his refrigerated, rock-walled home. He ushered us to synthfur chairs around a black crystal coffee table, loaded with bowls of fresh vegetables, chips, crackers, and dips. We gazed dazedly around the cave-like room while we tried not to visibly shiver during our introductions.

"I'm Giemsan Fane and this is Tajen Jesmuhr. You can just call me Giem."

"And you can call me Taje," I said, happy to scan the thoughtfully simple supper awaiting us. I could just nibble and not seem impolite, while Dr. Bioh covered the oh-so-thrilling details of our summer assignment.

"It was very nice of the University of Olecranon to send me two interplanetary veterinary students," Dr. Bioh said, as he served us tall carbonated versions of Giem's magenta breakfast juice. "Incidentally, this beverage is made from locally farmed, native krava fruit. Most humans find it quite enjoyable. Anyway, I wasn't sure Dr. Hako would even look at my job offer."

Dr. Bioh climbed into a seat opposite us, and his brow wrinkled as he absent-mindedly straightened the already beautifully groomed fur on one knee. "Unlike you, who must learn how to treat all animal life, I am fortunately limited to the study of the life of just one planet, a world which has not even evolved the concept of endothermy. And I still find more than enough work here for many lifetimes. I look forward to your help this summer."

"As do we," Giem said politely, as she hungrily grazed on the array of food treats before us. I couldn't keep up with her. I tried my best. It was tasty stuff and nice light fare, on top of juice fizz which helped settle my stomach.

"Why a parasitology survey?" I couldn't resist asking. Of all the exciting projects which he might consider for a relatively new FIL colony, why did he have to saddle us with this one?

Dr. Bioh nodded human-style for us, and leaned back in his chair. "I have to rather stretch my job qualifications at this post, since we lack a variety of personnel. In the process of setting up rudimentary meat inspections, I discovered this whole field no one has studied.

"I'm sure you've noticed we're rather on the fringes out here. We have a limited amount of station territory, generously donated to us by the Pios. And we're starting to develop a reputation as a first-class stopover for the culinary-minded. And because the majority of Pios don't seem to care much for trading with us—I suppose that helps protect their culture—we mostly grow our own here.

"In short, production has become increasingly important to our local ranchers and farmers, and I'm certain that internal parasitism is damaging our native livestock. Not seriously yet, mind you. If we develop a good understanding of the problem early, maybe we can head it off before production methods intensify."

"How much have you quantified the situation?" Giem said.

"I know quite a bit about indigenous wildlife parasite loads. I've recorded detailed descriptions I've transmitted into your hotel room coms. I've only run a few spot checks on local domestics. However, it's enough to discover, not too surprisingly, that they are infected with similar parasites. I just haven't had time to carry it any further. That's how you can help me."

"That's a fairly broad task." I had to work at suppressing a convulsive shiver. I hadn't worn a coat because it was so warm outside. "Do you have specific tests you want us to run, or do we just jump in and see what we can find?" I dipped a conical purple vegetable, and forced myself to enjoy it.

"All I really need at this point is a thorough set of fecal scans run on a representative portion of station livestock, and some comparison parasite counts on any of the animals that go to slaughter."

I could see it dawning at last on Giem's horrified face. "This station doesn't just produce eggs, cheeses, and riding stock. People butcher animals for meat?"

She wasn't usually this slow. She must have led a very protected life on Ballophon.

Dr. Bioh sneezed politely into a napkin. "We're simply too small and too new to afford clone cell vats. Of course we'll pursue them when we can—"

"You only want us to look at parasites that live in digestive tracts?" I said as a quick, polite diversion, and cringed at any hint that we might do more.

"At present, that's the area of most economic concern for us, and I think beginning there will give us a good solid start." Dr. Bioh sipped his drink. "The problem doesn't really merit more at this point. I hope it will give you sufficient work to fulfill your summer externship requirement. I don't want to get you into any trouble. I am very pleased to have merited your services. If you should come across any other question or subject of personal interest to you, I feel certain we can also fit it in. You just need to let me know."

"I'm sure we can figure out a way to keep busy," Giem muttered, tempting fate right from the start, while I evilly daydreamed about backpacking, and had at last a grin to suppress despite my worse-than-usual pallor. Giem must have only noticed the latter.

"We've really enjoyed this meal," she added after glancing my way. "I'm afraid we must leave. We've had a long day, and we want to feel ready to start working for you tomorrow."

"Oh, you mustn't rush." Dr. Bioh dabbed at his whiskers with his napkin, and slid down from his seat. "Our satellite system not only protects our planet, it also provides an excellent network for calls and downloads. My reports have already arrived at your hotel deskcoms, where you can also download them to your wristcoms if you wish. Furthermore, I've allowed a couple days for you to study my reports and work out the details of your survey, before I've scheduled you for any farm or ranch visits. Tonight you can relax and experience why your work is so important to us. Feel free to bring your drinks into the next room."

I stood up, exchanged puzzled looks with Giem, and hesitantly picked up my half-empty glass. Dr. Bioh proudly led us into his dining room, and to the biggest banquet I'd ever scanned, lavishly arranged on a huge wooden table.

"We know the microfloral exchange tanks make most humans ravenous." Our little host smiled human-fashion, revealing tiny, amazingly sharp teeth. "And you came such a long way to help us. I received many generous donations for tonight's feast. I'm especially proud of the skitsh steaks from Ziehl Ruck's ranch, gratis in greetings to our two veterinary students. She produces some of the finest station livestock available."

Skitsh reach the size of some of the largest Earth dinosaurs. Giem and I stared at each other, and even Giem's normally golden face turned pale. I asked for the bathroom. While I sat on the little toilet, I had to tell myself sternly that I'd have to politely sample a steak, even if it was from a live animal, not a cell culture. Ick!

CHAPTER 7

"Hors d'oeuvres—the first course was just hors d'oeuvres. Why didn't I com it promptly?" I wailed, as I tottered down the muggy street late that night.

"Why indeed, oh spoiled traveler." Giem shoved me, narrowly rescuing me from a trampling by a herd of tourists obviously new to local lizard mounts. "You could have warned me—crap!" She wasn't kidding. She stopped and leaned heavily on my shoulder while she scuffed reeking reptilian feces off from her boot onto the curb. "And I suppose you've visited plenty of fringe planets where they still have to kill for meat. Disgusting!"

"Fecals and necropsies," I added to her rant, as crowds surged around and jolted us. "Our summer externship *stinks*. Literally. Have you heard about the great assignments some of our classmates received? Sakk and Jekkan get to help record normal anatomy of the primary domestics on CVT IX. How did they rate? Dr. Hako must hate us."

"Dr. Hako doesn't hate us." As usual, Giem immediately leaped to the Bright Side.

"Then why did he hand us an assignment that will prove worthless when they get clone vats here?" I emitted a foul burp, which I barely kept from becoming a spew.

"We can still help the egg, cheese, and lizard producers," Giem said in her annoyingly positive way.

"Blast it all, how am I supposed to help devise a survey, much less study the anatomy and handling techniques we'll need to know, when I feel like someone ought to dump me in a recycler? Within a couple days, I won't feel ready—"

"You don't look like you'll ever feel ready." A stocky, roguish, dark-haired man with a scar on his hand flashed me a mocking grin as he pushed past us.

"You again," I said angrily.

"Who are you?" Giem called after him.

"Wouldn't you like to know," he said, as he disappeared into the bright, noisy interior of a tavern.

"Why, that—"

"Wait a micro." Giem hauled me back from the open doorway, vibrating with the spirited sounds of a live band. A holo outside advertised <u>The Rock Forming Minerals</u>. During a brief pause in the music, someone announced their next song, "Hey! Watch Out for That Asteroid!"

I swung again for the doorway, and Giem grabbed my sleeve.

"He deserves a comeback!"

"Scan where we are, Taje." Giem pointed, with the hand not restraining me, across the street at the station's lit-up police department.

I relaxed, and a grin twitched on my pale lips. "I had you that worried?"

"I never know about you, Taje." Giem held her ground, and her grip on my sleeve. "You have a somewhat checkered past."

"Humph." I broke her hold with a very basic move from our self-defense class. "Why don't you go in there and introduce yourself? You've still got your eye on him, haven't you?"

Giem gave me an impatient look. "You don't just go barging into a saloon to meet someone. At least, I can't. Anyway, the music's too loud to talk. Besides, I don't feel much better than you do right now, and probably all we need is a good night's rest."

It sounded like a nice theory. I have a vacful sense of direction, and Giem navigated us with ease through the interminable, noisy streets and back to our wonderful hotel room at last.

I dropped onto my bed and into a restless, sweaty nightmare. An automatic banquet table was stuck on endless production of massive waves of food, all contaminated with monster parasites that dropped off the giant table to relentlessly chase me around it. Nausea woke me up to grope my way into the bathroom and empty out my stomach the fast way. I felt such great relief that I wondered why I'd fought it off for as long as I had.

My noise didn't seem to bother Giem at all. She was out cold, and only got up a couple times later on, to do it the right way.

CHAPTER 8

The only fun part over the next two days was room service. We felt like we were cramming for finals all over again, studying Dr. Bioh's hyper-detailed parasite reports, picking out ID info for our fecalyzer, and writing up a husbandry survey to com what was working and not working for livestock production here.

Our deadline, our first working day, would come too fast. We looked at our schedule, and guessed Dr. Bioh had started us off easy with just three stops the next day. We guessed wrong.

The pony-sized "lizard" whacked its muscular tail across my chest, almost knocking me to the ground.

"I'm very sorry." Mikk Keljo struggled to regain his hold on the lizard's tail, while I fought to hang onto my hard-earned odiferous sample, instead of pitching face first into it. Fortunately I happen to possess fewer than average human breast pain receptors. I didn't faint. I just doubled over for a moment, gasping and choking.

"How many lizards do you own altogether?" Giem tried to fill in more of our survey, after glancing my way to make sure I wasn't permanently damaged, I supposed. Somehow I managed to insert the fresh stinking specimen into our fecal analyzer.

"I don't know, don't know exactly," Karr Keljo said, from his position at the lizard's head, where he hung onto her halter with the three grey stubby fingers typical of his species, while somehow losing none of them to her beak-hard lips. "Mikk, how many of these animals do we have?"

"I don't know exactly. We can count them today for you. You want to set up practice here after you graduate?" Mikk asked for about the sixth time that morning. "We don't have any vets, just Doc Bioh and our MD, Doc Devlin."

I made the mistake of trying to change the subject by asking again for some sort of animal ID code to feed into the analyzer, and got an argument between the two elderly Nandrusian ranchers over whether her name was Jet or Rocket.

"How's the test going?" I asked as I thrust my gloved arm into our portable sterilizer. Giem had switched her attention from her scribescreen with our survey questions to the analyzer's little monitor screen. We'd crammed Dr. Bioh's vast parasite data into the small machine's memory, and we'd still have to be ready to catalog any new parasite species.

"Okay." Giem brushed a dirty lock of hair out of her face. "This one is almost done. I've seen nothing new here."

"She's a fine animal, isn't she?" Mikk said, as the two spindly brothers struggled with the arcane controls of their homemade restraint chute. "What do you think? You know more about animals than we do."

I was looking at the lizard from her butt-end, of course, and about all I could scan was that she was brown-scaled, irritated, and just as pot-bellied as her grey-skinned keepers. Because it was our first morning on the job, I was hardly in any position to judge.

"A fine animal, Rocket is." Mikk released her tail as his brother released the latch at the front of the stocks. "Right, Karr?"

"Old Jet is very fine," Karr managed to brag, even as the lizard almost bowled him over in her haste to escape us. "I found another egg in her stall this morning."

"What do you think, girls? Do you think she's worth keeping another year?" Mikk prodded me in the ribs to make sure I heard. Karr snagged her halter and both Nandrusians wrestled her back down to a set of ramshackle stalls.

"This is a vacful prison sentence," I muttered the moment they were out of earshot. "I guess the idea is why bother to train a lizard you'll never ride?"

"Great Galaxy, Taje, for safety!" Giem hissed at me, shaking her head.

"How many have we done?"

Giem glanced down at the fecalyzer. "Eighteen."

"When was the next ranch expecting us?"

"It doesn't matter. There's nothing we can do about it." Giem stood up to stretch, and we both gazed at the makeshift cluster of pens and sheds, which emitted some crashing noises. "I doubt there's more than twenty stalls altogether down there. Home stretch—you want to switch jobs again?"

"Nah." I sighed. "You did the first ten. Besides, I wasn't able to get any straight answers for our husbandry survey."

"You think I'm doing any better?"

We heard more banging, some loud cracks, and the two brothers managed to emerge with another lizard, a green-scaled critter this time.

I returned to the rear end of the chute while Karr backed the balky beast into it. Giem and I exchanged relieved looks when he announced this was their last layer. She kicked at the rear restraining bars and I hoped she wouldn't slip her razor-clawed feet between them.

"This one's not so fine." Mikk nodded at the beast. "She hasn't laid an egg for over a week. We're going to sell her this year, right, Karr?"

"I don't know, Mikk. Her last egg was extra large. What do you think, girls?"

"I don't know. What's her production rate?" Giem tried valiantly to get another survey question answered, while I wondered uncharitably if the two elderly ranchers would promptly retire if we suggested it. "How do her stats compare with your average production rate?" Giem looked up, noticed me doing a dodging dance while the two brothers discussed possible answers, and Giem stood up to grab the thrashing tail for me. I ducked under it, and found I had to reach into the rectum as far as my armpit to get anything from this animal.

I don't think I'd ever signed up for such a fun-filled summer. Just why was it I wanted to become a vet? A rickety chute lever fell off and almost smashed our analyzer.

Karr dropped his grip on the lizard's halter to slam the lever back into place, and I hastily fed our analyzer our last reeking sample while the lizard let out a hiss more like a shriek, and tried to reach around to bite me. Karr grabbed her halter again just in time.

"What do you think of her?" Mikk persisted while I stuck my trembling arm into the sterilizer.

Giem shook her head, and remembered to say "I'm sorry. We didn't bring a diagnostic bioscanner, and we haven't yet learned enough to tell from external signs—"

"How many years of vet school do you have left?" Mikk asked his first truly sensible question of the morning.

"Three planetary years," I said, peeling my glove off. "Uh, that's about four and a half standard years." I sighed. I couldn't imagine life beyond school. Or beyond this day.

"Do you think she'll lay us another egg soon?" Mikk said.

"As Giem said, we'd need more equipment and training—" I began, and the lizard kicked a rear limb between the bars. Giem and I rushed to untangle her, and we frantically dodged dagger claws to stuff her leg back inside the stocks before she fractured it.

"Let her out!"

Karr obeyed us, and this time the lizard mowed right over him as she launched from the chute.

"She might be looking for a good nest," Mikk said, as he lurched after their bucking escapee.

"Or she may not lay again this year." Karr fussily brushed dirt from his genital sash, revealing its bright pink color, before he slowly stood up again. His brother's sash, when cleaned off, was neon orange. The bright colors signified they had reached the end of their fertility period. Probably a long time ago.

"Sorry we don't have time to help you catch her," I said cheerfully, as we began to shut down our equipment. "We must get going. We still have two other ranches—"

"Don't you want to see our babies?" Mikk's translator voice sounded crestfallen.

"Babies?" I gasped. "I thought this was an egg production facility."

"Yes, we must replace the layers too old to produce, and we keep some extra hatchlings until they're old enough for trainers to purchase," Karr said.

"You have young lizards here? How many?" Giem said wearily.

CHAPTER 9

Giem and I at last escaped down the road that afternoon, after we'd sampled over two dozen calf-sized "hatchlings" even more difficult to restrain in the oversized chute. We each had a small krava fruit in our day packs, from the Keljo brothers' orchard, as a reward. We were eating the six large perfect ones they'd told us to take back to Doc Bioh. The day had turned hot and muggy, we'd had nothing to eat or drink since breakfast, and the sweet, tart, lobulated, magenta fruit tasted so wonderful I could hardly believe it.

"These seem much too large for a person of Dr. Bioh's size," I said between greedy, pulpy bites. "I'm sure the smaller fruits will suit him much better."

"It's nice to see at least your appetite has recovered, even if your attitude hasn't." Giem chuckled, swiping red juice from her chin. It made her look like a sated carnivore. Half her fluffy hair had escaped from her work ponytail. "What silly old ranchers."

"They're silly old ranchers who have made us very late. Shouldn't we call the next two ranches to warn them?" I chucked a thick lime green krava peel into a nearby bush, and something screeched back at me. "Hey, I'm sorry," I said, startled. When was I not going to make an animal angry here?

Giem shrugged. "The next ranchers are nearby neighbors and should understand, and we can call the third ranch from there."

We spat out our last shiny black krava seeds as we arrived at the Happy Lizard Ranch. A human foreman greeted us with a nod. We apologized for our late arrival as we wondered how long he'd had his first dozen restless lizards tied up outside in a courtyard. I thought it a welcome sign of efficiency, and thank the Galaxy he didn't seem bothered or surprised by our late appearance.

While we called our third scheduled ranch—only to find that owner remarkably unperturbed as well—the foreman rounded up several other tough-looking ranch hands of various species. Each clutched a rope, halter, or some other piece of tack with their multiple limbs. That should have tipped us off right from the start.

We soon discovered we faced something far worse than the fat, untrained Keljo lizards, and that was the thin, quick, smart, nasty lizards of Happy Lizard Ranch.

CHAPTER 10

The sun began to set over the tops of tall thick-leaved trees as we departed, amazingly unscathed, physically anyway, from Happy Lizard Ranch. Thank the Universe many of their lizards had become so enraged by the very idea of restraint—much less by anyone touching their anuses—that they'd spontaneously spewed out samples for us.

When my adrenaline wore off enough to calm my breathing rate and heart rate, I called the Ruck Ranch again, only to have the owner once more decline rescheduling and insist it didn't matter how late we arrived tonight. Giem and I stared back at each other with grim, dirty faces.

We hadn't thought to pack food for eating on the job—we'd planned to try lunch in town, between ranches. And we'd have to pass up dinner and hurry on through town to reach the third ranch. Giem dug into her day pack, and started peeling her last little bruised krava fruit. I followed suit, picking a green worm off of mine as we approached the town perimeter.

When we reached the busiest streets, we needed all of our remaining willpower to walk past all of the mouth-watering restaurant aromas wafting out amongst the cheerful crowds. We distracted ourselves by concentrating instead on dodging the onslaught of evening traffic, a chaotic mix of peds, aircars, and various work and pleasure mounts. The latter attracted our jealous notice. Even mutated dwarf grieshnags would have served better than our feet aching in our boots.

Then a particularly obnoxious, ritzy-looking open bushcar slid to a stop right in front of us, blocking our way. I scanned the cocky grin on the fortyish human driver, and I briefly considered what a sweaty, generous hug in my odiferous coveralls would do to his expensive evening suit.

"Hey—" I yelled instead, about to launch into a curse with the force of my day's frustrations behind it.

"You young women look like you could use a lift." The big pale blond man confounded my attack with his generous offer. "Where are you headed?"

"The Ruck Ranch," Giem sputtered, beaming him a surprised look of gratitude.

"Ah, everyone knows the famous Ruck Ranch around here. No problem—hop on in."

"We're awfully filthy," I had to admit, and got a swift elbow in my ribs, right where Mikk had poked me ages ago today. "Ow!"

"Well, I can't say my car is the pit of cleanliness, either. Come on, climb in. I'm headed for one of the restaurants on that side of town. I can just drop you two off on my way."

We hesitated no longer—angry traffic had backed up behind him, and we just couldn't refuse our tired, perspiring bodies. With all the crowds about, we commed we weren't running much of a risk. Giem sat down alongside the man, I clambered into the dusty back seat, and he ordered the bushcar to maximum town speed.

"By the looks of your clothes, you must be Dr. Bioh's newly imported vet students." He nodded at Giem's conspicuous shoulder patch, with its serpent-entwined Aesculapian staff, "FIL Univ of IP Vet Med on Olecr" crammed around the border, and a stinky brown splotch in the middle of it. We had looked so smooth this morning, in our nice crisp new coveralls.

"Word travels fast." Giem laughed nervously.

"It's a small town." He smiled at both of us. "My name, by the way, is Garth Riddock."

"My name's Taje—Tajen Jesmuhr—and this is Giemsan Fane."

"I hear it's quite a challenge, getting into a FIL interplanetary vet program."

"There aren't many schools available," I said, happily feeding my ego a bit after more than a standard year of getting it smashed into subatomic particles.

"And I should think those schools would have to be extremely selective. How does one memorize the treatment of every possible problem of all the animals in FIL?"

"We don't." I snorted. "We can't."

"We are taught how to learn deep biology, as fast as possible," Giem said, in response to Riddock's puzzled reaction. "We also learn how to practice general principles of diagnosis and treatment. Most of the animals we study in vet school are presented as exercises, rather than as cases we have to commit to memory."

As they chatted on I stared at the back of the man's slightly sunburned neck. He was even paler than me, a real rarity among humans, and he must have slipped up a bit on his systemic UV blocker. I was very careful about it here. What with the dirt and debris also tracked into his aircar, I guessed it had some genuine use beyond showing off the Adventure Look. What was this person doing here?

"We did have to pass a very difficult test and have excellent grades and references to get in," Giem said, as an understatement, and revealed her own curiosity. "Do you live here?"

"No, I'm just a visitor—and a student, like yourselves."

"A student—of what?" Giem said eagerly.

Garth chuckled. "Currently, I'm studying people. I'm on vacation."

I was too tired, perhaps, to scan that properly. I made some comment to the effect of "Oh, people-watching—I like to do that too."

"Do you now?" Garth's aircar sped up as it left town lights behind, and next it swerved around numerous bends and before pulling up in a dirt driveway. "Then maybe we'll see more of each other. Here's the Ruck Ranch."

"Thank you." We both jumped out and waved as he raced off again. We walked toward the lit-up ranch house in the gloom ahead, and admired green and blue glow-bugs fluttering over pale fluorescing blossoms on the bushes lining the driveway.

"Nice guy," Giem commented on our way to the ranch house.

"Hey, and another smooth looker," I said. "Did you notice those arm muscles?"

"Would I miss a detail like that? Unusual blue eyes and blond hair too, and a handsome if rather pallid face—"

"Hey—"

"Sorry. Sensitive, aren't we?"

"You would be too, if you'd ever been mistaken for something not human." We stepped up onto the front porch, and to the door. "Okay, why can't I ever find a buzzer or sensor around here?"

A dog started barking inside. Moments later, a tall, slender, very dark woman, with short, dense, curly black hair, and almond eyes like Giem's, opened the door to greet us. She was quite obviously the same woman who'd caught me calling this world a backwater planet, our very first day on Big Maxson. And now we'd arrived at her door—reeking, exhausted, and hideously late.

"Hi, my name's Ziehl Ruck." The woman grinned at us, her hands on her hips.

Giem matched my appalled look, while I fervently wished I could just vanish beneath Big Maxson's crust.

CHAPTER 11

Instant total mortification. On Ziehl Ruck's doorstep, I gulped dryly, since a pit stubbornly refused to slide open beneath my boots, nor could I quite master instant teleporting to the other side of the Galaxy.

Yet the rancher didn't act at all surprised or angry as she scanned us. In fact, the insufficiently masked look of amusement on her smooth brown face reminded me of Dr. Hako.

"Why don't you peel off those coveralls and come join me for some dinner?" she said cheerfully, as we slowly stepped inside. Immediately her canine companion gave each of us a disgustingly thorough scan with his cold wet nose. I considered dogs a rather trite human pet, and I had tired of all our canine lecture material. Nevertheless I caught myself absent-mindedly patting his soft head.

From the entryway we could see the sitting room of a rustic, very neat and rambling home. We could also just catch a glimpse of a dining table in another room, and some mouth-watering smells reached us where we stood. On Big Maxson it seemed like I never got the right amount of food.

"If you want us to get our work done by a reasonable bedtime, we'd probably better not take time for dinner," I said reluctantly, while Giem remained mute.

Ziehl's laughter bubbled up out of her throat, even before she opened her wide-lipped mouth. "I've spoken with Dr. Bioh, and I know all about your supposed schedule. I didn't expect you to do any work here today."

"Then you invited us over just for dinner?" I said, dazed.

"I commed you could use it."

"You supplied the steaks at Dr. Bioh's dinner for us too, didn't you?" Giem said, dumping her day pack in the entryway. My filthy coveralls, boots, and pack rapidly joined hers in a heap there. We had both overdressed in shirts and shorts underneath our coveralls. Not exactly company clothes, and we still stunk from penetrating angry lizard secretions.

"The skitsh steaks?" Ziehl said. "Don't worry, I won't try to feed you so much that you can't enjoy your food tonight."

We all laughed on our way to the dining room where, as promised, a simple meal awaited us. We sat down and gratefully went to work on it. The dog wrenched himself away from the delightful bouquet of our belongings, to sit under the table and beg from each of us in turn.

He didn't make out as well as he would have at Dr. Bioh's feast. After I'd engulfed enough of my vegetable omelet and bread to silence the loud growling in my belly, I remembered to pay attention to Ziehl. She didn't look much older than us, and her self-confidence and sense of humor impressed me. Especially since I had to com she'd grown up with as much teasing as I had, not matching the blended racial norm of human appearance.

"This is rather nice treatment for a rude foreigner," I said to her. She had even avoided challenging us with uncloned meat.

"Ha ha! Someone's got to look after the latest set of innocents. Have your impressions of this 'backwater' changed at all? Or have today's experiences forever confirmed your worst fears?"

"I meant that comment more as a compliment, at the time—"

"Tell me," Giem broke in, "are they all like that?"

"The ranchers? How could anyone else resemble Mikk and Karr Keljo? I hear you've developed a very complete husbandry questionnaire. Did you get any straight answers from them?"

"What do you think?" Giem matched wry looks with Ziehl. "At least the Happy Lizard Ranch crew handled our questions efficiently—a lot better than they can handle their lizards."

"Did they really? Can I see what they told you?"

Giem and I glanced nervously at each other. Was our host asking us to reveal rival trade secrets? Maybe we shouldn't feel too trusting too promptly.

"You don't seriously think I'm in competition with that outfit, do you?" Ziehl immediately recognized our consternation. "If it will help you to hear it, I put my main efforts into quelsh egg and skitsh meat production. My lizards are more of a sideline, and the people who come to me for them would rather do without native mounts than save credits at Happy. I can understand— client privacy and all that."

Giem and I nodded at each other. Giem got up to retrieve our scribescreen, and Ziehl scanned it only a moment before snickering.

"Well, no business secrets there." She handed it back to Giem. "Not much of anything at all."

"What do you mean?" Giem demanded.

"You don't know all that I do about Happy. Fortunately you included questions which should result in some cross correlations."

Giem checked the screen again, and frowned.

"Can I see?" I asked Giem.

"This data doesn't make any sense at all—in fact, it looks practically random."

"Let me see," I pleaded.

"It probably is random." Ziehl chuckled in an infectiously musical manner, while I snatched the screen away from Giem and peered at the figures. "Image is everything at Happy. No one there likes to admit they don't have all the answers."

"They just faked it. Vacful jerks," I cursed. "How are we ever going to produce a decent study at this rate?" Suddenly I didn't feel good. The day began to catch up with me all over again. "I hate this assignment." And I was doomed to it all summer long.

Ziehl flinched and raised her eyebrows, while Giem rolled her eyes. "Don't mind Taje. She's behaved like this ever since our last day of freshman classes."

Ziehl leaned forward and nodded thoughtfully. She reached once more for the screen. I barely restrained myself from throwing it at her. She studied it for a little while longer and looked up at us with a serious expression.

"Listen, you two want some good insider advice?"

Giem nodded and I said, "Sure."

"Right. This looks like an excellent questionnaire." Ziehl handed it back to Giem. "I'm sure you worked hard to make this a very thorough study. As you may have guessed, I'm good friends with Dr. Bioh, and I've heard more than a little about you. Anyway, I'm guessing maybe you're working too hard at this."

"You mean we'll find all the ranches and farms this difficult?" Giem said anxiously.

"Oh, no, not at all. You've just had the misfortune of experiencing some of the operations with, shall we say, the loosest schedules today."

"Some?" Giem said.

"There's more?" I said.

"Only a few others come anywhere near those two, and I can give you tips ahead of time for handling them. None of us has been at this work longer than about fifteen planetary years max, and our years here don't last much longer than standard. Although your study can help us, it doesn't have to be perfect at this point. Let me guess—instead of random sampling, you attempted to check every lizard from both ranches today, right?"

We both nodded numbly.

Ziehl shook a finger at us. "Don't you two want to have any fun this summer?"

That argument definitely caught our attention. "We're guaranteed two weeks of vacation at the end," Giem said, making one last feeble attempt to remain noble.

"A couple weeks? With all this planet has to offer? What about all those evenings you'll feel too tired to even notice the night life? I suppose you plan to just dock your noses into your work every day of the week, straight through to your measly vacation?"

"You sound like an ex-student yourself," Giem said, sounding amused.

"I have done more than enough time there, and I know what happens. You start working for grades, and quit working on life. You come out a highly trained social misfit."

"I think we were already misfits—"

"Hey, speak for yourself," Giem interrupted me.

"Seriously, what are you suggesting we do?" I said. "Cut our hours, and run out and play every night?"

"Why not? Although I didn't mean to get you so worked up about it. You just need to know there's more than one option here. Dr. Bioh would never tell you this directly, but I know you'd satisfy him if you worked like black holes to obtain a decent minimum database, and consequently also earned some extra free time for yourselves."

"We'd really make him happy with that?" Giem said, startled.

Ziehl grinned with the obvious delight of getting to be the one to tell us someone else's secrets. "Look, why do you think Kiernan went to the trouble of applying for such high level students to come here? If he just wanted you for a little study like this, he'd save time, bother, and expense by hiring and training locals for the job.

"Our biologist isn't fuzzy-brained. He invites students like you because he hopes you'll enjoy Big Maxson enough to consider returning here with all your knowledge and skills once you graduate—or maybe you'll at least talk us up to some of your fellow classmates. And you won't do that if you don't have fun here the first time."

"Ha!" I said. "Mikk and Karr kept saying how much they need a vet. They probably drove Dr. Bioh nova."

"Dr. Bioh's dreaming," Giem said. "Most students don't bother to get into a FIL interplanetary school just to settle down on one world right after they graduate."

"Some don't originally intend to," Ziehl said. "Besides, we aren't nearly big enough to build and support a local vet school. How else can we get any real help between FIL SEAR Ship visits?"

"You're truly serious about this, aren't you?" I quit smiling.

"Of course. Although my more immediate motive is to get a little refreshing company out you. Speaking of which, you look—and smell—nearly as fresh as your coveralls."

"We do feel quite done," Giem said, before I could counter the insult.

"Yeah, we lucked into a ride here, or we might not still do this well," I added, as a hopeful hint for a ride back. Giem frowned at me.

"I thought I heard an aircar. One of the Happy people haul you out here?" Ziehl said doubtfully.

"No, some guy driving through town." I yawned. "What was his name, Giem? Barth? Karth?"

"No, it was Garth—"

"That's it. Garth Riddle—"

"Riddock. Garth Riddock. Know anything about him, Ziehl?" Giem said.

"Know anything about him?" Ziehl gave us the most amazed and appalled expression. "Great Universe, you two must live very protected lives. You'd better stay in good with those of us looking after you."

"Why?" Giem said, as an involuntary shiver ran up my spine.

Ziehl groaned over our ignorance. "Garth Riddock is only infamous throughout FIL for his mysteriously vast wealth. Presumably he's obtained at least a good portion of it through very murky sources. Although no one has ever managed to prove much of anything against him. And that's despite the fact that he doesn't seem to care much about avoiding publicity."

"Hiding out in the open," I said to myself. "A clever ruse."

"Huh? It caused quite a stir here on poor little Big Maxson's Planet when he arrived some months ago," Ziehl said. "He does claim quite openly to be on vacation, period. We don't possess any fantastic sources of income, or any significant criminal element— at least not yet. Many of us fear he'll attract the latter by his mere presence here. I suggest you both give that man a wide berth. He simply can't be up to any good here."

Giem and I exchanged puzzled looks. Why would anyone like that even bother to notice us? I wondered if Ziehl could have it wrong. Perhaps the poor guy was just looking for a break—from a lot of vicious rumors.

"If you two feel ready, I'm glad to give you a lift back to your hotel, if only to make sure you don't get into any more trouble tonight."

We accepted her offer gratefully, and got up stiffly to retrieve our belongings. We yanked our boots back on sore feet, put our packs on sore shoulders, turned our coveralls inside out, and rolled them up to carry them. We followed Ziehl out to her airtruck. In short order Ziehl dropped us off with a final urging to consider her earlier advice. "It's not too late to cut a few corners on your study, as long as you still produce decent stats. Oh, and one other suggestion—"

"What?" we said, pausing in front of the hotel doors.

"Reschedule your appointments tomorrow, and come over to my place instead for some lessons."

"Lessons?"

"I raise the three main native domestics. I'll teach you the right way to handle them."

"Leave it to Dr. Hako to find us a planet with people to look after us," I said as we reached our room.

"Dim Side Cynic," Giem said. We raced each other to the shower. I swear I got there first, but Giem won by brute force.

CHAPTER 12

Ziehl spent the next morning teaching us the rudiments of dairy quelsh handling, with her herd of waist-high, blue and green scaled native ungulates. Only one quelsh rammed hard into me once in the process. Over lunch sandwiches in her house, she made us promise not to retrieve eggs from quelsh nest boxes for farmers—not everyone bothered to dehorn their layers.

She also taught us to not directly risk handling her trained, two-story tall native skitsh. I felt gratefully impressed. It didn't seem wise to get anywhere near the immense feet of these bluish-grey reptiles, whose thickly scaled hides provided another whole ecosystem for insect life and small reptiles.

And we didn't find skitsh difficult to avoid—what with their foghorn-like calls, and the way they made the ground shake with their footsteps from nearly a kilometer away—fortunate, since even a shedding scale could cause an innocent bystander serious injury. We followed Ziehl upstairs, where she called her skitsh in with a loud horn and food trough reward controls on a second story balcony.

A ridiculously small, segmented, bright green tree snake cut short our skitsh lesson. It sent the herd stampeding away from their feed and back into the woods.

Lastly Ziehl threw in a lizard riding class, after we learned basic restraint, grooming, and tacking to her satisfaction. "You might as well understand why we raise and train these critters." We had no objection to the fun lesson. Afterwards she suggested we go out for dinner.

"I don't know. I think we'd need to shower and change before—"

"Forget that," Ziehl said, interrupting Giem. "I'll take you somewhere informal, where all us smelly ranchers hang out."

"I'm afraid of the cost," I said. I still had a stash from the sale of my mother's farm. It felt like eons before I'd earn anything more, and I'd had a scary glimpse of station prices.

"We'll receive a discount," Ziehl said. "Places that serve my produce give me a price break. Come on, let's drive into town. Or have you two missed out on socializing for such a long time that you're afraid?"

Maybe I was. After that challenge, I refused to admit it, and Giem agreed to Ziehl's plan. We hopped in Ziehl's airtruck, and as we rode towards town, I looked all around.

"Ziehl, don't you have restaurants near your ranch? Or are they too expensive?"

"What are you talking about? We have to go into midtown to eat out. I don't live near any restaurants."

Giem and I glanced at each other. Riddock had lied to us. Why? Just to act nice?

Ziehl drove us to a small, rustic restaurant and bar, and worked to find an empty spot for her airtruck a couple blocks away. We walked back, ducked inside, and joined a rowdy group at a large central table. The owner hand-delivered a pitcher of a local brew to our table and took Ziehl's orders for us.

Ziehl knew everyone sitting at the table. She loudly introduced us to too many people to keep track of names early on. Most were dressed in coveralls and other work-dirty farm clothes. I did a lot of nodding and listening as I hoisted a heavy mug and cautiously sipped at a huge bitter drink passed down to me. When my dinner arrived, even with a voracious appetite I was only able to make a small dent in the huge slice of quelsh egg, cheese, and vegetable quiche.

While I chipped away at it, table talk focused on sex and scandal, lesser station gossip, and the local economy, in that order of emphasis, with Ziehl leading the way in the raciest stories. My ears began to burn, and Ziehl started in on parties at the U of O.

"You also attended the FIL University on Olecranon?" I interrupted Ziehl, with a subject I could add at last a vector to. Small galaxy.

"Yeah, sure. Got my bachelors there in ranch management. Giem and Taje can confirm just how vacfully desolate the whole planet is. One of those bombed-out worlds some vac-heads had to quit warring over to join FIL. Must have been a cheap bargain for the campus. Nothing to do there except study, so we used to become rather nova after finals."

As her audience gradually coaxed Ziehl into revealing increasingly lurid details, and our tablemates became louder, I scanned the room. Most customers seemed to consider this normal. Two traders at the next table over seemed too engrossed in their own dealings to even notice us, and I couldn't help eavesdropping.

"You've got to commit to grueling sixty, eighty hours of trade per week, if you want to succeed here. If you have family, don't ship them out here with you. You won't have time for them. I'm talking real success—not just subsistence—even very early, wealthy retirement, if you dock into this with me."

I couldn't make out the potential recruit's answer, and I could tell this conversation had even caught Giem's ear.

"I mean it," the trader said. "If you just want to get by, go partner with someone else. I'm looking for total commitment—like a Big Maxson breakfast. Scan it this way—you order quelsh eggs and skitsh sausage. The quelsh is involved, but the skitsh is *committed*."

Giem and I exchanged looks of horrified amusement. Neither of us could imagine sacrificing life that intensely, just for business. It did make me think. Maybe I had chosen a better path.

Not everyone in the room enjoyed or ignored our ruckus, however. One scowling Kralvin, at a small table near the door, slammed his unfinished drink down and stomped out, lashing his dark furry tail behind him. The three of us got up from our table late, enjoying rather silly spirits.

"Where's your better half tonight, Ziehl?" An older Altruskan cackled, showing his thick yellow teeth. "We missed her."

"Since she's not here, she probably worked late again," Ziehl said cheerfully, as she led Giem and me to the door. "Maybe dehorning her new quelsh calves," she added, pointing at her forehead in obvious mockery of the elderly Altruskan's two short, neatly trimmed horns, poking out from his yellowed bangs. "I'll tell her you missed her when I see her tonight."

The remaining customers laughed as we exited. Ziehl strode between us, and offered to drive us back to our hotel. "Was that so scary?" She put her arms on our shoulders.

"I had a great time, Ziehl. Thank you." I still chuckled, remembering all the jokes and yarns.

"It's a miracle," Giem said. "Taje is smiling."

"I told you Big Maxson has a lot to offer, and that was just a taste of it. The best part about this place is the people."

"I think the best part is your stories," Giem said teasingly. "And I thought I led a wild life before vet school!"

"Speaking of which," Ziehl said, swiftly guiding us around a corner and down a side street, "we didn't get much in the way of tales out of you two. We'll have to remedy that. It's only fair."

"Well, I don't think we can live up to yours," I began, hoping I wouldn't have to explain.

"No problem. I'll listen anyway. And you obviously need practice socializing—"

"Thanks a lot," we both objected.

"Glad to know you care so much for our welfare," Giem said, with little sincerity. "Speaking of which, are you sure this is the right way back to your truck?"

Ziehl's laughter bubbled off the walls as she led us around a dimly lit corner shop window. Pink and purple glow-bugs tapped its surface, the only other light sources for an especially gloomy little alley. Then Ziehl abruptly reversed course.

Giem and I stood blinking at each other in dumbfounded horror, as we heard the sounds of a scuffle and a body hitting the ground, hard.

We dashed back around the corner. Luckily, we found Ziehl still standing, over someone with dark furry features in the dim shop light. Ziehl had a boot on the Kralvin's chest.

"Who are you?" she demanded as he squirmed ineffectively, and then lay still. "You don't live around here. Why were you following us?"

When he didn't answer, she bent down, searched his belt pouch, and found half a dozen different wristcoms in it—probably with different ID's. She gave them a shocked look, and slipped them into her pouch. "Clear out of here on tomorrow's shuttle, or I'll have you jailed by tomorrow night." With that, she released him, and he silently leaped up and padded swiftly down the street.

"A wristcom thief—or forger—on Big Maxson." Ziehl led us back up the side street. "I can't believe it."

"The criminal element has moved in." Giem tried to gently mock her, in a shaky, breathy voice, which made me realize I was still trembling and swallowing against my pulse. My sweat smelled almost as bad as it had for my parasit exams. It takes extremely sophisticated tampering to forge or use someone else's wristcom. Maybe Big Maxson was a little less slow than it seemed.

"It sure coms that way," Ziehl angrily agreed with Giem. "To think I'll have to be more careful now about walking town streets late at night. Your experiences here must have you wondering about my enthusiasm—"

"How did you even know we were being followed?" I said, amazed, and a little abashed and disappointed that neither Giem nor I had noticed. Hadn't we learned anything in self-defense?

"I heard him sneeze a couple times." Ziehl almost sounded amused again. "Kralvins are usually quite silent when they want to be, yet not on Big Maxson, at least until they see Dr. Devlin. A lot of Kralvins seem to develop allergies here. They claim it's the reptiles, which I doubt, and I don't think they like it here very much."

"I heard that noise and I thought it came from local wildlife in the bushes, angry and hissing at us," Giem said.

"You'd have to stomp on a Big Maxson reptile rather hard to get a reaction like that, when the temperature drops at night," Ziehl said. "A noisy walk won't do it.

Besides, when you've lived on Big Maxson as long as I have, you can hear the difference."

I wondered if the Kralvin who'd left the restaurant in a huff had put on an act. Then he could hide outside, waiting in the shadows for us—why? Comming us for a couple of naive, vulnerable offworlders? Thank the Galaxy we'd had Ziehl with us.

"How come you've lived here for years, instead of planet-hopping, with your FIL training?" I found a chance at last to ask Ziehl.

"I started out on an ag team, on a FIL SEAR Ship. We orbited here a couple times for shore leave, and the last time, I decided not to sign on again. I felt like I'd found home."

We climbed aboard her airtruck and rode in silence. Her encounter with the Kralvin footpad had obviously disturbed Ziehl's mood, and Giem and I felt too tired to make any good conversation. When we reached the hotel, Ziehl scanned her wristcom with sudden alarm, and apologized for keeping us up late.

"I hope you two don't have a busy schedule tomorrow."

"It's not too bad," Giem said. "We took your advice. We're going to try for representative sampling."

"We're still going to cram some," I said. "We'll get a day off each week, and a little more time for our vacation at the end of our study." We had carefully plotted it all out. We didn't want to finish too fast, and have to take up Dr. Bioh's suggestion of a second project, which might fill all the rest of our time here.

"Good. Let me know how it's going near the end of this week, and I'll give you more riding lessons if you wish."

"Our two Intrepid Spies were followed tonight," Giem teased, as she toweled off after her shower.

"For a few micros there I was fused enough to wonder about Ziehl," I said, as I undressed for my turn in the shower. "That's about the third time I've misjudged her."

"Just as the ever-devious Other Side would have us do. And thus the Adventure begins, ruthlessly drawing us into a Tangled Web of Intrigue. We Must Proceed With Caution."

"Hey, I'll say. Look at this bruise I got from Samson."

Giem was impressed—Ziehl's most rambunctious quelsh had smashed capillaries over most of my right thigh that morning. Ziehl had taught us to approach quelsh from an angle, to avoid being rammed head-on. Unfortunately, clever Samson knew how to butt sideways. Ziehl had forgotten to warn me.

I also had a rainbow across my breasts from my encounter with the Keljo lizard's tail. Ah, the gratitude of Veterinary patients. And the worst torture imposed on us over the next several days—from the Other Side, no doubt—became escalating cases of saddle-soreness from our first lesson, to which I was never quite sure how much my bruises contributed. I found it kind of entertaining, however, trying to guess what new colors I'd sport each time I undressed. It turned out, this was only one of the most minor diversions Big Maxson's Planet had in store for us.

CHAPTER 13

"Too bad no one has started a taxi service here," I said, as we turned onto the busiest street so far. Once again, we were running late.

"Always complaining." Giem frowned as she expertly wove between milling tourists and busy station residents. "Dr. Bioh will understand."

"I know. I just hate to foul up the timing of his lunch." Today I truly felt ready to do justice to a second meal in Dr. Bioh's home, and I lengthened my stride to catch up with Giem. "I'm starving. How about you?"

"I hope we can talk and eat at the same time. I'm hungry enough to eat a skitsh—"

"Perhaps then you would accept an invitation to lunch, on me?"

"You again?" I said rudely. Garth Riddock flashed a cheerful smile as he braked his aircar in front of us, repeating his trick of rapidly backing up traffic behind him. His clean clothes and neat, sun-bleached hair contrasted even more than last time with his muddied bushcar.

"Is that any way to answer a luncheon invitation in this town? Name any restaurant within station borders, and I'll put it on my wristcom."

"No thanks," Giem said curtly, with little effort to cover up a look of disgust on her face. We had both learned enough about station prices to understand the generosity of his offer—whatever his motive—which was consequently even more questionable. Giem must have bought Ziehl's story from port to starboard. Now that I knew Ziehl better, I felt inclined the same.

"Dr. Bioh has already invited us to lunch," Giem added coldly, when Riddock didn't immediately drive off.

"Well, I can at least offer you another ride, as a courtesy from one offworlder to others."

Very pushy. My hackles rose, while Giem shrugged and got in, so I jumped in back again. At this point, shouts and honks and screeches from behind did make it the most expedient move. I also wondered whether Giem's sudden supposed indifference covered up a Deliberately Bold Move in the Adventure. Riddock promptly set a straightforward course for Dr Bioh's lab, which Giem and I both observed with relief.

"Not very talkative today?" Riddock commented smoothly, after a minute or two of awkward silence. Apparently Giem didn't feel bold enough to start grilling him. "Have you had a tiring morning? At least you've stayed a lot cleaner today, not that it matters in this piece of junk. You are presentable enough for any bar or café along this street, if you'd like to stop for a quick refreshment along your way."

"We spent all morning on necropsy work, and we're only clean because we took time out to shower and change. That's why we're late," Giem said. Riddock had no prompt comeback. Noting the growing pallor on the back of his neck, I immediately followed up on a malicious hunch.

"Yeah, you can hardly tell that we were drenched in purplish skitsh blood and guts, not too long ago at all," I said. "You should see what a mess it makes to butcher an adult skitsh. Clouds of insatiable insects chased after a dozen meat trucks while we untangled countless meters of oozing bowels, to scan all the writhing worms inside of them. Did you know that skitsh possess seventy-two digestive compartments? That's twice as many as quelsh." And that proved to be a real conversation killer, right up until our curt goodbyes in front of the lab.

"I think we really made him queasy," Giem said the moment Riddock's car whooshed out of earshot. "Taje, you may be the worst liar I've ever met, nevertheless you're sure good at diversions and embellishments. You started spraying it on so thickly I almost felt sorry for him."

Frankly our necropsy work had made us both increasingly uneasy, and I decided to swear off real steaks forever, regardless of social situations here. I understood new colonies couldn't afford cell culture technology, and I didn't have to participate in the alternative. Eating infertile eggs were one thing—actual living animals were another.

"I just invented a new defense against the Other Side," I said, as we made our way around the lab to Dr. Bioh's front door. I picked up Dr. Bioh's door gong mallet, used it, and dropped it. "We'll have to get this defense published in our Operations Manual." We both snickered, and slid promptly into polite smiles when Dr. Bioh swung his door open.

"You're a bit late," he said, ushering us into his living room. "Did the skitsh dissection go alright this morning?"

"Fine," Giem said, choosing a synthfur chair near the black crystal rock coffee table. On it lay a simple wooden tray with plates, napkins, a small platter of sandwiches, and three glasses of krava juice. "It just took us a bit longer than expected."

I sat in the seat next to Giem's, and observed the decidedly conservative display of food. Whether Dr. Bioh had commed it for himself, or it was under the influence of a certain rather talkative rancher, I didn't know. I still felt disappointed. "The ranchers became annoyed with the time we took for our counts, until we pointed out a number of parasite-induced injuries in some of the most valuable stomachs, which provide enzymes for cheese production."

"That's helpful." Dr. Bioh nodded politely as he climbed up on his seat. He urged us to begin our lunch. "I decided to make this very informal today. We can talk while we eat." I shared secret smiles with Giem.

"I understand you're due at Ziehl's this afternoon for another riding lesson?"

So he didn't mind the lessons. Ziehl must have talked to him about that too.

"That's right," Giem said, scooping up a hefty share of vegetable sandwiches, while I tried not to look too conspicuous loading up my plate with all the egg salad sandwiches. I still carried the stink of skitsh blood in my nose, and I inhaled the wonderful bakery bread scent of my sandwiches.

"Ziehl has taught us a lot of helpful techniques for handling the native domestics," I said. My first sandwich vanished in a micro.

Dr. Bioh eyed us a bit nervously, delicately selected a fish sandwich, put it on a plate, and set it on his furry lap. "And your study—I assume it is going smoothly? Have you found any new parasite species?"

"No, not yet. Possibly a few new subspecies," Giem said. Dr. Bioh's "preliminary" studies had proved disappointingly thorough. Nothing had appeared on our scanner that we could name after ourselves, although I must confess I hadn't lost any sleep over it. "We haven't gathered enough data to see if there's any correlation between necropsy parasite counts and fecal egg counts," Giem said. "There often isn't. We have started to see a direct relationship between inadequate farm sanitation and parasite loads. And a few particular parasite species seem to be associated with the worst stomach wall damage, along with a general lack of host health and productivity."

"Good, good, that's important to pursue. These are the sorts of findings that can truly help us." Bioh stared at the empty platter and our empty plates, and stood up. "Excuse me for just a moment."

When he left the room I worried about our pacing again. If this was just the nose of the space liner, we could be in deep vac, and after a few minutes Dr. Bioh simply returned with two small packages.

"You two must be working very hard indeed," he said. "I'm very pleased. It sounds as if you have made an excellent start on your project. Once you become more certain of your sub-species identifications, I can run confirmatory genetic analyses for you. Of course, keep up your data transmissions, and unless any of us notes any special problems, we'll wait to meet again in two weeks. Does that sound okay?"

"Fine." We got up from our chairs.

"We mustn't keep Ziehl waiting." Dr. Bioh gave us each a warm packet and ushered us to his front door. "Maybe these will you keep you from eating too much at her dinner table tonight." He smiled shyly—his brow wrinkled—and wiggled his fingers in goodbye to us.

We waved back as we headed on our way, and tore into his packages.

"Cookies!" Giem said.

"Fresh-baked," I added gleefully.

We devoured them all before we even reached the middle of town, and we inserted a special thank-you note at the tail end of our data report that night. Life, I thought, had become surprisingly tolerable on Big Maxson's Planet.

CHAPTER 14

After a month on Big Maxson, Ziehl graduated us to trail rides. We spent most of a day on one of the longer local trails. It led our lizards on a winding, peaceful course through the almost tropical forest on the outskirts of town, and for the moment I could pretend I was totally free. Free of all homework and worry. Free to go where I wanted, when I wanted.

If only I could search for Shandy, or visit with Aerrem on her FIL Scout Ship, or see Krorn playing his flute at the music school on Tardeam. I succumbed to lustful daydreams, and I had lost all track of time when the nearly daily warm deluge struck. The others laughed when I was last to notice. We snatched raingear from our saddlebags and raced our lizards back to the edge of town.

Ziehl won, of course, pulling up right before the first busy street. Giem was close on her lizard's tail, and she beat Krome, Ziehl's girlfriend, a pleasant, bluish-skinned, younger-looking version of Dr. Hako. I arrived last.

"You took your time." Krome gave me a human smile, while I struggled to keep my lizard standing peacefully with everyone's mounts. As long as we kept the antisocial beasts properly supervised, I knew I could do it, at least in theory.

"I have a morbid fear of falling—stop it, Lizardbreath," I ordered my mount. "I'm not going to let you bite Krome's lizard."

"Let's go to Kaxsie's," Giem said to Ziehl.

"Sure—good food and drinks, at a discount since they're one of my customers." Ziehl shifted around in her saddle. "What about you two? Kaxsie's sound okay?"

"I need to trot on home," Krome said. "These studious visitors have scheduled my ranch for early tomorrow morning, and I don't want the place to look neglected when they arrive."

"Krome only raises cattle and some pigs. She sold off her quelsh. What are you two checking on, her one lizard?" Ziehl gave us a shocked look.

"We're running fecals on nonnative livestock, when we have time for it," Giem said. "And, yes, while we're at it, why not check Krome's lizard for her?"

"You need another lecture about wasting time we could spend having fun instead?" Ziehl said. "What do you expect to find? FIL membership has always required certification of disease-free status for all animal imports, as well as for canned gametes and zygotes—and it requires intra-transit rebugging of imports, and complete sterilization of cans."

"Everyone knows the health certification process was far from perfect, especially in the early years of FIL," I said, more hotly than I intended. Shandy had ended up at my Orphan Center after nearly dying from a foreign plague which had slaughtered his family and everyone he knew on Istrann. "Your earliest nonnative domestics may have brought along their own parasites, and their descendants could still harbor them. Or, even worse, they could be vulnerable to invasion by native parasites, without rebugging to stop them. Without time for host adaptation, local parasites could cause lots of damage."

What I didn't say was that the colony here was probably too new to encounter any serious certification failures of the past—increasingly paranoid FIL export/import restrictions had seen to that. Furthermore, Big Maxson parasite biology probably differed too much from primarily warm-blooded imports to stand much of a chance. And even if local parasites managed to invade alien hosts, such a problem was even less likely to show up in a fecal. Abnormal parasite infections tend to wander far afield in host tissues. I wasn't going to admit to Ziehl that Giem and I were really trying to make our assignment last long enough, and hoping we might stumble on an exciting, rare finding.

"Sounds awful," Krome said, with an exaggerated shudder. "I'll see you all later." She wheeled her lizard around and made it trot away.

"Well, I guess I'll let this pass." Ziehl tried to sound stern, and couldn't completely hide the teasing look on her face.

"You'd better." I worked to get my lizard uneventfully between hers and Giem's. "We com we're collecting our data fast enough, anyway, to finish with almost a month to spare." What Dr. Hako might think of that, Giem and I dared not wonder. We craved time off too badly to not try for it.

"That's smooth." Ziehl allowed her smile to spread across her beautiful face, and she urged her lizard into a brisk walk towards the busy street ahead. Giem followed suit, and I swallowed hard and tried to keep up between them.

"I guess we're riding to Kaxie's?" I said, not mentioning that this meant our first lizard ride on busy streets.

"Unless you want to suggest a better place?" Ziehl grinned evilly.

"Uh, no, Kaxie's is fine—stop it, LB!"

"Pull on your upper reins like this." Ziehl demonstrated yet another complicated maneuver on her lizards' triple reins. "What will you do with all your free time here?"

Giem and I exchanged looks, and I shrugged. Well, we couldn't avoid it. We'd have to tell her sometime.

"We'd like to go backpacking," Giem confessed.

Ziehl tried to look shocked again. Instead she laughed. "Despite all my efforts to socialize you two, you just want to run off by yourselves—hey, it's your choice." She noticed the anxious looks on our faces. "What's the matter?"

"We weren't allowed enough baggage to bring our own backpacking gear," I said. I had to jerk my lizard's face away from an attempted nip at an oblivious pedestrian tourist's rear end, and we all had to muffle our snickers.

"We com we can rent what we need for some extended hiking, if the off-station trails are safe enough," Giem said, as we made it the rest of the short distance to Kaxie's without serious mishap. We used emergency release clips to fasten our lizards' halter lead ropes to widely spaced posts under the eaves. We stuffed our raingear back into our saddlebags.

"I wouldn't worry about the trails out of here. But you'll pay dearly for rentals," Ziehl said, as Giem ordered her mount to lift a front foot for inspection. "What's the matter?"

"I thought so. Cracked claw—see?"

"Not too bad—it hasn't reached the quick," Ziehl said. She kept her lizards' claws clipped and polished, for rider safety as well as to reduce cracking. "Remind us to walk them home. Then I'll show you how to trim it—and cauterize it if needed—and I'll rest her for a week. Now let's get dinner. I'm starved."

Ziehl led our way up a couple wooden steps, across the covered porch, and into the dimly lit restaurant. We sat down in the first empty booth and menus lit up at our places.

"The Pios limited FIL to enough land for an R&R station and outlying support. That doesn't mean they discourage travel," Ziehl said as she scanned the drink menu. "As long as you go on foot—your own, or a mount's. The Pios decided they didn't want major roads cutting through their forests, or flight paths that might disturb their villages or wildlife. And don't worry about wristcom calls out there. The FIL satellite fleet here works great."

"Perfect," I said. "Pios fall under an unusual FIL category, don't they?" I scanned the drinks for something that wouldn't affect my brain, which felt feeble too much of the time anyway.

"Nonindustrial natives yet full FIL members, with cultures judged able to withstand the polluting influence of offworld visitors, right?" Giem reeled off.

"Right," Ziehl said. "Incredibly minimal restrictions apply to travelers here. No aircars beyond station boundaries, except FIL emergency vehicles. No weapons anywhere on the planet more sophisticated than what the Pios have, except in the hands of station police. And, of course, no tampering with the environment, littering, or violence of any sort—the usual FIL standards for tourist behavior, no matter where you go. You don't even have to refrain from telling the Pios about any of the scientific material you've learned in vet school."

"Like the Mumdwars," I said, amazed.

"Like who?"

"Taje is rather well-traveled," Giem said, as she studied her menu.

"Oh. Anyway, the Pios even have a hostel system," Ziehl said. "It's set up mainly for their wandering adolescents, and it's open to anyone with reasonable manners. Hmm, I think I'll start with Kaxie's beer."

The small station tried to put on a big luxury act, and a real waiter delivered our drinks. Thank the Galaxy we did get a discount here. Ziehl and Giem sipped at a local brew, while I indulged in a pink krava shake.

"As for hiking the wilds of this continent," Ziehl confessed, "I've done some myself, and enjoyed it. Big Maxson has a lot of great scenery, and the natives haven't overrun it, at least in South Maxson. They seem to prefer a very specific type of river bank for their villages.

"Kiernan also suspects the Pios eliminated dangerous predators sometime in their evolutionary past. That's fortunate, because visitors are more or less on their own beyond station land," Ziehl warned us. "The station isn't large enough to provide routine patrols beyond its borders. As long as you use some common sense, you should do okay. Besides, Krome and I can loan you a lot of good equipment."

"Hey, that would be great," Giem said, in the middle of making her dinner selection.

"You'd really do that for us?" I said.

"Sure. It's worth it just to scan the happy anticipation on your tired faces. Although I still don't understand why, after a year of grinding away at your studies, you aren't ready for a little more company—or are you two already an item?"

Giem's golden face flared red as we looked at each other. She laughed, startled, while I just shrugged. I'd known since nearly the beginning of the school year that Giem had no interest in female sex, so I'd never tried anything with her. "It's not that way for us," Giem said.

"You sound very antiquated," Ziehl said.

Giem sighed. "We're just vet school roomies who haven't throttled each other. And I haven't scanned many prospects, male, that is, around here—"

"Although we're a lot more common than these two penal colony releases are used to," commented a stocky black-haired man as he walked by, waving a scarred hand. Giem developed a silly distant smile. Ziehl gave us both bewildered looks.

"I can't stand it." I shrank down in my seat. "Everywhere I go on this planet, I'm humiliated."

"Do you know that man?" Ziehl asked.

"I was going to ask you that," Giem said.

"He's a lone trader, and not too respectable about it, from what I hear. A petty opportunist. His name is Davin Mohrogh. He hasn't stayed here long, and I don't know much about him. It looks like you know him better than I do." Leave it to Ziehl to know all the gossip.

"Not really," Giem said. "We've just run into him a couple times."

"Humph. Don't you ever try to stay out of trouble? Have you also managed to just randomly vector into Garth Riddock again?"

"We've passed him several more times on the streets in town," I said, trying to sound as guileless as possible. A smile twitched at my lips as I watched Ziehl's reaction. "He always acts very nice. He remembers our names, says hello, and asks us about our work."

"Great Universe, maybe you two are better off escaping into the woods, before your nova hormones lead you both to destruction. We have plenty better prospects than those two around here—"

"The problem is, the vast majority are transients, just like us, and Taje believes in love first," Giem interrupted, before Ziehl could offer another objection, although Giem politely left out the first-before-what part.

"And I don't want another crush on someone just passing through my life." I sighed.

"I'm no big expert on love, either." Giem shook her head mournfully. "How about sharing a pizza?"

"Sounds good. I recommend number sixty-four—"

"With krazzle claws!" I said, finding them at the bottom of the list of topping add-ons.

"No," Ziehl and Giem snapped back.

"Just a few, on just a portion?"

"No!"

"On a tiny portion?"

"Order them on the side, cover them with your napkin, and eat them fast on your pieces." Giem finally gave in, with her usual demands.

"It's not the same. Oh well." I submitted as usual.

Our steaming-hot pizza and my fragrant side order arrived promptly.

I picked up a krazzle claw from underneath a napkin on my side plate. "Did you know they can really grow these in vats? A miracle!"

"Put that back or in your mouth!" Giem held her nose.

After some silently intense ingestion—interrupted only by brief exclamations as we burned our mouths or dropped toppings in our haste—Ziehl's curiosity got the better of her. I could see it growing on her dark, beautiful, intelligent face. I should have realized we hadn't the skill to keep her redirected from our hot gossip for very long.

"What happened to your love life, Giem? Or would you rather not discuss it?"

Giem swallowed her last bite with difficulty, while my knuckles turned white. "I should learn to start talking about it," she said at last. "I might get over some of my embarrassment if I did."

"I don't even like to think about stuff that embarrasses me, much less talk about it," I said sympathetically, around a mouthful of pizza. A moment ago I'd savored the blend of local cheeses, vegetables, and exquisite Naridian-style crust, topped off from my bowl of krazzle claws. It was light years ahead of dorm fare, yet now it tasted sort of like ship hull. Tourist class.

"That's right, just bury your problems, and let them putrefy," Giem retorted. "I simply feel vac-brained that I ever felt attracted to him, and that I didn't have the sense to cancel our contract right away. I guess maybe I lacked self-confidence to believe I could do any better."

"That's hard to believe," I said. "You always seem so confident in school."

"That's school. Real Life is another matter—"

"School again," Ziehl interrupted Giem. "Can't you two ever dock at any other station? You still haven't told me what was so fused about this guy that you needed to break a marriage contract with him—"

"I didn't break it," Giem said softly.

"Put it this way," I said, as Ziehl tilted her head in puzzlement. "I won't let Giem give me a tour of her glorious home planet until she permanently engraves certain self-defense lessons into her motor neurons."

That shocked Ziehl into silence, while I thought Giem might attack me for mentioning self-defense.

Giem did turn on me. "Thanks a lot, Taje."

"Just trying to help you talk about it." I sunk down in my seat again. "Thought that's what you wanted."

"You might give me a chance to speak for myself."

"Hey, I didn't mean to start a fight," Ziehl said. "Are you two sure you're not a couple?"

"Fights are rather your specialty, aren't they, Taje?"

"Giem—"

"What's the matter?" Giem said with mock innocence. "Don't you want Ziehl to know all about your sordid past too? It's only fair, although I must admit at least I know who and where my parents are, and I don't have a criminal record."

"Giem!"

"A criminal record?" Ziehl's shocked look returned, and she replaced it with an evil grin. "I had no idea I was asking such leading questions. Taje, you always look pathetically innocent. I would never have thought to add you to Big Maxson's new list of criminals."

"It's just a juvie record," I said. "Some minor mischief in my distant youth. No big deal."

"Yeah, nothing big," Giem said, "just micro items like starting a full-scale Orphan Center riot and illegal tech exchanges with non-FIL aliens. That theft of a FIL ship never even got on her record—"

"She's distorting all of it. As a FIL pre-ecology student, I had to help take a ship, and we ran into an unexpected and rather tricky First Contact—"

"A First Contact? As an ecology student? How did you ever end up in vet school?" Bafflement overtook the impressed and astonished looks on Ziehl's face.

"I realized I was more into promoting survival of the unfit." I grinned.

"That would create rather a conflict." Ziehl smiled, and made an exaggerated sigh over her empty glass. She and Giem ordered second drinks. "Speaking of unfit," Ziehl gazed at me again, "where did you get that limp? Right knee, isn't it?"

My turn for surprise. "I didn't know it still showed. I'm usually not aware of it, unless I've recently and rather thoroughly abused it."

"It's subtle. I've had to learn a lot, raising various critters without a vet to call on."

Another hint for our services?

"Taje busted her knee back when she stumbled on a Lost Race." Giem laughed at her own pun, while I choked.

"I didn't want to go through rejuve, with prevet training about to start. I settled instead for orthopedic surgery and some fake parts," I said, another rapid and useless attempt at redirection.

"You stumbled on the First Contact, huh? Recruit them for FIL membership?"

"Uh, yeah, with the help of my pre-ecology class. Although I guess if I don't tell you that this wasn't my only discovery, Giem will. I've played a part in finding two intelligent species. In both cases, it was mostly just being in the right place at the right time."

If you could call it that. Philiki's pet had nearly fried my pain receptors before I commed that one out, trying to restrain the creature for Dr. Korax aboard *Onnarius*. It hadn't occurred to anyone else in the Veterinary Care Unit that an intelligent species might communicate via electrical pulses.

I saw the fuel spilling out of Giem's next remark before she could even launch it. I felt like shrinking even more. Most of my prevet experiences were so humbling that I didn't feel I had a right to brag about any of it.

"Taje is famous for her discoveries," Giem managed to add in anyway. "She's been Commended twice. We just have to keep her out of trouble long enough that she doesn't die a virgin."

"Giem!"

"Well." Ziehl lounged back with a look of wicked anticipation. "I do believe I'm at last managing to extract some interesting stories from you two."

We enjoyed a long night—longer than we should have allowed it to get. I'm sure we were trying to prolong our day off, demonstrating a lack of self-control we knew we'd both regret, early the next morning. We just didn't realize how much.

CHAPTER 15

I felt ill from lack of sleep the next morning, and Giem looked worse, so we agreed to splurge on a rental aircar to get to Krome's ranch. After we ordered our destination, I curled up in the back seat and left Big Maxson's Planet altogether.

"Where are you, Taje?"

"Hmm?" I almost woke up.

"A million light years away." Giem started to shake her head, and abruptly thought better of it. "Just where in the Universe do you go, right when I need you? If we're truly going to do this, we need to get out and start."

Giem paid the car and we found our first project waiting for us on a picnic table outside Krome's barn. Giem collapsed on a bench and I sluggishly followed suit. The odor wafting from two rows of labeled cups was unmistakable.

"I see Krome went to the trouble to collect cattle and pig fecal samples for us," Giem said, muttering into her arms on the table. "Let's start with the swine samples. I don't think I could handle a bunch of screaming Earth pigs this morning. I had commed we'd just do her lizard and then excuse ourselves." She slowly rolled up her sleeves, laid her head back down carefully on her arms. "You watch the monitor. I've got a nova headache."

"It's all those poor brain cells, crying out in their death throes," I said. I dumped part of the first conscientiously labeled specimen into the fecal analyzer, gave it the pig's ID number, and watched the rapid flash of sampling views while it processed. "Why didn't you take an antidote?" I asked Giem. "You've got to help me out. Watching the screen makes me motion-sick."

"I thought I'd do okay," Giem muttered from under her bushy hair. "I didn't drink that much last night. Must be sleep deprivation. Besides, how can you feel sick? You only drank a krava shake at Kaxie's, and you didn't even eat any breakfast this morning."

"What's the matter—you regretting yours?" I said. "You know what lack of sleep does to me. Oh, Great Galaxy!"

"I don't believe that's quite what you're looking at. Are you sure you didn't sneak in a couple real drinks last night?" Giem said.

I ignored her question. The little analyzer screen had frozen on one view, and it flashed a red light and beeped at me. Giem didn't bother to look up. "What's wrong? Another false positive?"

After some early and very misplaced excitement, Dr. Bioh had taught us to program the analyzer to ignore certain ingested native parasite eggs that just passed harmlessly on through the digestive tracts of imported livestock—proven out by our necropsy work—sometimes we still had to add another to the list.

I shook my head. "I deserved that grade I got in parasit. This ovum looks vaguely familiar. Only the machine isn't programmed for it, and I can't ID it."

"What do you mean? Maybe you have discovered a native parasite Dr. Bioh hasn't cataloged yet?" Giem looked at our analyzer with a hint of hope on her bleary-eyed face. "Oh no. This can't be right. Large, yellowish-brown, ellipsoid, thick-walled—it looks like a Terran roundworm egg."

I scanned her through a dim haze of nausea. "That's impressive," I said, sincerely. "Blast. Does that mean we have to run all of these samples?"

"It's impossible! Pigs only carried ascarids like these before the big FIL quarantine and decontamination crackdowns. Which followed right on the jets of the Beta Two eco-disaster, and the plague wipe-outs on Drexus and Trikan. You might see a nematode infection on one of the oldest human colonies, and not get too excited—"

"Only here—"

"Here it's a disaster—a total disaster. Oh, my head. It feels like it's going to split open!"

Probably more than one explanation existed for this find. Our fused brains immediately docked at the worst-case scenario—that this single worm egg might represent screaming evidence for the first failure ever in the supposedly fool-proof FIL microfloral barrier program. We'd have to report it, and not just to Dr. Bioh. My head began to pound too.

CHAPTER 16

"You're sure you've depopulated every pig on Big Maxson's Planet?" The Head Interplanetary Public Health Agent pointed several accusing, cream-streaked, purple tendrils at Giem and me in Dr. Bioh's lab.

"Absolutely," I said, frowning. I asked myself was that their platitude for mass slaughter? That order from the FIL Interplanetary Public Health Agency team, before they'd even departed for Big Maxson, had made us less than well liked. After one angry farmer sicced her fiercest lizard on us, we'd learned to go in with a police escort. Crandall was lucky we hadn't pressed charges against her—for attempted murder—which would have only added to our lack of popularity.

"And you thoroughly necropsied every single one of those pigs?" Another team member clacked her chitinous orange claws at us.

"What do you mean? Wasn't that the purpose?" Giem had become frustrated enough for sarcasm. Our first euthanasias—an almost totally healthy population of dozens of innocent swine. The job had sickened us, even if it immediately controlled the primary disease vector.

"We could have easily treated all of them instead of slaying them!" I said, disgusted. Fused FIL bureaucrats. Giem looked ready to swat me. Of course we both understood that it was far more economical to eradicate a contagious disease—even a fairly benign and treatable one, like this—in its early stages, than to live forever with its consequences. Fortunately the same control tactic couldn't be used on humans, who were also susceptible to *Ascaris suum*.

"Too risky!" The human IPHA member scowled at us. "How do you explain only finding one other infected littermate, besides the two on Krome Meki's property? Where did this parasite come from? You didn't find it in any other cohorts or previous generations, even on the farm where all three were bred and sold."

"Among those still living, no," I said. The source farm sat right behind one of the largest station restaurants. "Either the original carriers were slaughtered, or these were the first."

"No doubt they weren't the first. Many nonnative domestic animals and colonists here pre-date the microbe exchange program. Someone must have fused a routine interplanetary canister disinfection, or gotten careless on an import health scan—"

"You're sure you can totally discount a microfloral barrier failure?" I said, interrupting the Head Agent.

"None of the three infested swine had been tanked, or descended from tanked pigs," the Kralvin IPHA said, before blowing her nose.

"Well, no," I said, "however, where did the infection come from? If the parasite infection pre-dated microfloral conversions, why aren't a lot more of the local pigs infected now?"

"Good husbandry could explain that." The angrily quivering Head Agent summarily dismissed my question. "We'll need prompt access to the stasis unit where you've stored the carcasses, and all your records. Yours too, Dr. Bioh. We understand you confirmed the diagnosis with DNA analyses?"

"That's correct." Dr. Bioh smoothed his elbow fur tiredly. His entire coat lay in disarray. "We suggest you retire these students from further station duties, at least for the time being, to clear the decks for us. We know all three of you have worked hard at this problem. Far more often than not, there's a very mundane answer for these sorts of questions, and we normally don't need to set off any planetary or system-wide alarms. We haven't even had time to check through your port security systems. Who's in charge of them, besides yourself?"

All the IPHAs gave Dr. Bioh quite stern looks, and he somehow shrank even smaller. Now I was glad I was still just a lowly student.

CHAPTER 17

"You must understand, they can't begin to consider a microfloral barrier failure," Dr. Bioh said quietly, after the four IPHAs, obviously space-lagged and annoyed with even being here, left the station biology lab to track down Dr. Devlin and the Police Chief. "If a barrier break-down did occur—"

"Which didn't have to happen with a pig, since humans can carry it—"

"They'd have to declare a station quarantine," Dr. Bioh said patiently over my interruption, "perhaps even a planetary or interstellar quarantine. Can you imagine the subsequent logistical and economic nightmares?"

"It's better to bury their heads in the mud?" I said. "While everyone complacently relies on their microfloral barriers, we may risk some truly terrible disease breaking through somewhere. Maybe even plagues, all over FIL!"

Dr. Bioh's mild brown eyes met my furious green-eyed gaze. "I happen to agree. The IPHAs are under orders to find answers, and they've taken the investigation out of our digits. Whatever the outcome, I do want you two to know how much I appreciate all the work you have done here. Although it may have provided you with uniquely vital experience, I'm quite sorry you had to get involved in all the challenging repercussions."

"So are we," I said.

Giem gave me a critical look, apparently lacking the energy to do anything more to me.

"What you need to focus on," Dr. Bioh leaned forward in his chair, "is how much of a report you can put together with what you've done. You realize you may not be allowed to collect any more data before you return to school?"

I gaped at him in horror, while at the same time giving him extra credit for even thinking of us at a time like this.

"We have gathered over half the information we planned on compiling for our report."

Well, just barely, and I made no effort to contradict Giem's ever-Bright assessment.

"Report what you can for me," Dr. Bioh said. "It will have to suffice, along with your IPHA report. I'm wondering what will you do with the rest of your break? Do you need to find some other project to fulfill your summer work experience requirement? Or perhaps you must return to school early, for another assignment?"

Ugh. That would completely fuse our summer! I had to think fast. Using the rest of our time here for a vacation probably wouldn't fly with Dr. Hako, and if we weren't allowed any more station work and didn't return, we could flunk. "Hey, what if we could talk a local Pio village into a comparison study? We could run fecals on some of their domestics and compare husbandry techniques."

"That might prove quite revealing." Dr. Bioh groomed his wrist thoughtfully. "How would you travel? You know you can't drive beyond station boundaries."

"We can walk," I said.

"Ziehl has a lot of camping equipment we could borrow," Giem added. We exchanged our first smiles of the day.

Dr. Bioh twitched his whiskers happily for the first time since we'd called him about Krome's pigs. "I don't see how anyone could object, if you're able to obtain permission from the Pios. Have you had any experience with interspecies relations? You'll have to approach this very carefully. The Pios may have serious trouble understanding what you're trying to do, and may become insulted by it if they do."

"Taje discovered and recruited a whole new intelligent species for FIL membership," Giem said, once again leaving out the fact that my classmates did most of the talking, and the Shielvellens just ended up feeling sorry for me, my broken knee, and my dead mount.

"I received my prevet training aboard a FIL SEAR Ship, which visited many planets," I said, instead. "I think we can handle it. What have we got to lose by trying?"

Giem and I shouted aloud with glee as we headed back through town to our hotel. Dr. Bioh had agreed to my idea, with delighted relief.

"Did you notice he didn't even offer the IPHAs any food?" I said, with shock. "I bet they left Dr. Bioh's lab ravenous!"

Giem and I looked at each other. "And recently rebugged!"

The first time we passed an open interspecies lunchtime restaurant, I peered inside the wide open doors and Giem peeked beside me. Sure enough, we saw all the IPHAs at a table, shoveling down their food and making wristcom calls. One looked up at us, banged the table, and we sped away.

CHAPTER 18

"All you'll need to buy is food. I should also download my special Winnett Wilderness trail instructions— they're the smoothest—and some topo maps, into your wristcoms. Where do you want to go?" Ziehl said, as we sifted through the splendid backpacking equipment heaped on her sitting room floor, gathered by her and Krome. We had just dropped our luggage off in one of Ziehl's guest bedrooms, to spare FIL further hotel bills during our absence.

"Isn't that data proprietary?" I wondered again about cost.

"She already owns the Winnett instructions and maps," Krome said, winking an eye. "Ziehl asked you a question."

"Where's the nearest Pio village?" I answered.

"Well, the closest is about three days' hiking from here," Ziehl showed us on her holo contour map. "You ride a Pio ferry across West Maxson River. That will take you to a well-used trail that tags along streams most of the way, for water supplies. There is a problem."

"What?" Giem said.

"Well, wouldn't you prefer a less popular trail? I can't guarantee you won't run into any irate pig farmers on this one." Ziehl downloaded an exquisite, extensive topo map into our wristcoms.

"Let's see." Giem studied the map. "Well, if we feel too harassed, we can always strike out cross-country to get to the village." Giem traced out a rough shortcut through the holo her wristcom projected, with her finger. "And the next nearest village along a different route, northwest of the station, looks like maybe two weeks of hiking from here. That's too far."

"Do you really have to work? Why not strike into real wilderness? Or even visit some of the beaches on the east coast?" Krome asked, pointing at her map.

"I doubt we'll pass our summer externship if we don't work," I said. "Besides, I want to meet some natives before we leave, and I hear the Pios who visit this station aren't typical."

"It's true most natives just don't seem interested enough in us to visit here," Ziehl said reluctantly. "I guess I'm going to have to admit the real reason I'm concerned about this trail."

"What's the matter?" Giem laughed. "Will we share it with Garth Riddock?"

"Well, I have to admit, the word is he and a few of his people headed out in that direction today," Ziehl said.

"Really? I was just joking," Giem said.

"Well, I'm not," Ziehl said, "and I'd rather hear you've decided to go elsewhere. Forget about extra work. You deserve a break, and everyone knows it who needs to."

We claimed we'd think about it. Truthfully, we didn't think we had much choice, and we still had trouble taking any warnings about Riddock seriously.

We left the next day after the usual early afternoon shower, and after we promised Ziehl we'd try not to attract his attention if we vectored anywhere near Riddock.

"You're getting a late start. You'd do best to trigger the tent before dark—there's a good campground just after you get off the ferry," Ziehl said.

"Yes, mother," we teased her, and hugged her goodbye. We knew right then we'd miss her terribly when it came time to ship back to school. Sometimes it feels like the whole Galaxy is just too blasted big, and filled with too many partings.

CHAPTER 19

Giem and I set out at an easy pace, with the benefit of top-of-the-line modern packs and gear for a possible month-long expedition, and we reached West Maxson River at sunset. The cloudy sky turned pink and orange above dark green foliage towering all around us. We stood on a grassy rise and admired colorful reflections on the quiet, wide river before us. Gold and orange glow-bugs swirled among the dark trees and over the water. Although we were strapped into full backpacks, a great weight seemed to lift from our shoulders.

"What's in your belt pouch?" Giem said, looking at it curiously. I suppose because our borrowed backpacks had plenty of room for all our stuff.

"Emergency food and my old pocket knife," I said, patting it.

"Emergency food, what for?"

"You never know," I said, from vacful experience. "Think the ferry still runs this late?"

"I don't know," Giem said. "Let's find out."

We walked on down toward the ferry dock, where a loud exclamation broke the peace of dusk.

"This is my fourth trip out this way! What do you mean, you can't let my horses across this time?"

"That voice sounds familiar." Giem quickened her pace.

"That's what I was afraid of." I followed reluctantly. Had we found more trouble this fast?

Well, what we found was Davin Mohrogh, having another argument. He stood near the dock along with a Pio and three bay horses. They faced a second, slightly taller, sort of a shriveled-looking Pio. Until we tramped closer, it was hard to follow both sides of the conversation with our wristcom translators.

The taller Pio was raking the air sideways with claws which didn't seem retractable. "I've heard it's a bad disease, a bad disease from foreign animals. I won't be responsible for letting you spread it," were the first words we made out over the Pio's hissing voice, which translated as an older male.

Giem and I exchanged amused glances. The IPHA folks thought they hadn't launched any big panics yet?

"You've let me do this before. What difference will it make today?" Mohrogh glanced over at us with annoyed distraction, which dissolved into surprised pleasure. "Besides, the parasite was only in pigs, not horses. Here are the two doctors who discovered the problem. They'll confirm I'm telling the truth."

"That was a vac-brained thing to say," I told him after turning my wristcom translator off. "You've lied!"

I realized some wristcoms and translator bracelets were still on. I wasn't particularly sorry.

"Besides, if you quit shouting, he might understand you better," Giem said. "How can he possibly hear your translations?"

"Look, I've got urgent business on the other side and I'm late. If you can't help me, get out of my way!"

With that, Mohrogh shocked Giem into silence. I hauled her forward. "Come on, Giem, we don't have to take this." I turned my translator back on. "Sir," I addressed the ferry Pio, "we didn't bring any animals. Can you take us across?"

"Of course."

"Wait a micro—what am I supposed to do?"

Giem and I glanced back at Mohrogh and the silent, probably younger Pio standing beside him. The latter wore a vest with multiple pockets similar to Mohrogh's, a slender translator bracelet, a belt with a sheath knife, and nothing else. Unlike humans, green-scaled Pios seemed to have nothing private to hide, beyond a subtle groove in their crotches.

I wondered how Mohrogh had managed to get any Pio to go partners with him. Peaceful co-existence, rather than teamwork, seemed to rule natives and aliens on Big Maxson. This didn't look like an average Pio. Offworld influence showed. This was only the second Pio I'd seen wearing any clothing, an extremely alien—and I should think useless—concept for a cold-blooded person.

The Pio gazed straight back at me with a colorfully striped face, until I realized I was staring. Embarrassed, I returned my attention to Mohrogh.

"Swim. Or leave your horses behind," I suggested nastily, and Giem snickered.

"May I run your payment, please?" The ferryman didn't have a wristcom, just a translator bracelet, and he still had a clunky old credit reader. As I downloaded our payment from my wristcom, I wondered what he spent FIL credits on.

He led us aboard the wooden ferry. We set our packs and sat down on opposite bench seats for balance. The Pio picked up a long pole to propel us across the river, with the guidance of a heavy vine rope passing through big wooden rings on the ferry and stretching from bank to bank. We could hear Morogh's curses for a good part of the way across the opaque, darkening, green-brown river.

"Are you really both doctors?" The Pio worked slowly and steadily, his lean muscles twisting under his green scales.

"We're studying to become animal doctors," Giem said. "We did discover worms living inside three station pigs, and we took care of them." She tactfully left out how. "We think we acted fast enough— we don't think this disease will spread to any other animals, especially yours."

She also didn't mention the problem of ground contamination with the sticky, long-lived, microscopic parasite eggs, or the possibility of human infection, and what she did say seemed reasonable to me. After all, the natives were probably in far less danger than humans, and the IPHAs had clearly kicked us out of the problem. I commed they had taken full responsibility for the whole nova mess, including any effects on Pio relations.

"That is good news," the Pio said, shifting a long-fingered grip on his pole. His green scales faded out to green skin on his palms and the inner surfaces of his limbs, chest, and colorfully striped face.

I found his slender hands especially interesting to watch. He had five digits which included two thumbs on each hand, and at least one more joint on each finger than a human had to work with. He possessed vestigial webbing between his fingers and toes, and long black claws on all of his digits. His feet also had five toes each—if I didn't count the dewclaw above his two rear toes.

"Out here, I hear a lot of rumors," the ferry Pio continued, "which often provide a lot of the amusement of this task. However, sometimes I find it difficult to sort out the truth. The group that talked about the disease yesterday couldn't tell me much—just vague warnings that frightened me."

"Who was in that group?" Giem said eagerly.

"I don't know. I've taken one of them across here a number of times before. A tourist. Human, like you."

"Was he pale in color?" Giem asked him.

"Yes, especially the fringe on his head—which was much shorter than yours—and he had sky-colored eyes. He didn't know as much as you about the station disease."

"Garth Riddock," we said to each other, feeling again like Intrepid Spies. Few other humans could match that description. Was he trying to slow pursuit? By whom? Or did he just indulge in innocent rumor mongering? To be fair, lots of wild stories had circulated ever since our discovery of the nematode outbreak, which had also kept us much too busy for further interactions with Riddock.

When the elderly Pio let us off at the far bank, he lit a lantern on the dock. He pointed out the trailhead and a nearby campground, occupied by several shelters, and we heard the low murmurs of other campers. Before parting company, we reassured the ferry Pio that bringing horses across shouldn't cause any problems.

The sun had set. Before we hauled our packs back on, we fished out lights to supplement the faint glow from nearby night blossoms and their pollinators, and stoves farther off.

"Where do you want to camp?" I said, assuming here somewhere, although I still felt fresh and energetic.

"The trail here is wide, smooth, and obvious," Giem said.

"You want to keep going?"

Giem projected the map holo on her wristcom. "There's another good camping area right about there." Giem sunk her fingertip into the image several kilometers up the trail. "I don't see any tricky parts beforehand. If we do become confused, we could always return here, or just pull off the trail and camp where we stop until morning."

"Let's try it. It sure zaps hiking under a hot noon sun. I feel like I could walk forever tonight," I said. "Only let's not tell Ziehl about this."

"And miss a chance to tell her how we avoided the crowds?"

We laughed as we set out on the night trail together. Finally it felt good to just be here.

CHAPTER 20

Having hiked well into the night, we slept in at our first campsite, between the trail and a stream. By the time we got around to packing up, Mohrogh rode up the trail. His native partner stood in shortened stirrups on the horse behind his, and their pack horse followed on a lead behind the Pio's mount.

"Getting kind of a late start, aren't you?" Mohrogh grinned, looking his usual ready-for-action, cocky self. Positively disgusting.

"You should talk," Giem said, laughing back at him. "Didn't the ferry return to the east bank until this morning?"

"No thanks to you."

"Hey," I objected, "it's thanks to us you have horses here at all to get ahead on."

"Well, think about that while you eat our dust," he said, as they rounded a bend in the trail ahead.

And that's what we did, as the dusty trail became rockier and steeper, the day hotter, and our packs somehow much heavier. We soon learned most people rode this trail, which meant we also had to work at avoiding fresh horse piles and a variety of other trail offerings typical of our summer. Carnivorous lizard scats with their hovering little clouds of sparkling insects stunk the worst, and all acted as taunting reminders of easier ways to travel.

Normally I would catch my breath, slow my pounding heart, and dry my sweat with frequent rest stops to enjoy the scenery. My new hiking partner set a fast pace, and I had to push hard to keep up with Giem. Nor did she let us dally much to chat with the few other travelers on foot, although some heading down seemed interested in exchanging news.

When we did stop off the trail long enough to remove our packs and eat lunch, our third camping meal confirmed a hunch we'd begun to suspect the night before. The colorful packaging was about the only interesting part, and at best bore only an imaginative relationship to the stingy contents.

"I hate to admit that Mohrogh is right about anything. This junk is worse than dorm food." I dug a hole where I sat, to bury my picked-over, thankfully biodegradable meal packet beneath the nearest bush. I was still ravenous, which was sufficient comment unto itself.

Giem frowned at her so-called lunch, nevertheless dutifully finished it before burying the container and sealed up her pack in preparation for our departure. "Come on. We've still got quite a ways to go, most of it uphill."

"Hey, I'm still recovering from murdering every pig on Big Maxson." I picked lethargically at tri-bladed blue-green grass carpeting the stream bank. "How about a little time for digestion before we move on? It's not as if we have a deadline here." The stream filled the warm air with rock-tumbling music, and my eyelids drooped sleepily.

"Digestion? I'm not waiting for that bush to finish your lunch." Giem picked a red fuzzy insect off her boot, let it crawl up one of her fingers, and carefully transferred it to a grass blade before heaving her pack back on. "Come on. We've still got quite a ways to go, and we made a late start this morning."

"What's the rush?" I stood up slowly, and gently plucked two coupled blue crawlers from one of my pack straps. I reluctantly shouldered my load while various sore parts of my out-of-shape student body tried to object. Strenuously. I had to reset some of my straps.

"Taje, don't you have any sense of adventure?"

"How can you ask that, after all the stories I've told you?" I felt stung to the core. "You do realize, by the way, that you can't have an adventure without pain and suffering?"

"Well, we obviously can't have an adventure with our quarry slipping ahead of us."

"The hot sun must have fused your brain if you think we'll ever catch up with Riddock today." I soon guessed her shallow plot. "And what will Ziehl say if she finds out?" I did hasten to finish my pack adjustments and fall into line behind her.

"Who's going to tell her?"

"Not that we've had any practical training for this either," I muttered to myself, sweating and questioning my own motives. "Besides, I suspect the adventure has begun, because it hurts."

"What's that?"

"Speaking of crooks," I said more loudly, between panted breaths, "did you happen to notice that crossbow strapped on top of the sleeping bag roll behind Mohrogh's saddle?"

"Yeah."

"That's illegal, isn't it?" And totally vac-brained, I wanted to add.

"It's at least borderline," Giem seemed oddly reluctant to concede.

The afternoon went about the same as our morning— more hard hiking, mostly up through dense green forest. A stream tried to entice us from around nearly every other bend, especially when we had to step off the trail to allow riders to pass. We also had to side-step more fresh manure on the rocky path.

I enjoyed the forest shade. Nevertheless I was still soon drenched in sweat. I tried not to suck in any bugs while I breathed hard in rhythm with each sore stride. I kept wondering which switchback would take us up the last of the climb over a cruelly deceptive ridge. It kept growing taller the closer I thought we'd got to the top of it. At least the worst of the heat started to lose its grip on us.

Various little chittering reptiles began to vacate their shrinking sunning spots. When I looked up from one of my carefully placed steps on the rocky trail to comment about it to Giem, I nearly ran into her, stopped abruptly in front of me.

"What?"

"Shhh. Look."

Three bay horses—two saddled and a third pack-laden—picked their way, riderless, down the trail toward us.

"Davin Mohrogh's horses," Giem whispered, hitting her pack strap releases. The geldings stopped in a tight bunch, twitched their ears, swished their dark tails nervously, and snorted at us suspiciously.

"He decided to spurn his advantage after all," I joked.

"Hush. Take off your pack and help me block the trail with it. Let's try to catch them."

I slowly slid my pack down and we leaned our packs together in a triangle in the middle of the trail. The horses glanced nervously over their shoulders, and obviously thought about turning back, despite clearly wanting to head home. If they did turn around, we stood little chance of ever catching them.

We climbed forward, and between Giem's coaxing approach, and the horses' obvious reluctance to turn around, she managed to catch each one. Only the pack horse dragged his lead rope. Giem turned them over to me one by one, until she had Mohrogh's in hand.

I stood between the Pio's horses as I held onto their halters. "Look at all the gear on these horses. It doesn't seem like anything is missing. What do you suppose happened?"

"I don't know." Giem absent-mindedly stroked the neck of Morogh's horse, who'd played hardest to catch, only he'd handicapped himself by not wanting to leave his two cohorts. He tossed his head at her first touch, and then began to rub his dusty forehead on her shirt. "I suppose some local reptile may have spooked the horses badly enough to throw both riders. The Pio seemed especially clumsy—I'm not sure he could sit down, with his tail in the way."

"Mohrogh at least looked like he had a decent seat."

"Maybe they tied their horses up together for a break, and they broke loose together," I said.

"So why was only the pack horse dragging his lead rope?" Giem pointed at neatly coiled ropes, clipped on the saddles. "And it seems awfully coincidental that all three horses broke loose at once, the saddle horses still wearing their bridles over their halters, and all three carrying their gear."

"What on Big Maxson do you think happened?"

"Great Universe, Taje, I think we'd better try to find out." Giem turned on her wristcom transmitter. "Giemsan Fane, calling Davin Mohrogh. Davin Mohrogh, please respond if you're receiving this."

"You know," she said, with her hand clamped over her wristcom, "everyone in the area with a wristcom can hear this. I'm not sure calling him is such a good idea."

"Suspecting foul play?" I teased, but then blood drained from my face. A deliberate, very efficient attack of some sort could explain all of this. I remembered Ziehl's warning.

My wristcom emitted static when I tuned it for reception. I held it up to my ear after increasing amp didn't help. "I think we're getting an answer, it's just not very clear. What did he say?"

"Shhh, Taje," Giem said. "We found your horses," she said into her wristcom. "What happened? Do you need help?"

"Help! From us?"

"Quiet, Taje! Okay, Davin, where are you? . . . I meant map coordinates. . . . Alright, we'll try to home in on your signal. We'll get there as fast as we can."

Giem swiftly led us back down the trail to our packs. She handed over Mohrogh's horse to my already full hands, and went to work on our pack frame controls Ziehl and Krome had shown us, which I'd ignored.

Nearly tugged off my feet by three horses who wanted to go home, I said, "Giem, what on Big Maxson are you doing?"

Giem just silently loosened our pack frames into pack horse mode. She moved sleeping bags and Mohrogh's crossbow onto the poor pack horse. She strapped our pads on behind the two saddles, and strapped our packs on the pads.

Giem neatly mounted Mohrogh's large bay horse, and gathered his reins. "You get the Pio's horse, and can lead the pack horse."

"No!" I said. "I've never ridden a horse." So high up!

"You've ridden mounts—what are they called?—on your home planet—"

"Not the same." Low slung yusahmbuls. Fortunately Giem knew better than to mention my similarly low slung, deceased sann on Shielvelle.

"You've had great riding lessons from Ziehl."

"Yeah, on pony-sized lizards."

"Lizards are bigger than ponies!"

"Not much, and they're not as big as these horses."

"I'm leaving, Taje. Hurry up. Just remember you mount a horse on the left side. We must help a fellow human out here. Ziehl did tell us everyone is on their own out here."

Ugh. I didn't need that reminder.

Giem nudged her horse up the trail, leaving me standing there, staring at the Pio's saddle.

I could see right away I'd need to com how to lengthen the stirrup leathers. After my best effort, I gathered the reins and the pack horse's lead rope, grabbed the saddle horn with my left hand, and I used my right hand to hold the left stirrup for my left boot. Once astride high up (I hate heights) on "my horse," I didn't have to urge speed to catch up with Giem. My horses made strides to join their buddy even though they had to climb a series of rocky switchbacks. I learned to lean forward and grabbed the pommel to keep from sliding backwards in my saddle. I have to admit I enjoyed watching all the difficult terrain swing by. Until my horse began to trot.

Lizard riding had taught me the wrong habit—dangerously swaying from side-to-side—until I realized I needed to try to bounce up and down with the horse. Double ugh.

"Taje, you made it!" Giem called down from her horse from near the top of the next ridge. "Hurry up! Davin needs help!"

"Two heroic veterinary students to the rescue," Giem shouted, after we topped the ridge. Ahead lay a smooth stretch of dirt trail through a long meadow, and Giem launched her mount into a full gallop, leaving me behind. My horses abruptly lurched into a full run to catch up.

I yanked on my reins and yelled, but my horse only twitched his ears around at me once or twice. I couldn't pull back with enough force—I had to work too hard at keeping my seat in the jouncing saddle. The ground tearing under his pounding hooves looked so terribly far away.

My lizard-riding instincts again tried to take over, and I almost twisted myself right out of my saddle a couple times. Finally I just stood up in the stirrups, hung onto the pommel, and leaned forward. At the end of the meadow I was almost thrown over my horse's withers, when he jerked back to a walk along with Giem's horse. The pack horse skidded to a halt beside us.

I grabbed my horse's thick black mane stiff-armed, to keep from flying into the back of his neck. I sat down with a pommel-bruised crotch, and long strands of black horse hair clutched in my dirty, sweaty fingers.

Giem laughed. "Sorry, I just couldn't resist it. I'll behave. I'm sure these horses have worked hard enough to get us this far."

"This far?"

"Great Galaxy, Taje, we must keep moving!"

I groaned, and my heart began to pound. What would we find?

Giem led the way, slowly climbing a rocky, winding, up and down trail through the woods. It followed a creek on our right, which receded from sight. It remained audible, gushing over its rocky bed. We passed foliage-enshrouded outcroppings.

A meter winged reptile erupted from a trail-side bush. It soared screaming across our path. Our mounts jumped back and sideways and neighed shrilly.

I ended up almost hanging off the side of my saddle. Ironically, I think only my lizard-riding instincts saved me from falling. Giem had to grab both sets of reins to keep the horses from running off with us.

CHAPTER 21

"Big Maxson's Planet to Taje, Big Maxson's Planet calling Tajen Jesmuhr." Giem laughed again at me. "Saddle up, Taje."

"Like I did that balancing act on purpose?" I wondered again when my heart would quit pounding, and now my head hurt, probably from hanging down and collecting a lot of blood in my brain.

I refocused on our green and rocky surroundings, and looked up at the sky, still a bright blue, although the sun had sunk below the treetops, putting us in deep shadows. After I looked up, my heart and head settled down, thank the Galaxy.

"How much farther do we have to go? Do you have any idea?"

"I'm fairly certain Davin is close. We should ford another creek soon, and find him nearby."

"Why the puzzled look on your face?"

Giem shrugged. "I'm just surprised they didn't make it any farther than this."

Minutes later our mounts splashed across a wide, shallow section of the stream. Some olive and pink shelled reptiles, sunning themselves on the far bank, seemed to consider us very rude. They hissed, leaped into the water downstream, and swam off. We rode around a prominent outcropping of greenish-grey rocks, stacked like irregular, flat bricks. Our wristcoms crackled.

Giem studied this landmark briefly, reined in her horse, and mine stopped alongside hers. We looked all around and scanned no trace of human, Pio, or any other person. Only the creakings of little amphibians, using the rocks like miniature balconies, and horse snorts and whuffles broke the eerie silence. A shiver tingled up my back.

Giem spoke into her wristcom again. "This is Giemsan Fane. Where are you, Mohrogh?"

"I'm right here!" came a shout, from a hillside opposite the creek. Giem and I looked at each other.

"We're here with your horses!" Giem yelled back.

"You'll have to come up here!" Mohrogh hollered.

"A trap?" I asked quietly, baffled, feeling ridiculous when the question launched from my mouth. After all, this was supposed to be Real Life.

"I don't know," said Giem, looking equally mystified, and evidently considering my question seriously. "I suppose we'll have to find out sooner or later. Come on," she said, as she rode into the woods on the left side of the trail, and my horses followed.

How about later?" I mumbled.

She dismounted and clipped her mount and my pack horse to tree trunks, out of sight of the trail. I slid off my saddle and stumbled to a nearby tree to anchor my horse. Back down on the ground I felt extraordinarily short and bow-legged. We snuck awkwardly together up the slope. I exchanged an excited smile with Giem, while my heart hammered in my chest. Maybe we had stumbled on a real Adventure. "Too bad we don't have any FIL-licensed weapons yet."

"I have my pocket knife," Giem whispered, as she patted a pocket.

"I have mine too," I whispered back, feeling one of my mementos from ecology class in my belt pouch. "That's rather against common-sense rules of self defense, you know. 'Any weapon that can be taken from you can be used against you,'" I quoted my first self defense instructor.

"Hush," Giem hissed, and shook her head. "It's also completely vac-headed to not 'always avoid potential danger,'" she quoted our self defense teacher.

"Are you coming?" Mohrogh gave an agonized shout.

Now I found it difficult to keep up with Giem's long stride uphill. When I'd at last caught up with her, she'd followed Mohrogh's voice to the edge of a small open area among the trees and bushes. I joined her to peek through dark green shrubs with oily, star-shaped leaves, at an astonishing sight. Mohrogh and the Pio were tied up to adjacent trees at the other side of the clearing. They were trussed up quite efficiently, standing with their hands tied behind wide tree trunks. No wonder Mohrogh couldn't adjust his wristcom or see his map coordinates.

CHAPTER 22

"Maybe this is some sort of trick," Giem whispered, with enough alarm to temporarily suppress the brief amusement I felt from our discovery. We glanced around, suspicious of the smallest noises.

"Hey, what's the hold-up?" Mohrogh bellowed. "Get up here and help us out!"

"If you've called us into an ambush—" Giem pretended to shout back, while we stayed behind cover, and prepared to flee the moment we scanned anyone else.

"The trap sprang hours ago! It's okay—they're long gone!" he yelled.

"Who's gone?" I said, as I pulled back out of the bushes and left Giem. I circled the shrubs around the clearing, checking the ground for every noisy dry stick and loose rock that might tumble downhill, while I scanned for attackers, even in the trees.

"Great Universe, Taje, where have you been?" Giem whispered anxiously.

"No need to swear at me. I just finished patrolling the perimeter, for any Bad Guys. All clear."

"Shhh. How sure are you?"

I turned my back on her. Giem never seemed to think I was quiet enough. So I pushed noisily through the bushes into the clearing.

"Come on, help us get loose," Mohrogh said, obviously embarrassed. I tried not to snicker. This had become too much like my idea of a perfect plot.

"Not until you tell us who did this to you," Giem said, giving up her cover to join me, after no one tried to jump me. Together we slowly approached the two bound victims, while still scanning for trouble.

"A Pio band," Mohrogh said at last, looking away. "I was just lucky they didn't know to turn off my wristcom."

We stopped in front of him, gazed at the blue synthetic rope bindings, and looked at each other.

"Let's steal his clothes, and see if he's just as good-looking without them," I whispered into Giem's ear.

"Taje, I'm shocked," Giem said aloud, grinning. "I thought you'd just suggest we steal his horses."

"What did she say?" Mohrogh demanded. "And what are you waiting for? This isn't fair." He began to struggle against his bonds, uselessly, and just made himself appear more ridiculous.

"Since when do you play fair?" I stepped over to the Pio. I admired emerald eyes, striped by thin red, orange, and yellow lines of pigment that swirled across the Pio's green, scale-free face. I turned on my com translator.

"Who did this to you?" I said. The Pio didn't move expressionless, pale green, keratin-edged lips; just twitched both arms a bit and stared back at me.

Frustrated, I returned to Giem's side. She had a thoughtful look on her face, while Mohrogh seemed to grow even more uncomfortable.

"You want a deal," he said, at last.

"Right," Giem said, a slow smile forming on her wide lips. "Well, if you won't tell us more, you at least have to promise to share your dinner with us tonight. That okay with you, Taje?"

"Sounds great," I said, startled, while my stomach growled with involuntary agreement.

"Okay," Mohrogh said, obviously astonished by Giem's terms. "Could you *please* cut us loose? My hands are going numb."

We stepped behind them and made quick work of it with our knives, not bothering with all the knots. We neatly picked up all the pieces of rope, while Mohrogh and the Pio massaged their hands. Giem led us back down to the horses. The traders insisted we ride double with them across the creek and down into the woods below, until we reached a hidden clearing big and level enough for a joint, well-used campsite. If Mohrogh was still willing to camp this close here, I commed his marauders must be long gone.

He and Giem took charge of unloading, watering, and feeding the horses, while the Pio unpacked their tent. I picked out a spot and triggered our tent, and when I scanned the Pio gathering up two large water containers,

I grabbed our empty bottles and followed the native back up to the creek. Time for another little Bold Move.

Mohrohgh's partner had a filter pump hose in the creek by the time I arrived, panting, and the Pio lounged on the bank, waiting for the first container to fill. I sat down nearby and decided to turn on our bottle filters, as backup for our rebugging. I knelt on a rock, and dunked my first bottle into the roaring creek.

A splash immediately struck nearby, and another a micro after that, even closer. I gasped and pulled my bleeding hand out of the water, while the Pio, crouched beside me, hefted a large, limp, blue-scaled, beaked, dripping fish. One of the Pio's long nails was buried in the back of the creature's skull. Instantly pithed. I gaped.

"You're either very brave, or very foolish." The Pio finally spoke aloud, and my translator gave him an amused male voice. A smile was anatomically impossible for his horn-edged lips. I thought I could see it instead in his colorful eyes.

"Uh, wow, thank you," I stuttered. I looked down at my hand, and put some pressure on a fresh cut in my right thumb. I was lucky I still had a thumb. And my hand.

The Pio flicked the tip of his tail, and squatted back on his haunches. "It's a gelssk. Very good eating. Do you want it?"

"Uh, if you want it, you deserve it." I gazed back at the rapid current, and realized I now owed Ziehl a water bottle.

"We'll have plenty to eat tonight." The Pio unskewered his catch, dropped it on a rock, and pulled his sheath knife out to seemingly clean the gelssk. Why hadn't the attackers taken his knife away? A Pio conspiracy? He ate the entrails as he removed them. Perhaps he'd bury the rest? No, he scraped the scales off, and handed the carcass to me.

"We'll share it. What's your name?"

"Tajen Jesmuhr. Thank you." I politely accepted the dead prize that had nearly sent me into thumb or hand rejuve. "My friends just call me Taje. Taje the foolish. What's your name? And can I fill the rest of our bottles from your container?"

The Pio made a sound like a sneeze, which my translator turned into a laugh. "Sure. My name is Skorrelsk Tak Grekkan. My friends call me Grek." He switched his hose to his other container. Of course now I noticed he kept his hands out of the stream. He lounged back again on the bank. Clearly he couldn't sit human-style; his thick tail base didn't bend far enough.

I set the reptilian fish down, rinsed my hands in a shallow puddle, and filled our remaining bottles under the Pio's steady gaze. I cleared my throat. "Uh, Grek, can I ask what you're doing with Davin Mohrogh?"

"I'm on vacation, and one of my teachers suggested I visit the station. It was boring." His tail switched restlessly, while I gave him a sympathetic look. I didn't know if he could read human expressions. He just kept staring at me.

"Everyone works hard there, I suppose because you can't get anything at the station without working a lot," he said. "Davin offered me some adventure"—that insidious idea again—maybe chosen by my translator because it had camped out in my head so much, recently—"and some payment if I'd be his guide on a trading expedition. That's how I earned this translator and the vest. I think pockets are a great invention. Looks like you've finished."

"Yep. You might want to top off this container again."

Grek finished filling his second container, sealed it, and switched the filter pump hose back to the first.

"Grek, who tied you two up?" I tried one more time, before we had to head back to camp, in case Davin had somehow inhibited him.

"I don't know."

How could he not have any idea who attacked him? Maybe my translation was too literal or too specific. "Was it really Pios, or aliens?"

"Humans," he said at once. "My people didn't do it. I don't know why Davin would lie about us."

Ah, now we were getting somewhere. "Strangers?"

"Yes, though I've seen them before in the station town."

"Did one have light-colored—uh, stuff, growing from his head?" I didn't know if Pios had an official word for hair.

"No."

"I'm talking about this." I tugged on a wavy lock of my own short hair.

"I know. They were both darker than you, and their fringes were brown, not pale red."

"Both? Only two of them? How did they stop you?"

"They hid in trees over the trail, and they shouted and pointed foreign instruments at us when we rode close. Davin told me they had weapons, and that we must stop."

Foreign weapons and an ambush? I swept up my bottles by their clasps in one hand, and the dead gelssk in my other hand. "Come on. Let's go see what else we're having for dinner."

"Okay," Grek said, as he hefted his containers.

"Did you get enough adventure today?" the wicked part of me couldn't help asking, as I hurried us back down to camp.

"More than enough. I may quit when we get back to my village tomorrow."

I returned anxious to have a private talk with Giem. However, she and Mohrogh had managed to arrange log benches around a low, almost level rock to make a combined kitchen and dinner table. Mohrogh had laid out elaborate cooking gear, along with various spices, sauces, wine, fresh vegetables, fruits, and imported vat meats, which he was busily slicing, mixing, and marinating. I stared at it all, amazed, my mouth watering traitorously. A civilized feast in the middle of a pack trip. No wonder he needed an extra horse.

"Have a seat, Taje," Giem said, bemused. "Looks like we've found ourselves a real cook—are you okay?"

I had wrapped my thumb tightly in my kerchief, and held up the dead culprit. "Did you know you shouldn't stick your hands in the creek?"

"You caught that with your bare hands?" Mohrogh said, impressed. "They bit right through my fishing lines."

"No." I sighed. "Whatever you do, don't stick any body part into water without checking it first. Grek speared it, to save my hand."

"Who?" Giem said.

"Skorrelsk Tak Grekkan is his full name. Grek, meet Giemsan Fane, my—" I was about to say "partner in crime," and decided that might not translate well, "—my teammate."

"And that's a gelssk," Grek added, when he saw Giem eyeing his catch. "Very good eating."

"I see you've eaten your favorite part." Mohrogh nodded at Grek.

"Can you use the rest in our dinner? I'd hate to see it go to waste." After all, the poor gelssk had died for the sake of my uneducated vac-brain.

"I don't see why not." Mohrogh promptly filleted it, and I didn't miss the secret smile that passed between him and Giem. Somehow the atmosphere had grown distinctly friendly in my absence. I excused myself to go use our first-aid kit on my thumb and arrange my stuff in our tent, and I took my time doing it.

I never did get to talk to Giem alone that evening. The warm glow of a stove light, and low merry voices guided me back to dinner, an elaborate fondue. We each got to build our own miniature shish-kabobs from Davin's spread, which even included a pan of large dried insects for Grek. He insisted that I try one and I found it tasted like cultured crustacean, despite grimaces from the two other humans watching me.

Our loaded skewers went into a pot of boiling oil, reminding me uncomfortably of one of Dr. Hako's odd expressions. Were Giem and I getting ourselves into some hot oil of our own out here?

CHAPTER 23

After dinner Giem and I got stuck with doing the dishes, since we hadn't cooked. I thought dinner should include the whole package. Somehow I lost that battle. I felt exhausted afterwards, and left everyone murmuring by the warm stove to go to bed. At least I thought I did. I found Grek, rolled up in a thin brown woven blanket, sound asleep in our tent. Poking, prodding, and loud exclamations did nothing. At last I gave up, remembering what Ziehl had said about cold native exotherms. I sealed the tent from inside, yanked off my hiking boots, and used my sleeping bag as a blanket over my clothes.

I felt strange waking up the next morning without Giem with me. The sun was up, it was warm, and Grek had vanished from my tent with his few belongings. Not wanting to join him, I yawned and pulled out my scribescreen. I couldn't possibly repair the huge black hole that vet school had punched into my journal. Instead I'd decided to try to resume it on our supposed vacation.

I folded up my scribescreen thoughtfully, and was surprised to find Giem yawning as she exited Davin's tent, as late as I left ours. Though probably for very different reasons. . . . Unfortunately we both missed our chance to share in a real breakfast. Mohrogh and Grek had saddled, loaded their horses, and were almost ready to depart.

"Business really presses, huh?" I remarked sarcastically, as I pulled the heat tab on my vac-pack breakfast. At least I still felt partly full from last night. I wondered how Grek felt, having to work hard again. I dropped down on one of the logs at the rock table.

Mohrogh retrieved his tent, and he and Grek checked over their gear on the horses one last time, and they mounted up. I watched Grek curiously. He stood up in his shortened stirrups, presumably to accommodate his tail. He didn't look at all comfortable.

"Well, business is what I'm here for." Mohrogh grinned, somewhat nervously, I thought. "And it won't wait around for me."

"Just don't get jumped by the wrong people again," Giem said, smiling back.

"I'll try not to." He reached back to release his crossbow, slung the strap over his shoulder, and urged his horse up the wooded slope. "See you later, maybe."

"Bye," we both called out.

"Bye!" Grek called back, waving the tip of his tail, and they left.

"Think you'll really see him again?" I asked Giem.

"Why? Jealous?"

"Why should I be jealous?"

Giem saw the look on my face. "You think he used me."

"It had crossed my mind." And perhaps the new microfloral protection program made these kinds of decisions far too easy. I stood up to gather my tent gear for packing, abandoning the rest of my breakfast to the dirt it looked and tasted like anyway.

"What makes you sure it wasn't the other way around?" Giem crammed clothes and dishes into her pack. "Maybe I used him."

"Because I'm on your side." I collapsed our tent and gently shook the fuzzies from it. "Remember? We're friends?"

"I've been celibate for almost two standard years. It's enough to make anyone desperate." She sealed her pack, heaved it on, and began adjusting straps. "Maybe we both used each other."

I rushed to get our tent stashed and my pack sealed up. "You're desperate? I've only been celibate for nearly two whole decades."

"Well, whose fault is that?"

Had either of us slept enough last night? "You're getting mean." I hauled my pack on, while Giem waited impatiently, and a bunch of my muscles cried a chorus of complaints.

"Well, sorry," Giem said in a falsely contrite voice designed to induce guilt in her opponent, without any guilt on her part. I'd heard it before, and fortunately I didn't fall for it this time. I wished I could make myself as impervious to guilt as she was. "Where's your second water bottle?"

"I lost it. Instead of my hand."

"Wonderful."

I stiffly followed Giem back up to the trail, which seemed nastier today too. "How did you get Grek to switch to our tent last night?" I said, as I began to pant.

"I thought it was Grek's idea. You two made friends, fast."

"Are you sure it wasn't Davin's idea?"

"There was no ulterior motive on your part for getting Grek to join you in our tent?" Giem asked, as we crossed the creek on a fallen log.

"What—you mean, to try to have sex with him?" I said, startled. I knew Grek even less than Giem knew Davin, and I knew nothing at all about Pio reproductive anatomy and behavior. Maybe I seemed more desperate than I felt.

"No," Giem said impatiently. "I meant just plain nosiness. I know how fascinated you are with alien cultures."

"Well, it wouldn't have worked anyway," I mumbled, not really listening to her as my brain went to work on the problem.

"You tried?" Giem gasped.

"I'm surprised, Giem. Once again, you're forgetting basic Big Maxson physiology. Being exotherms, Pios can't perform at suboptimal temperatures. It wasn't even a question."

We hiked on in silence for a while after that, until I couldn't stand not asking. "Was it fun?"

"What?" Giem looked around at me vaguely, pulling out of some deep thought. Our hiking made her breathe hard too.

"With Davin? Last night?"

"Oh." She let her breath out in a huge sigh. "It was wonderful." She smiled as her face reddened. "The problem is, it makes me want more."

"What's he up to, anyway? Did you learn anything, oh Intrepid Vet Student Spy, or were you too busy?"

"Hush—someone might come riding right around the next bend, Taje." We hiked around a vine-entangled tall rock without encountering anyone. Giem answered me quietly and a bit grudgingly. "Like Ziehl said, Davin's a freelance trader, with his own little ship parked up at the orbital station."

"What does anyone trade for here?"

"Mostly food. Davin says the most precious items are the native cheeses, though most traders find the Pios rather difficult to work with. That's why Davin went to the trouble of hiring one from town, to help him with negotiations."

I snorted. "The way Davin acted towards the ferry Pio, it's no wonder he has trouble with the natives. And he may not have help for much longer. Grek got a little more excitement than he bargained for yesterday. Cheeses— don't they have to be thoroughly sterilized before export? And doesn't that greatly reduce their value for offworld connoisseurs?"

"Not if you don't export them," Giem said. "Because the Pios are so reluctant to do business, and won't tell station people their production secrets, the prices are fabulous locally. If you can manage to trade at all, you can easily make more than double what a vacation here will cost you, which is also part of the attraction. It's fun here. The weather is good and the wilderness is fairly safe—" I snorted again, and that didn't faze her—"and it's not overrun by tourists. What's this about Grek quitting?"

"He comes from the village we're headed for, and he's thinking about leaving his job when he returns home."

"Why?"

"He didn't like being threatened by foreign weapons or being trussed up to a tree." Since I'd had to wait all night anyway, I'd saved that one up for Giem's reaction, and she didn't disappoint me.

"The Pios have already obtained illegally imported weapons? Are you sure you set your translators correctly?"

"Giem, he said it was humans who attacked them. That means Davin was lying to us yesterday."

"Or Grek lied to you."

"What about that synthetic rope they were tied up with?" I said.

"Pios could have bought or bartered for it. It's not as if they totally refuse to do business with outsiders."

"Well, whatever. I'm just getting kind of concerned about all this."

"I am also," Giem said.

"Maybe we should slow down, savor the scenery, and let some real distance fall between us and these nefarious characters."

"Did he say whether Garth Riddock attacked them?" Apparently Giem couldn't entirely discount Grek's story either.

I grinned "No, two other humans occasionally seen in town. You have Riddock imprinted in your brain."

"Well, what do you think he's up to out here?" Giem said. "Trading innocently for cheese?"

"Uh, somehow I just can't holo it."

"Neither can I, and I want to see if we can find out the real answer."

So much for Ziehl's hope of keeping us out of trouble.

CHAPTER 24

After covering the ground we did the day before on horseback, Giem and I resented trudging a long hard day on foot. We sweated over the rolling, winding trail through green sun-dappled woods, beautiful and rarely shady enough. Hiking with a full pack is about the only time heat makes me suffer, and we cautiously refilled our water bottles at nearly every stream crossing. Fat little trail reptiles couldn't eat up the insect swarms fast enough to keep them from goading us along. Thank the Galaxy I barely tasted my dinner before I fell into my sleeping bag that night.

Giem's assurances of a short remaining hike the next morning boosted my morale for a little while, but it soon sank altogether. I rounded each bend hoping to scan the Pio village directly ahead, only to have to climb another tough segment of trail. We also passed a number of discouraged traders on their way out, which didn't help my mood.

Shortly after we broke down and spent over two hours on a lazy lunch stop, the trail widened into the main village road.

"It coms." We laughed, and picked up our pace. The road soon led us to the outskirts of the town, nestled along another river.

Giem's map unimaginatively called it "Pio River," and pictured the village as a network of tiny bumps along its banks. From a distance, I could tell this river didn't stretch as wide as West Maxson. Unnaturally neat, small hills overgrown with vegetation dotted both raised banks. Beyond the mounds lay gardens and livestock pastures, and along the banks I scanned a few small docks and boats.

The first earthen domes we came upon were set closer to the road than to the river, and looked like businesses, surprisingly enough. From the complaints of passing traders, I'd begun to wonder whether any Pio besides the ferry operator had any concept of commerce.

People of various origins haggled over fruits at a counter in front of one wide doorway. I could see others perusing wood, stone, fiber, and scaled leather products in other open burrows. More Pios and aliens sat at outside café tables, including Mohrogh, who was arguing again, of course.

When we got closer I recognized Grek, opposite Mohrogh, along with a more shriveled Pio with duller facial stripes. All three had their translators on, and Giem and I halted in our tracks to listen in shamelessly.

"Grek made an agreement to help me on my expedition," Davin said to the older-looking Pio.

"You didn't warn him you'd be involved in any criminal activity." The Pio's voice translated as an older female, and she spoke between crunching bites into a large hard-boiled egg cupped by a wooden bowl.

"How was I to know I'd get jumped by a jealous rival? I didn't do anything wrong," Davin said.

"Be glad of that, or you'd do worse than lose your guide. I should call in FIL Station Guardians immediately with what Grek told me."

Davin leaned back and took a sip from his drink. "Well, if I'm to lose my guide, perhaps you could at least give me some advice."

"And what would that be?" She broke off as Grek noticed us and waved us over with the tip of his tail. Giem and I stepped forward hesitantly.

"Hello, Taje and Giemsan," Grek said. "Mother, here are the two Humans who rescued us."

"Pleased to meet you." Grek's mother tapped her black claws, not quite as long as her son's although even sharper, lightly on the table. "Sit down. You must feel thirsty. I'll get you drinks." She stood up with her empty bowl and disappeared through a dark arched doorway in the nearest herb-covered mound. With sweaty relief, we dropped our packs against the nearest tree trunk and dragged carved wood stools up to the tree-shaded table.

Davin nodded at us with a sickly smile. "Hello, Giem, Taje."

People—including my mother, before she disappeared—tend to use my full name only when I'm in trouble. But Giem doesn't immediately encourage most people to shorten her first name the way I do. I studied her happy face out of the corner of my eyes, and wondered grimly if I'd lose her entirely to the mindless desires of her endocrine system. Reproductive physiology is so complex and confusing that we don't study any of it until junior year.

Grek's mother reappeared with two tall wooden cups for us. My dark red drink tasted like a fruit mixture dominated by krava juice, with a tinge of some sort of sharp spicing. It was dilute enough to quench my thirst, and I gulped it down gratefully.

"What advice do you need? Other than to be told to stay out of trouble?" Grek's mom sat back down, her stool accommodating her tail quite nicely. We laughed as Davin tried not to squirm.

"I just want to know why your people are so reluctant to trade your better products, especially your cheeses," he said. He stared down at an orange fuzzy slowly following the edge of the table in front of him. He poked at the insect curiously. "I know a few traders succeed. What's their secret?"

"There's no secret," the older Pio retorted. "Cheeses take a lot of hard work to make. It's not worthwhile making more than enough cheese for ourselves and good friends to eat. Why should we? What have you got to give us that we want that badly?"

"You take credits right here at your restaurant from foreigners. Why don't you just set appropriate prices for your products?" Davin began to tease the fuzzy, using a finger to block its path, and it kept crawling back and forth in front of him.

"Very few of us take credits," Grek's mother said. "And those of us who do usually get something more than just credits in the bargain. I get more interesting company, for myself and my customers, usually."

I snickered at the pointed tone in her translated voice, and Davin frowned absently at me.

"Speaking of which," the Pio turned her frank gaze to Giem and me, "I'd like to invite you two to dinner. I'll serve it about sunset tonight, and I won't charge either of you."

"We'll be happy to pay," Giem said politely.

"I won't take credits from my son's guests—will you quit toying with that?"

"Huh?" Davin looked up at her blankly.

Grek's mother reached across the table, deftly lanced the fuzzy with a sharp claw, and it immediately went limp. She unskewered it into her mouth and swallowed neatly. "Didn't your mother ever teach you it's cruel to play with your food? If you'll excuse me, I have more customers to serve." She got up to attend to some bedraggled Altruskan tourists who looked as if they'd never ridden lizards before, and never wanted to again.

"Well, that's just great," Davin said morosely after our laughter subsided. "My guide has quit on me, one of my horses has gone lame, and I can't even get any decent leads. And I'm falling further behind financially every hour I stay on this planet."

"One of your horses went lame?" Giem rapidly turned sympathetic.

"Giemsan grew up with horses," I said. "Maybe she can help you."

"That's right, you're both FIL vets." Davin perked up.

"We're just vet students," Giem said. "But maybe I can help, if it's an obvious problem."

"Okay. I've got them penned in a corral behind my hostel room. I can show the lame one to you right now." Davin got up from his stool, and Giem followed him. I stayed on my stool.

"Will you come too?" she said.

"No, thank you. I've seen enough horses in pain to know that I don't know how to handle them safely." I also guessed Giem would prefer to be alone with Davin, probably in that hostel room, afterwards. A loyal friend, that's me. "Go on, I'll be fine here."

"I can give you a tour of our village," Grek said to me.

"And maybe I'll get a chance to explain our study," I said.

"Okay, we'll meet you back here for dinner," Giem said cheerfully, and promptly walked away with Davin, leaving me with twinges of disloyal envy.

CHAPTER 25

Grek helped me stash our packs just inside his mother's restaurant burrow. In the dim cool room a gentle flapping approached me, and I felt something land lightly on my right shoulder.

"What?" I fought my natural instinct to flinch and brush it off, even as Grek rushed to explain.

"Don't worry—that's just Skelner, my pet karc."

I felt a gentle little blunt nose and fine tongue investigating my cheek. I moved my hand slowly, to touch cool, smooth scales. "Can I bring Skelner outside to see better?"

"Sure."

Out in the sunlight I found one of Big Maxson's smaller flying reptiles on my shoulder—one of the critters that filled an avian niche here. This one was light-boned and delicate, though facial ridges gave it a fierce little expression. Skelner kept a careful grip on my shoulder with the clawed toes of four feet. It must have evolved from one of the six-legged beasts of Big Maxson. Glossy dark blue scales blended to pale blue underneath, with some lines of red and orange on face and wings.

"What a beautiful creature." I stroked Skelner tentatively under the chin. The karc responded by leaning into my hand.

"Thank you. I raised her myself from a hatchling."

"Do many of you keep these as pets?" I asked.

"Only those of us with enough patience. If you don't raise them right from the egg, they will try to fly away young."

"How long have you had her?"

"I guess about ten years."

"That's great. Is she at all useful, or is she just a pet?"

"Karcs supposedly hunt and eat small pests. I convinced my mother to let me raise her to protect our food supplies. But Skelner's so spoiled from my mother's handouts that I don't know if she remembers how to hunt."

I laughed, and forced myself to part ways with the pleasing little reptile. Grek led me past shops and other restaurants, and a cluster of four large mounds, two just beginning to sprout greenery, which comprised the local hostel. It was full today. Oddly, I saw few Pios about, even when we wandered on towards backyard crops and livestock.

The Pios here raised mostly quelsh, and a smaller domesticated species I hadn't scanned before. Grek called them minskis. They ran around in flocks and sort of reminded me of giant reptilian, featherless chickens, raised for meat and "small" eggs. Amongst them wandered some tame, spiky carnivores, krellas, allowed to run loose to keep down vermin populations. I patted one knee-high, dagger-lipped krella, after it sniffed me over and sat up appealingly on its powerful hind legs. Grek rambled on about some local food plants. I interrupted with a question.

"Grek, back at the creek with the gelssk you saved me from, you mentioned you have teachers—what do you study?"

"Agriculture. I suppose that's rather obvious?" he said, somewhat embarrassed.

"How old are you—do you mind me asking?"

"Twenty years."

"Wow, I'm almost as old as you—at least in FIL standard years. And you're still stuck studying too?" I said sympathetically.

"I think," Grek paused a bit, "from what little I've learned about Humans, we start our schooling later, and take a lot longer for it. Life for us here . . . is not difficult . . . and I think we live more slowly than you. I know we live longer, so maybe that's why. Am I making any sense?"

"I think you've learned a lot about us," I said, impressed, while the scaly beast at my feet nudged my leg for more attention.

"Not enough," Grek said. "Shoo, Kraka. Leave!" Grek spread his claws and hissed ferociously. Kraka just gave Grek a resentful look, waited until it seemed like its own idea, and sauntered off.

"I studied crops at Big Maxson Station," Grek said in a calmer tone, "and I must have missed something. I know other FIL people possess a lot more knowledge than us. You can even travel in boats between the stars. Surprisingly, station crops didn't seem very advanced, and I think some aren't even doing as well as ours."

"We haven't the centuries of experience your people have had with the plant life on your world." I gazed at an orchard along our path. Krava was the only fruit tree I recognized among about half a dozen different species. "Have you met Dr. Kiernan Bioh?"

"No. Who?"

"The station biologist. He could probably explain what's happening with station crops, or send you to the right people for more information. You should talk to him—I'm sure both of you could learn a lot. Speaking of which, there's something Giem and I would like permission to try to learn here."

"What?" Grek said.

"If your neighbors will agree to it, we'd like to check the stools of some of your domestic animals for parasite eggs, to compare the problem with results we got back at the station."

"Worm eggs? You mean from those disgusting, slimy little creatures found in livestock guts?" Grek squeezed his eyes shut.

"Yes," I said, frowning heavily, as I thought about horrible humans who describe reptiles—totally inaccurately—in a similar manner.

Grek opened his beautiful eyes and I smiled.

"Our village doctor says some kinds of worms can make animals sick, if they get too many from crowding and filthy housing," he said. "She also tells us how to avoid infection. We've never seen any eggs from them."

"They're too tiny to see," I said. "That's how they cause infections—by having eggs too small to tell when anyone touches or swallows them. They grow inside, to become the worms you can sometimes see when they're expelled. When we use a special machine to see their eggs in stools, we can assume there are worms—and can even tell what kinds—without having to look inside of animals to find out. And that's a good first step toward treatment and prevention."

"I have a friend who'd probably find this very interesting—she's studying livestock production—and I think I know where she is," Grek said. "Would you like to meet her? She should know how to get permission for your work."

"Sure. Lead the way."

Grek took me straight down to the river, and I learned why I'd seen few natives out and about. With their outstretched bodies, Pios of all ages nearly obliterated the more level rock outcroppings along both river banks, out of the forest shade, in the sunshine.

As we walked closer, I noticed most of the Pios looked like females, and I scanned both sexes casually slipping in and out of the water. All had crotch grooves which sometimes seemed to widen as they hit the water, and obviously the webbing between their fingers and toes must be far less vestigial than I'd assumed. This also explained the scarcity of boats and docks for a river village.

I fervently hoped Grek's friend sunbathed on this shore. I knew how to swim, but I doubted I could keep up with anyone built like Grek in the river's swift current, and I still felt very leery of aquatic wildlife.

"Turn off your wristcom," Grek said.

"Why?" I asked, wondering if he was worried about it getting wet. I found out I was all wet.

"We don't consider it polite to talk to others or pay attention to devices when visiting with each other," he said. "Just leave your translator on."

"Okay," I said, as I turned off my wristcom screen and call reception.

"This is my favorite sunning rock," Grek said, as we approached a large, flat, Pio-covered stone, jutting out above the water from the near bank. I smiled with relief, while the nearest Pios politely shifted to make room for us. "Most of my best friends come here. I hope you enjoy becoming warm more than most Humans—we like to spend as much time here as we can, midday. In fact, it might interest you to know our doctors say we avoid certain illnesses with this habit."

I'd kept up dutifully with my systemic UV blocker on Big Maxson, and unless I was trying to haul all my belongings uphill, my skinny frame made it difficult for me to stay warm enough most places, like Olecranon. I was about to express my delight when another Pio face, with duller stripes, exploded from the water just below and beyond the jutting rock. Grasping the edge of the sunning rock with one hand, she swallowed whole the gelssk skewered and wriggling on the claws of her other hand. She silently eyed me and Grek.

"Tajen Jesmuhr, this is my friend, Korrel Tek Skilmelsk," Grek said, as he and I took lounging positions on the nicely sun-warmed rock. "Skil, this is my new friend, Taje."

"Hello," Skil said, after she finished swallowing a lump that went visibly down her throat.

I watched with open amazement. "Hello." I remembered my manners and helped make room for her among the mass of sunbathers, assisted by a male and a female who abruptly dropped, coupled together, into the water from the opposite side of the rock.

"I don't get it," I said.

"What have you not gotten?" Grek said.

Oops, human expressions don't always work. "I don't understand how everyone here keeps from getting bitten by gelssk when you go swimming!" Spear them all? Or were Pio scales more like armor?

All of the Pios on the sunning rock snickered—quiet sneezes.

"We have very tightly woven nets stretched across upriver and downriver. A few fingerlings get through. Yum! If a few grow up, they learn we have weapons!" Grek flared his sharp finger and toe claws along with everyone else on the rock.

After that, I settled in to explain our parasite project, and in turn learned some of this town's gossip.

CHAPTER 26

By the time Grek and I returned to his mother's restaurant for dinner, I again felt impatient to give Giem a private report. However, once more Davin was also present, paying his own way.

Giem glanced at me and I pointed at my blank wristcom screen and shook my head.

She didn't understand.

"What's wrong with your horse?" I asked Davin, as I picked up a sort of free-form utensil. Smoothly carved out of a small branch, presumably a Pio invention to assist less fortunate species. Each human at the dinner table had one parked by their plates, while Pios used their claws.

I used the various carved prongs and scoops to enjoy an exquisite dinner served by Grek's mom. She started us off with a huge salad of greens and pieces of boiled quelsh egg.

"Just needed some rocks picked from his feet, I think," Giem said while we gobbled up our salads. "Hopefully Davin's horse escaped any stone bruises."

"She's good with horses," Davin said.

"When the problem's that simple, it makes me look good," Giem said. "Promise me you'll never again forget to pack a hoof pick when you take horses on your trips."

Next Grek's mom brought us fish in a thick cheese sauce, which I suspected was a sign of special honor for us, difficult to refuse, regardless of the lack of cell culturing. We ate it politely, and washed it down with tall glasses of quelsh milk, which was also poured over several kinds of berries.

After that dessert, I still didn't get a chance to talk privately with Giem, because she hastened to share Davin's hostel room. Neither could I get Grek to tell me where I might politely trigger our tent. Instead he insisted on taking me in, and I laid out my sleeping bag next to Grek and his mom in a comfortable, shallow, blanket-lined sleeping pit that filled one section of their home burrow. I couldn't tell if I should consider this average, expected treatment for a guest, or another special honor, which made it difficult to know how much to thank them. Giem didn't know how easy she had it.

I set my wristcom for an early alarm and managed to wake up the next morning before my Pio hosts did. I dug a breakfast packet and some biodegradable TP out of my pack. I ducked outside to find the nearest public outhouse. I met Giem just exiting.

"Got a breakfast with you?" she said.

"If you could call it that." I took a rushed shift at the pit in the small, noxious burrow. Despite open windows,

I found the mingled smells from too many different species almost overpowering, especially this early.

"Fine. Join me when you're done in there," Giem called from outside.

I hurried back out and we headed down a sloping path to the nearest dock, where we sat down to eat. The morning air smelled like wet pilings and alien grass, a definite improvement.

"Where's Davin?" I ventured.

"He left." Giem couldn't completely hide her disappointment.

"Blasted out early again, huh? You shouldn't have fixed his horse so fast for him."

"Thanks a lot, Taje. I knew he had to leave today. Anyway, why are you up this early? Bored with the Pios so promptly?"

Ouch. "No. I needed to talk with you—alone. It just doesn't make sense, unless he has something to hide." I squinted at the sunrise, and down at its colorful sparkling reflections on the smoothly flowing river, reminding me of Grek's face. In the green depths below us, I scanned a couple of gelssk nibbling innocently at a water weed–encrusted piling. I watched lacy blue and green insects flirt with the river's surface. The gelssk began to glide slyly towards them. I crossed my hands, and made a sudden shadow full of fingers over the gelssk. The gelssk shot upstream. They were afraid!

Giem flung a stone in the water too late. "How did you do that? And who has something to hide?"

"The Pios have gelssk running scared in their Homeriver." I looked up at my friend. "But why is Davin in such a hurry? He even told Grek he really likes you."

"He did?" Giem looked startled.

"Such confidence," I teased her, and from her sad expression, I realized I'd zapped uncomfortably close to home. "I think maybe he's up to something odd," I said, changing the subject. "Yesterday one of Grek's friends said that Mohrogh has asked around about Pio cheeses, and also about the whereabouts of Garth Riddock."

"Riddock—I think Davin's afraid of him—maybe Davin's just trying to find out how to avoid him. Does anyone here know where Riddock has gone?"

"I didn't think to ask," I had to admit. "I can try to find out today. I discovered he spent a fairly long time in this village, demonstrating unusual patience for a human, and consequently learned more than a little about the Pio art of cheese-making."

"He learned about cheese-making?" Giem looked quite puzzled. I could see her trying to fit that into some Dastardly Scheme, without much luck. No more than I'd had.

"Not a particularly worrisome pastime, is it?" I said. "Giem, I think it's time to focus all our efforts on our study here. The Pios make fun company, and I think I may get permission today to run some demo fecals."

"Oh, that sounds like grand fun!"

"Well, it's supposed to be our project here."

"Taje, if you're feeling so responsible, don't you also feel at all concerned about what's happening out here? And by the fact that no one else seems to care?"

"What do you think is going on? Someone with a bad reputation is getting along well enough with the natives to learn about their cheeses on his vacation. Is that any excuse to practice playing spy on him? I do feel responsible for the research we promised everyone."

"I thought you hated this whole assignment," Giem said.

"Oh." I rubbed the side of my nose and smiled. "I guess it has kind of grown on me."

"What about the weapons aimed at *your friend* Grek—doesn't that bother you at all?"

Something about the odd emphasis she placed on "your friend" irritated me. "It's up to the Pios to report that incident to station authorities. We're not witnesses. Nor have we been trained to deal with outright crime between rival offworld traders."

"Not unless it involves the 'health or safety of animal life, wild or domestic,' on this world," Giem quoted stubbornly.

"You think it does?"

"I have no idea what to think," Giem said. "We need more information first."

"Well, maybe we should split up to get both jobs done," I snapped.

"Maybe."

Giem returned to Davin's hostel room for her belongings, while I left to dig our study equipment out of my pack, and find Grek and Skil. After the Pios' slow breakfasts and casual morning chores, Skil took us to see her teacher.

Once again I carefully explained our parasite survey. With Grek, Skil, and the teacher helping, I obtained samples from half a dozen of her well-mannered animals, enough to demonstrate my procedure. That gained the teacher's interest, trust, and approval—my results confirmed some of her own theories. She agreed to explain the idea to other villagers with livestock, to get their permission for my study. Grek and Skil took a break for their daily sunbath. In the interest of good human-Pio relations, I joined them.

"Hello, Taje." A human hand gripped my shoulder and shook it. I startled awake, to find Giem squatting beside me. I propped up on one elbow, peered at her wristcom blearily, and discovered I'd dozed off for several hours. Kraka slept on my numbed feet, and the sun headed for the tips of the tallest trees.

"You're not answering your wristcom," Giem said. "Find anything more about where Riddock went?"

"Uh, no. I forgot to ask," I admitted, abashed. Grek slowly peeled open his eyelids. He'd left his arm lying across my waist, and a foot over my ankle. Giem eyed us, unable to hide a look of disapproval on her face. Were we too lazy or too close? I frowned.

"Well, I did," she said, impatiently. "I've talked to several villagers, including Grek's mother, about Riddock. Apparently his last inquiries, before leaving this village, involved the locations of certain wildlife. He particularly wanted to know where he might find wild quelsh herds."

"Has he gone hunting?" I wondered aloud, gently pulling my feet out from under Kraka's belly. "That might zap a little closer to home for us, especially if he hasn't bothered with any special permits. "Did he give the Pios any reason for his questions? Maybe just wildlife watching?"

"No, and he even turned down a willing Pio guide," Giem said. "It's suspicious enough that I don't think it would hurt to try to find out more. I'll check into it. If it's an innocent lead, I promise to come right back and help you here."

"You're leaving? You don't want me to go along with you?" I sat up. "If you could just wait until we run some sample fecals, and maybe get in a few butchered carcass inspections—quit it, Kraka." My numbed feet were at the painful tingling stage, and the beast insisted on trying to lay back down on them.

"The evidence and the people may be long gone by then."

Including Davin, I thought to myself. We both guessed he could somehow be mixed up in this, and I suspected Giem might simply be looking for an excuse to run into him one more time. "How will you ever catch up with Riddock on foot?" I said.

"I can't. Grek's grandmother will loan me a lizard— she and his mom are both worried now too."

"When will you leave?" I resigned myself.

"When I've finished packing—whew, it's still hot out here." Giem wiped beads of sweat from her forehead. "How can you stand it? I'll take my backpack along with our tent, stove, and part of our food, if that's okay with you."

"I suppose I could arrange to put off our study here for a bit."

"Don't break your promises, Taje—I know you don't want to. And don't worry about me. I'll call you every evening with a report. Promise me you'll turn your wristcom back on for reception after dinner each night."

"Sure," I said.

"I'll probably return promptly anyway, after chasing down a false alarm. Maybe Riddock is just doing some wilder sightseeing."

"Well, okay," I said. Although deep down, I suppose we both knew that if we felt concerned enough to want to investigate Riddock's motives, we shouldn't have split up. I guess we didn't fully believe anything was seriously wrong, except perhaps our overactive imaginations. That's how I justified it, anyway. At the time I simply felt relieved that I could satisfy Giem without having to cancel my plans with the Pios. I laid back down on the warm rock and fell innocently back to sleep.

CHAPTER 27

After a week in Grek's village, I had gathered enough data for preliminary parasite comparisons, which revealed surprisingly few differences from our station statistics. I could only conclude the Pios must make up for a lack of technology with a better overall feel for their livestock, gradually acquired over a shared evolutionary past.

I didn't feel too shocked by my results, and I became eager to report them to Giem. Perhaps she'd get interested enough in what I was finding out—and bored enough with what she wasn't discovering—to ride back soon. She could help me evaluate the efficacy of Pio anti-parasitic treatments, which might also prove useful to station ranchers. The problem was, I never heard from Giem that evening, even when I tried to call her.

I felt like I hardly slept that endless, ghastly night. I must have, because I kept waking up from gruesome dreams covering the worst possibilities: Giem stomped flat by a stampeding skitsh herd, or attacked and shredded by a vicious, wild lizard. In one dream, Riddock tortured and murdered her. In another, a giant orange segmented tree snake nearly throttled her, and a deranged band of Pio outlaws kidnapped her. All sorts of ridiculous scenarios chased through my zapped brain, and had me sweating, numb, and sick to my stomach by morning.

I woke up early and quietly escaped outside. I sat down miserably at one of the café tables and gave myself a harshly bitter review, with a flunking grade at the end of it. Focusing on all my losses this summer, I'd completely failed to appreciate what I did have. I was gaining the knowledge I'd craved more than anything, while over half my prevet classmates aboard *Onnarius* had failed to get this far. My success had in turn given me Giem, a good and loyal new friend, and all I'd done during our last few encounters was fight with her.

Worthless fights did seem to be my specialty. One of my brawls with Branem had led to my ill-fated ride on Shielvelle. And I'd let a girl I didn't even know goad me into a vac-brained Orphan Center food riot. No wonder I kept losing friends. It was a wonder I ever made any to begin with.

I made more useless wristcom calls to Giem. I also considered calling Ziehl. Sure, ask her to get me out of this fused mess, when she was the very friend who'd warned us to stay away from Riddock in the first place. She'd be furious, and rightly so. She'd have to call station authorities to request a FIL search and rescue team, which I could very well do myself.

I called the station police department instead. I had to summon some courage, even in my frantic state. I knew from mutual encounters with irate pig-owners that station police had limited staff and resources to spare, and I couldn't guarantee I had an emergency on my hands. Could I afford to risk guessing I didn't?

I was referred to "Missing Persons." "Name? Address? Relationship? Length of time missing?"

Only when I got to the fourth question was I told I'd have to wait longer before I could declare my friend missing. How much longer? A week! Was I talking with a real person, or a comsec? A comsec, and no, I couldn't ask for an emergency supervisor. The staff was completely tied up at the moment with an extremely serious station emergency. Please call back in one week, if your friend is still missing. What station emergency? Please call back—and I hung up, wondering if the FIL IPHAs had at last faced the unthinkable. If they were in the midst of setting up a serious quarantine, I might never get help.

Ziehl was too right—we were truly on our own out here.

Grek came outside and found me a little later, staring vaguely at the main road and trying not to cry with frustration.

"I can borrow two lizards and show you the way to the quelsh valley," he offered, after dragging the story out of me.

"It may be very dangerous." I looked up at him, startled out of my misery. "More dangerous than your little incident with Davin Mohrogh."

"You think Giemsan Fane has been hurt?"

"Unfortunately, it's a possibility I have to consider. If Giem's too injured to answer her wristcom, she's in real trouble." Or dead. I swallowed with a dry, numb, foul-tasting mouth, while I tried to come up with other answers. The problem was, all I could think about was a frighteningly realistic search and rescue lesson back in my pre-ecology class, where I'd had a lot more help and equipment. Near the end of our final exam I'd almost died, because no FIL technology could locate where I'd fallen. Instead Shandy had somehow mastered his normally out-of-control esper ability just enough to find me. I wished I knew where he went.

"Maybe Giemsan just lost her wristcom. Don't lose hope."

"I don't want to hope," I snapped, before I could stop myself. "I'll feel too disappointed, if I do, and she's— gone." Like my mother had vanished, years ago, without a trace. I didn't want to face that again. Is this how Aerrem and my other classmates had suffered, when I went missing on Shielvelle?

Grek's nostrils flared, and he hissed. "You are confusing expectation with hope, Taje," he said. "Or else your species is more superstitious than I thought. How can you live without hope? Your wristcom translator is giving you separate words for these ideas, isn't it? Or do Humans fail to make this distinction?"

I gazed at him in a state of confused and impatient agitation. "Yes, those are separate words for us. What difference does it make? Giem—"

"Is one of your friends. So you're probably just not thinking very clearly. We can discuss this again later. Giem may be okay, and we don't have to take any chances, or wait any longer. I'll go borrow a pair of lizards from Skil."

Grek ran off—the first time I'd seen any Pio run—and he moved surprisingly fast for an ectotherm. He shortly returned with a pair of fully tacked, lean, dark-green lizards. A moment later Skil panted up to deliver a scaly pouch of grooming tools. She checked over halter, bridle, and girth adjustments. My hands shook as I packed and strapped my pack over my sleep pad behind one saddle. Grek dashed back inside his home to retrieve supplies for himself. Skil strapped the grooming tool pouch onto the other saddle.

Grek returned carrying what looked like a bedroll under one arm. He wore his translator, his vest, knife belt, and carried two bows and a quiver. His mother followed him with a scaly sack.

"Give me your outer-skin," she said to her son, reaching for his vest.

"Mom!"

I felt like shouting too, growing totally impatient.

"I have food in all the compartments," Grek said.

"You don't know how long you will be gone," she said. "Let me take care of it." Grek's mother took his vest, used its contents to top off her sack, cinched and tied it closed, and handed the bag and vest back to him. He rolled the bag and vest in his thin blanket. He folded up an oiled, scaly tarp, rolled the bundle up in it, and lashed it on the back of his saddle, along with his bows and quiver. I was about to ask if anyone had a tent to spare, when I heard horses on the main road before us.

I glanced over my lizard's low saddle, and got blasted by my next fused surprise—Davin Mohrogh rode past us with a look of nova terror on his face. As soon as he saw us he urged his mount and his two pack horses into a gallop, without a pause or a hello.

"Wait! Come back!" I tried to run after Mohrogh, and he neither answered nor slowed down. Horror-struck, I stood in the road and watched him disappear down the trail back towards West Maxson River.

CHAPTER 28

"Want to chase after him?" I nearly jumped when Grek asked that from behind me.

"No," I said, wondering what had put that nova look on Mohrogh's face, and guessing at morbid answers. "I guess we'd better. Come on!"

We ran back to the lizards. We flung ourselves onto our scaly leather saddles. A sudden challenge, in my case, as I found myself grappling with a padded hook on each side instead of stirrups. We waved goodbye to Skil and Grek's mom, and took off at a lizard's gallop.

I discovered lizards can't run as fast as horses. All we did was fall farther behind, wasting precious time we might better spend on a direct search for Giem, in the opposite direction. Mohrogh wouldn't slow down, nor did he respond to wristcom calls. I tried repeatedly.

I barely managed to stay in the Pio saddle, with no stirrups, and a forward-facing padded hook on each side, one far enough back to beat the back of my right knee whenever I slid back. The other one hit my left kneecap whenever I slid forward. I cursed back tears while I goaded my lizard into maintaining its top speed, and squeezed my thighs into a death-grip on the saddle skirts between of the hooks.

Grek kept pace on his lizard beside me, and a better seat than I'd seen him use on a horse. And no wonder—now he could sit side-saddle, his tail hanging over and braced against the right hook, while his right leg rested over his left leg, which rested in the left hook. He remained silent until we reached a particularly woodsy, winding part of the path. There he insisted that we stop, and as I sat listening to the open-mouthed wheezy respiration of both lizards, and felt the trembling in my lizard's limbs, I understood why.

"We'll never catch up with him," I said, after everyone's breathing quieted down.

"Not if we stay on this trail." Grek blinked his green eyes with amusement. "Come, follow me." With that, he reined his lizard off the trail and plunged it down into the leafy-floored forest.

"Where are you going?" I called after him, as I urged my mount to follow him.

"A shortcut."

The lizards moved out at a fast walk, on a nearly straight line down whatever terrain got in our way—through gullies, across streams, between trees and shrubs, and right over logs and rock outcrops. Our mounts had clearly entered their real element. Here they excelled over any horse, and didn't balk once, even when small reptiles burst from disturbed bushes and loudly hissed insults at us. Our mounts found perches with their claws that I couldn't even scan. On some of the downward climbs they made, I was glad I was riding close to the ground, and they moved so smoothly that I found it almost easy to keep my seat.

After a while, however, the novelty wore off as my useless worries began a renewed onslaught, and once again the ride felt endless and interminably slow. Moreover, all my lizard-riding muscles, mistakenly thinking I'd put them on permanent vacation, began to complain again. When we returned to the trail at last, I had to check my wristcom twice to believe we'd spent only an hour to get this far.

"What do we do next?" I said, as we halted in the middle of a narrow part of the trail, right after a sharp bend. "Is Morogh ahead or behind us?"

"He must be behind us." Grek jumped down from his lizard and unstrapped his quiver and bows.

"What are you doing?" My voice rose in sudden panic. Was my Pio friend capable of shooting at people? Maybe his species wasn't as peaceful as I'd begun to assume. How much did FIL really know about the rest of Big Maxson's Planet, anyway?

"I'm guessing you want Davin to stop and talk to you, right?"

"Uh, yeah—"

"If this worked on him once, it might work again, with a few changes. Dismount from your lizard," Grek said.

I tried to convince myself to trust him, as I slid out of my saddle onto quivering legs.

It was silly to think Grek would resort to violence over this. If nothing else, he hadn't any incentive. And I had no better plan. Grek efficiently tied our lizards up loosely on opposite sides of the trail. They could almost nip each other. He selected a handful of arrows from his woven reed quiver and offered them, along with one of his carved wooden bows, to me.

"Do you know how to use these?"

"No." I kept my hands pointedly at my sides. Maybe Giem was in more danger than I thought. "Why do we need them?"

"The lizards will stop Davin's horses. What's to keep him from turning around or leaving the trail?" Grek continued to hold out the second set of weapons for me. "Take them anyway. I've never used them before to scare anybody either. I've seen how Humans do it. Maybe if we pretend we're very serious, Davin will halt long enough to tell us what went wrong."

I took the bow and arrows from Grek, and listened humbly to the rest of his plan. It all reminded me of holo thrillers I'd watched as a kid—almost an Adventure, except for the cold slimy feeling in my stomach. Which renewed itself every time I thought about why I was doing this, and how much trouble I could get into for doing it, especially if we ambushed the wrong party. I couldn't remember any of my childhood story heroes feeling this sick over the plot. Was I even going to find Giem in the end, and if I did, would she still be alive and okay?

That question did goad me into following Grek's example, although I'd never held a bow in my hands before. I watched curiously while Grek braced one end of his bow in the dirt with his foot. That end of the bow string was tied in place, and he had to slip the opposite loose string loop up the bent bow shaft to hook it over the other notched end. This took him just a micro. When I tried to copy the simple-looking maneuver, I found I couldn't coordinate it or bend my bow enough.

Grek snickered as he took the second bow back from me. "This way is easier for some beginners." He stepped one leg between the bow and its loose string, braced the end on the ground with his other foot, and used both leg and foot to gain more leverage.

To my dismay, he promptly took the bow apart again and handed it back to me. Before I could complain about wasting time on archery lessons, he scrambled up a tree, to a swaying limb nearly four meters up. There he kept his grip with his front and back toes and tail, and casually shoved a small brown segmented snake out of the way. He pulled an arrow from his quiver, positioned his bow free of snags, and watched me awkwardly struggling to master stringing my bow.

I also took much longer than Grek to find a secure fork to sit in, after a couple of meters of slow, shaky climbing in a tree opposite his. My simian ancestors would have been ashamed of me and my fear of heights. It didn't matter. We ended up waiting almost another whole nerve-wracking hour before we heard horses approaching.

Mohrogh trotted his sweaty horses around the sharp trail bend, nearly into our alarmed lizards' open mouths before he hauled to a stop.

"Get off your horse or it'll die for my dinner," Grek called out coldly and clearly enough for everyone's translators. Mohrogh had no time to even think about turning around or detouring.

I didn't need too much effort to suppress a hysterical laugh, since I felt like I was choking on my pounding pulse. I only pretended to aim at Mohrogh, so I couldn't possibly hit him by accident. Grek had an unmistakably professional and deadly grip aimed at the trader's mount.

Mohrogh dismounted, cursing under his breath, and glanced back at the crossbow strapped on his sleeping bag. I scrambled out of my tree so fast that I barely made a controlled fall, and Mohrogh chose that moment to try for his bow.

A swift arrow from Grek tore open the trader's sleeve. In the reaction time that it took Mohrogh to freeze, Grek had another arrow trained on him. I backed Grek up by aiming at Mohrogh's belly, from just beyond kicking range, a distance I commed should make up for my inexperience. His golden face turned pale.

"Hey, watch it with that." He stared at my trembling weapon fearfully.

"Tell me where Giem is, right now!"

"How should I know?" Mohrogh didn't take his almond eyes off my bow.

"Liar," I said. "She went after you and Garth Riddock. I know she did."

"Garth Riddock? Oh, you fools." Sweat made Mohrogh's black hair shiny.

"What do you know about Riddock?" I demanded.

"Nothing. And I want to know nothing. I'm leaving this fused planet just as fast as I can, before I get involved in any more vac-headed trouble. You and Giem should do the same."

"Giem is gone—looking for you and Riddock. She was supposed to call me last night and didn't, and I still can't reach her this morning. Quit stalling and tell me how to find her."

"How can I, when I haven't seen her since I left Grek's village a week ago? If you intend to kill me, do it now, because I can't help you find her."

Feeling defeated and rather ridiculous, I slowly lowered my bow. While Mohrogh was watching me, Grek slithered down out of his tree, and retrained his bow tightly on Mohrogh's horse.

"What do you know about Riddock?" Grek said. "Maybe that will help us."

Morogh didn't reply.

"Answer him." I raised my weapon again, with aching arms.

"Go ahead and shoot me," Mohrogh squinted his brown eyes at me.

"You think I wouldn't?" I dared him. In my loner life I'd made and kept few friends. The ones I have I realized I'd risk almost anything for. I liked to think that wouldn't include shooting an arrow into someone's gut, but it looked like maybe I would. My arms shook with fatigue.

"We know you asked about Riddock," Grek pressed him, "and something scared you off. Did you find him?"

"Yes," Mohrogh's barely audible reply came at last.

"And you didn't see Giemsan Fane?"

"No. But if she's found Riddock, she could be in a lot of danger."

"Why?" My hands were growing slippery with sweat. I wanted to throw down my weapon and strangle what Morogh knew out of him.

"Because Riddock and his people are stealing wild quelsh," Mohrogh blurted out.

I gave him an incredulous look. "You mean illegal hunting, right? How can anyone steal something wild?"

"The next villagers to the west of us select and capture quelsh from wild herds, to trade to villages needing fresh breeding stock," Grek said, without removing his attention from Mohrogh and his horse. "They've done this for many generations, so it's theft to hunt without their permission."

Giem had ridden straight into this fused mess. What do we do next? My friend could be lying anywhere between Grek's village and the wild quelsh, badly injured in a freak accident. Or she might be wandering around the countryside after accidentally dropping her wristcom in a river. However, if I played the odds, I'd have to seek out Riddock too.

I could call Ziehl for help, even if I did have to admit to her what trouble we'd gotten ourselves into. However, even with Ziehl's help, help would take more time to get here, especially if the station was embroiled in the threat of quarantine or some other dire emergency. Besides, what could I ask for that I didn't have, besides expensive scanners and elaborate first aid equipment I might not even need? I still had nothing definite to report, to justify any official station assistance.

"Taje, I think we should forget this scale-scum and go look for your friend ourselves," Grek said.

"I agree—I don't think we should waste any more time here."

We untied our lizards, tightened their girths, and checked their feet before we mounted. Mohrogh just stood there, with reins and lead ropes in hand and a stunned look on his face. "You really think Giem's chasing after Garth Riddock?"

"I know it." I picked a loose scale out from under the edge of my saddle pad, and my lizard grunted with itchy relief.

"Why? You and Giem aren't traders. What are you two up to out here anyway?"

"That's what we wanted to know about you," I replied impatiently, trying to find a comfortable way to sit on my lizard. I'd rubbed the inside of my knees raw on our frantic ride to intercept Mohrogh. Was it possible to teach myself side-saddle in the middle of all this? And did I have any other choice?

"Two FIL vet students—you must be FIL spies!"

"No, we're just students," I managed to choke out that half-lie over my own surprise. "If you want to keep on running, by all means go ahead. We won't stop you." With that I shouldered my bow, stuck my arrows under some pack straps, and turned my mount back up the trail. Grek did the same behind me, and Mohrogh had to jerk his horses out of our way.

About half an hour later, we heard horses trotting and snorting behind us. When Mohrogh caught up with us, he muttered something about at least heading us in the right direction, toward Riddock's destination.

CHAPTER 29

Horses and lizards make a miserable combination for speed. We had to slow to a walk anyway to keep from driving our mounts into the ground. I spent my time practicing side-saddle. The technique did seem to better match the sideways pitching of a lizard's back, even if it didn't make as much sense for my anatomy.

I resented any stops we had to make, for hasty snacks or meals, consults over our wristcom maps, quick visits behind bushes, and exhausted sleep at the end of each long day. Mohrogh got us up in time to use every possible bit of daylight for our warmly tangled forest route, which was formed from his general directions, modified by Grek's wild shortcuts, and we bypassed his village altogether. We were limited only by what the horses could tackle. If we'd had a third lizard, I'm sure Grek and I would have demanded that Mohrogh abandon his worthless equine mounts.

After three days of hard labor, strained conversations, and frequent futile attempts to call Giem, we at last arrived just short of the top of the ridge overlooking what Grek

called a wild quelsh valley. We didn't want the wrong
people scanning our silhouettes at the ridge top, and it
was too late to spy from there anyway, so we triggered
Davin's tent in a flat spot below and crowded into bed.

Grek woke me up the next morning. Davin had
disappeared. Before I could get angry, Grek led me to
him near the top of the craggy ridge. I found it barren,
hot, and windy. Davin crouched behind a rock formation
and peered into the valley with a field scanner.

"I think Riddock's people have left," he said softly,
after we crept up to him. "I've seen no sign of them for
the past couple hours. I have scanned lots of Pios."

"Maybe they can tell us what's happened." I accepted
the scanner from Davin, and saw nothing besides close-
ups of trees. "Grek, are they friendly?"

Grek sneeze-chuckled. "My neighbors and I have
many relatives in this village. We shouldn't have any
problems."

"I don't know." Davin rubbed the back of his scarred
hand. "I've never seen so many Pios carrying weapons
before."

I couldn't scan any choice in the matter, for myself.
"Are you coming with us?"

"I suppose . . . I can't let an inexperienced fellow
human go bungling around in this wilderness all alone.
But if you decide to ride on after Riddock, you can count
me out."

I shrugged. At this point I didn't care what he decided.
Maybe we might even find Giem with these Pios, and
it wouldn't matter anymore whether Davin could help

us find Riddock. We had to work hard to convince him to leave his crossbow conspicuously strapped on his sleeping bag behind his saddle, as we did with our bows, a condition Grek rightly insisted on before he would lead us to the main trail heading down into the valley.

"You may consider it normal to aim weapons at each other. We don't. If Humans have tried to steal quelsh here, people will be very upset."

Within ten minutes of plodding down the switch-backing trail, about two dozen lizard-mounted Pios, bristling with bows and arrows, accompanied by half a dozen ferocious, spiky, waist-high krellas, slipped silently out of the forest and surrounded us.

CHAPTER 30

"Grekkan!" One startled voice among the Pios made sense to me. My wristcom translator was on, as it had been for days. I heard too many voices to follow hardly anyone except Grek, and concentrating on translations was difficult, with lizard discipline threatening to launch into vac.

"Skikkan! What is this nonsense, with all your nastiest krellas?" Grek asked the Pio who recognized him, and hissed and waved his clawed hands at the spiky krellas. They stood their ground and hissed back up at him. Skikkan answered Grek, and after some minutes of heated conversation, Grek gave his lizard a swat with his tail to force it close to mine. "Did you hear that?"

"Not enough," I admitted, as I barely restrained my nervous mount from trying to sidestep off the trail. I didn't think even an unintentional appearance of trying to escape would look good here.

"She says groups of aliens, mostly Humans, have ridden away with several quelsh herds from the forests around here," Grek said. "Her village formed a large number of patrols to protect the remaining herds. Trackers failed to hunt down any of the thieves or stolen quelsh— strange weapons froze anyone who got close."

"Stunners. Those are illegal weapons here. Witnesses should report all this at once to station authorities." Wasn't the station controlling anything? Perhaps the IPHAs correctly thought Port security needed closer scrutiny!

"These villagers sent off messengers two days ago to Big Maxson Station. It takes time," Grek said. "They've become very suspicious of any strangers who show up here, particularly Humans, and they've captured one."

"Giem?" I could hardly wait for the answer.

"It sounds likely."

"You're not a stranger. Have you convinced them we're okay?" Davin said anxiously, giving his sweating horse a comforting pat on the neck. All our beasts snorted and hissed at the crowd of Pios, lizards, and carnivores hemming them in.

"If we hand over our weapons, your wristcoms, and my translator, they're willing to take us to their village. There I'll have to convince others of your innocence," Grek said.

"Better do a good job of it." Davin scowled as he watched a Pio take his crossbow and find his cooking knives, while another insisted he hand over his wristcom.

Grek and I hastily relinquished our camping knives, bows and arrows, his bracelet and my wristcom. I should have cared more about my wristcom. I just hoped I'd get my pocket knife back some day. It had seen me through some rough times in Tarnek's pre-ecology class. As I now listened to the completely incomprehensible, hissing voices of gesticulating natives, I consoled myself by comming this was one of the nicer explanations for Giem's mysterious silence.

We endured yet another half a day's ride to reach the other side of the valley. There a combination of caves and mounds formed a village along a more mountainous river with several roaring waterfalls. We had almost no time to admire the view. Our mounts were taken from us immediately upon arrival, and while Grek departed to talk, Davin and I were ushered into a room in the local hostel. Two tough-looking Pios squatted down just outside, and one closed a curtain across our doorway.

"Guards," Davin muttered disgustedly as we sat down in the gloomy interior.

I'm sure we'd both hoped to meet up with Giem inside. Not even a glow-bug awaited us. We sat on fiber blankets lining the shallow sleeping pit which filled most of the small room, and waited in silence.

After my eyes adjusted to the dim light from the curtained doorway, I spent some time covertly studying the man sitting across from me. Like most humans other than myself, Davin possessed wonderfully golden skin. Although his clothes looked dirty and rumpled, he had quit shaving, and he seemed to have forgotten to comb his thick, dark hair this morning, he was not only still quite handsome, he even seemed genuinely concerned about Giem. What else could have lured him this far?

Was this another person I had judged too fast? Maybe my opinion of him was simply clouded with envy—an absurd student rivalry with Giem. I still thought about Krorn with more longing than I had ever foreseen or desired. So perhaps jealousy wasn't the whole answer here.

Sure, Davin was fun just to scan, and seemed friendly enough, but I was still unsure of his motives. My admiration for Istrannian self-control climbed another level, as I realized how sorely tempting I'd find it to invade Davin's mind this evening without permission, if I could.

"What are you thinking about?" he said, with unfortunate timing. He grinned as if he knew it. He stretched out on his side and gave me his innocent brown-eyed look, from beneath eyelids with a hint of an epicanthic fold, like most humans.

I looked down, embarrassed to realize I'd been staring at him Pio-style, and I picked dirt from under my fingernails. After all this time away from civilized bathrooms and Grek's river, I was filthy.

"You're awfully quiet without your friends around," Davin pressed. "Are you afraid of me?"

I swallowed hard. Perhaps I was. "I have a lot of questions about you." I faced him. "I wonder what you're up to out here—why you were chasing after Riddock, and why you reversed course. And whether you will run off if Giem isn't in this village, or help me find her."

"You don't think she's here?" he said, making two of us who evaded questions.

"I don't want to get my hopes up too high," I said, comming that wouldn't elicit a philosophic diatribe from Davin. "Why won't you answer any of my questions?"

"Why won't you answer mine?"

We had reached a silent impasse, and dozed off. Grek and Skikkan, both wearing translator bracelets, arrived close to sunset, waking us up with the delivery of our water bottles and bowls of a very spicy vegetable and quelsh meat stew.

Davin immediately asked for his wristcom back. "Haven't they run my ID yet?"

The two Pios ignored him. Grek formally introduced his cousin, and they both lounged and ate with us in the pit. Davin angrily ate by hand. I literally picked at my dinner. The alien food simply tasted too weird for me tonight.

"I'm sorry I led you into this situation," Grek said. "I have gotten my translator back, and learned more about Giemsan."

"Is she here?" I blurted out.

"She was, until early this morning, when she escaped," Grek said.

"The guard became sleepy, and a noise in some bushes distracted him," Skikkan said. "Later this morning we discovered the Human and her lizard had left."

"Probably chucked a rock out the door," Davin said, between mouthfuls scooped up with his fingers, while I alternated between cursing and giggling with relief. "Good for her."

I dug in the dirt near the edge of our shallow pit, and sure enough, I found a stone.

"Are the villagers chasing after her?" I said, and dropped the rock back in the dirt.

"No," Grek said. "She escaped without any weapons. They were still afraid to go after her. Since they caught her sneaking through the woods, they mistook her for a member of the quelsh raiders, and they feared an ambush if they tried to track her. They're frightened of your weapons."

Irrational guilt stabbed me, as if I was personally responsible for every crime committed here by my species. "Have these weapons killed or hurt anyone?" I swallowed nervously. Stunners don't work the same on everyone, especially without careful tuning, an effort criminals might not bother with or care about.

"No," Skikkan said. "We thought at first some of our trackers had died. But they've always started moving again. So far."

"Did Giem manage to take anything with her?" Davin surprised me by asking a good question.

"Everything except her knife and her wristcom," said Skikkan. "We left the rest of her gear with her saddle and tack in the hostel stable, and she must have found it there when she took her lizard."

"Not bad." Davin said, delighted.

"Are these villagers willing to trust us?" I gave my tactless fellow human a disgusted look.

"They'll let you go, as long as Skikkan and I stay with you," Grek said. "However, they won't return any of our weapons or your wristcoms until they find out more from station authorities. They expect you to return to the station immediately, if you're truly not involved in the thefts."

"And if we don't?" I countered. "What if we decide to follow after Giem? Have you explained what she was really doing here?"

"I tried to. Giemsan told them the same story, before she escaped. So they've decided they won't stop us, and they won't assist us either," Grek said. He lightly brushed his face with his long black claws. "I'm sorry. I expected to do better." Skikkan gently touched his shoulder with the tips of her claws.

"You don't think Giem is on her way back to the station?" Davin said, startled.

I sighed. "I don't know what to think."

"We tracked the direction she took out of here," Skikkan said, "and she didn't ride back toward the station. She set out on the same route as the quelsh thieves. That's a big reason my people don't trust your story more."

"That settles it," I said. "Tomorrow morning I'm riding after her. Grek, are you any good at tracking?"

"Wait a micro, that's utterly vac-headed," Davin said. "Without a wristcom or weapons? Why don't you get real help from the station, like the Pios are doing?"

"That's just it—the Pios can report our ID's, and have sent for help. Why should I waste any more time on that? And I can't call anyone without a wristcom. Besides, Giem is probably in no immediate danger. If I find out she's just safely spying on Riddock from a distance, I can help her out. And if she does get into any more trouble, I'll arrive as a backup before anyone else can. As it is, I'll have to wait until daylight to set out after her."

"I haven't done much tracking. I know some of the theory behind it—"

"Forget it," Skikkan interrupted Grek's offer. "Your tracking ability is a joke. I have to escort you well beyond our border, and I might as well guide you too."

"You get any closer to Riddock and you'll regret it," Davin warned both Pios. "Why get involved?"

"Like it or not, my people are involved," Skikkan retorted. "The question is, are you?"

That at least shut Davin up, even if it didn't get a proper answer out of him. We sketched out a few more plans. The two Pios picked up our dinner dishes and left so we could all get plenty of sleep before tomorrow.

"Hey, you've got no right to keep us in here!" Davin shouted after them.

The moment I scanned Davin reaching for the stone I'd dug up, I had no time to think. I stood, leaped, and landed with one booted foot on his hand, driving it into the dirt right before he got his fingers on the rock. I snatched up the stone, and leaped back.

He gave me a look of astonishment and pain, and cradled his hand as if I'd broken every finger. "What did you do that for?"

"I won't risk letting you hurt any Pio in this village. They will let us go in the morning. Remember? Plus you outweigh me two to one." No use trying to tackle him.

I turned my back on him, perhaps the most dangerous thing I did that day. Davin just laughed.

I buried the rock as deep as I could in the darkness of the back of our little room.

My mind still ran full blast, and I wondered how I would ever fall asleep. When I tried to lie down and wrapped one of the thin fiber blankets around me, I learned the natives must not use these for insulation. Perhaps the covers were just another remnant of some sort of burrowing instinct? I should have asked Grek to retrieve my sleeping bag. The guards remained outside with a small campfire. I could see firelight flicker through our door curtain, but it provided us no real heat as night fell. To add to my misery, I felt more nervous about our plans than I had let on to anyone.

My teeth began to chatter, and I wondered how I was going to make it through another long night. Someone tried to steal my blanket. I angrily yanked back on it.

"Don't be so stubborn," Davin whispered. He snuggled up behind me and wrapped both of our covers around us. "It's not that cold, and it looks like you could use some help."

He'd forgiven me? I was shivering too hard to turn away his body heat.

CHAPTER 31

"Wake up and get your lazy butt moving," Davin called from outside the hostel doorway the next morning. "We never unpacked and we're ready to go." He began another loud, useless argument with someone over the unlikely return of his wristcom.

I groaned and slowly got up, uncomfortably aware of some rather uninhibited dreams. Just lying in the arms of a human had done that to me. I fervently hoped I hadn't talked in my sleep. I also desperately needed a shower and clean clothes. At least I'd slept better than I had in days.

I stepped outside after pulling on my hiking boots, and blinked in the sunlight. In answer to another urgent need, I grabbed some TP from my pack, and Grek directed me to the nearest outhouse. He met me back outside with our lizards. He handed over my reins, along with a pale chunk of tough spongy stuff, which tasted just enough like bread to seem quite strange. Davin waited impatiently on his horse, his other two on leads, and Skikkan sat impassively on a stout brown lizard nearby.

"You're coming with us?" I asked Davin, about to add "to chase after Riddock?" and too fearful of changing his mind. I wondered why I cared. Probably the Pios hadn't given him any choice.

"I'm totally fused," Davin said. "If I get into any trouble, it'll be your fault."

"It's always my fault," I mumbled around my Pio-bread. I held it in my teeth just long enough to pick up my lizard's feet one by one, and systematically check pads and claws.

"Huh?" Davin frowned with impatience.

"I said, it's no wonder you and Giem get along so well."

"What's that supposed to mean?"

I mounted up, and ignored his question as we coaxed our various critters into a ragged line behind Skikkan. I gathered my half dozen reins in one hand, freeing my other hand to unclip my water bottle from my saddle. Several swigs prepared my dry throat for more breakfast. I hung my left leg over the left hook, and swung my right leg over my left, and proudly sat sidesaddle Pio-style, as I worked on my rubbery meal and rode out and away from the suspicious stares of the villagers. Grek, seemingly unbothered, followed behind us.

"Really, I hardly know Giem, or you for that matter." Davin rode up beside me, as soon as we were out of earshot from the village. Caring whether anyone overheard him was seemingly a first for him—or was it just happenstance? Reins and lead ropes in his left hand, he rested his swollen, bruised, scarred right hand on his thigh. I looked away.

"Why in FIL am I doing this?" he continued. "I must be absolutely nova—"

At this point my lizard lashed out at his horse. Davin pulled his mount back just in time, while I narrowly avoided pitching out of my saddle or dropping my breakfast overboard.

"And how can you eat that fused junk?" Davin muttered. "I bet you don't even know what it is."

"It's probably just as well," I said, after regaining my seat and my grip. "Which reminds me, Grek—what about feed for our lizards?" I called back to him.

"We fed them yesterday afternoon. That should hold them for another week or two, if necessary. They're properly trained."

And have wonderful metabolisms, I thought. "I guess mine just doesn't like your horse," I glanced back towards Davin. "Why are you bothering with all three, anyway?"

He shrugged. "What else am I supposed to do with them? I'm surprised you're not begging me for a chance to get off that ridiculous saddle. Anyway, maybe Giem will need a fresh mount, and that'll still leave one for my gear. The real question is why I'm doing this at all."

I didn't disagree. Was sex truly such a powerful motivator? Well, I had to admit it was at least a very great torment.

We made our way up out of the valley via another set of switchbacks, and at the top of the ridge, Skikkan called a halt.

"This is as far as we tracked your friend yesterday." She and Davin dismounted, checked out the rocky ground ahead, and conferred on the most likely route.

I made no pretense of tracking ability or even a reasonable sense of direction. Instead I sat back in my saddle to admire the view of blue cloud-strewn sky and deep green woods sweeping down before us. Grek sat silently beside me, scratching his lizard behind its pale tympanic membranes, and idly peeling old scales from its neck. The lizard snarfed with pleasure.

Skikkan and Davin selected a way down that led us in among the trees again, and for the rest of the day they put their skills together to pick our way cross-country. The job became easier the farther we got, though we lost Giem's trail. Davin still seemed to have some knowledge of Riddock's nefarious destination, and to prove it, we came upon a far more obvious route midday. Now we could just assume Giem had taken the same easy path.

We urged our mounts along numerous quelsh claw prints deeply indenting muddier patches of ground. Even a light grey drizzle, which forced Davin and me into raingear, did little to the obvious signs. The latter included scattered evidence of accompanying horses, and the whole group appeared to join together with several others later on. Next we followed a freshly torn highway through grass and other ground cover, broken up only by stretches of flat rock strewn with quelsh droppings and occasional horse piles. This whole nova scene reminded me of the remains of a flat screen Western cattle drive.

I felt sorry for the quelsh. At this point, like it or not, I did know my stool specimens, and some of the quelsh samples looked more than just rain-soaked. I guessed some of the stolen animals had become quite stressed. I doubted Davin took any notice of this particular symptom. However, he did seem to grow increasingly nervous as the day wore on. Nevertheless, he steadfastly led us on until dusk.

We had passed through several smooth green meadows ribboned with lazy winding streams. We picked out a campsite among the trees at the edge of one such meadow, near a convenient creek. We all set to work taking care of our tired beasts.

Then Skikkan helped Grek lash down his scaly oiled leather tarp over a natural, brush-encircled burrow they built with dirt they mysteriously whisked around. I quit watching, testily set my tired muscles to work on finding a comfortably level spot to trigger Davin's tent, and stashed our bedding inside. Davin unpacked his cooking gear. The Pios and I refilled water containers, and we sat down to watch Davin fix dinner.

"No wonder you need extra horses, with all that stuff just for cooking," I said.

"I see no reason not to eat proper meals out here." Davin reached for a stasis containers filled with vat steaks and fresh vegetables, and frowned when he realized he had no chopping knife. "Grek, can you gather enough skinsh for a salad?"

"Sure," Grek said. The Pios taught me which wide, thickly veined, phosphorescing pale blue-green leaves to pick from a ground plant along the stream bank. By the time we were chewing away on the tart, glowing salad, we could watch two moons skimming in and out of the clouds overhead, and silver and gold glow-bugs dancing beneath.

I listened to small screams and growls of local creatures coming on the night shift. "Amphibians?" I asked, wondering if Big Maxson did, after all, have some night reptiles. Grek and Skikkan confirmed my guess, and yawned widely. "Yes, and we're up past any sane bedtime."

"What's the matter?" Davin asked when I slowed down even more than the Pios over our next course. It was a heartbreaking plate of perfectly prepared teriyaki vat steak, with a heaping serving of steamed vegetables and grains. "Don't you like my cooking anymore? I haven't seen you eat a decent meal since we set out to find Giem."

The sleepy Pios may have found his spices odd. I couldn't use that excuse. "I haven't had much of an appetite ever since Giem disappeared." I gazed at my plate sorrowfully.

"So that's your problem. You worry too much."

Perhaps he was just right for Giem, who didn't believe in worrying. "I thought you cared," I said anyway. "Aren't you anxious that we may be following too slowly—that we won't catch up with Giem before she gets into worse trouble?"

"And wouldn't that be her problem?" Davin smiled back at me.

"If you truly believe that, what are you doing here?"

"Aw, quit burning off all your fuel over it," Davin said. "There's nothing more we can do tonight. Skikkan and I commed a theory today about Riddock's general direction, which should help us do some short-cutting tomorrow."

"The thieves obviously have a lot of untrained quelsh to herd, which should also hinder them considerably," Skikkan said, between slow mouthfuls. She scooped with her claws from her plate. "Especially if they were unwise enough to try to move any females protecting nests, we stand a good chance of catching up with them soon."

"Where do you think they're going?"

"Following the direction they've taken, they seem to be headed for a rather small, isolated, unsettled valley."

"No major rivers there to attract Pios," Davin said. "A bit northwest from here."

"It makes a kind of sense. Why?" I said, agonized by the whole mysterious mess. "What is Riddock going to do with all those quelsh out there—set up his own dairy and cheese farm? Fly the whole lot off into outer space?"

Davin choked on his steak. I almost thought he was laughing at my sarcastic humor. Yet he was normally so serious about his food that I had to suspect I'd fired correctly at something. Besides, he began to look as sick as I felt.

"That does it." He dropped his fork on his plate. "I'm not even hungry anymore."

"Why?" I said. "What did I say? Just what is it you know about Garth Riddock that you're not telling me?"

"You'll find out soon enough, when it's too late anyway," he said.

"Tell me now, when it might still help," I said, frustrated.

"Riddock plans to smuggle quelsh offworld, without any rebugging. There, does that help you any?"

I was stunned into silence for a micro, until my curiosity got the better of me. "Why is that such a problem for you? Were you also involved?"

"No." Davin looked down at his plate. "I have—a borderline record. I'm a marginal trader, and if I occasionally pick up leftovers from bigger operators with fewer scruples, I consider that my business. Unfortunately FIL doesn't always agree, and if I get even indirectly mixed up in a crime this serious—if Riddock doesn't have me killed—it may not matter. I doubt anyone will believe I just hoped to find out if and how he managed to trade for Pio cheeses. If you're a FIL spy, I sure wish you'd hurry up, arrest me, and get it over with."

I almost laughed, until I saw he was serious. "You really must care, if that's what you think, and you still haven't left us."

"How else can I prove myself?" He snapped off his stove and slammed uneaten dessert ingredients into their boxes. "Besides, what should I think? Why else would two vet students go chasing after Riddock?"

"Excitement. Adventure. Romance!" I could tell, not too surprisingly, that he thought I was teasing him. So

I changed my approach. "Seriously, we're taught how important it is to avoid contaminating planets with alien microbes not genetically designed to stay exactly where they belong in their hosts. Plus we're concerned about any animal abuse."

"Lizard crap. Pure lizard piss."

"You realize those aren't the same?

"Humph. I'm going to bed. Maybe when I wake up, I'll just discover this was all a bad dream." Davin silently cleaned and put away his cooking gear, and retired to his tent after a brief walk in the woods.

That left Grek and me sitting and staring at each other, Grek with a confused expression on his face, and me feeling distinctly uncomfortable. Skikkan scratched a circle in the damp dirt with a toe claw, and traced it repeatedly between her stares at us.

"I don't understand," Grek said at last, in a quiet voice. "Is Davin a criminal?"

"I'm not sure," I said.

"Are you a spy?" he said.

"Not yet."

Needless to say, Grek did not appear enlightened by my answers, and he had the sense not to ask any more questions.

It began to sprinkle again, and we parted to do our own business in the woods. I expected Grek and Skikkan to bed down in their burrow after that. Instead they came to me while I was checking my pack seals one last time, and asked my preference.

"Don't you two want to sleep together?" I asked them.

"Sometimes I get very confused translations when you Humans talk about sleep," Grek said, in a tired, amused voice, while my face grew hot. I'd better work harder on fine-tuning my translator. "Even if we could do anything besides slumber at night, Skikkan and I are cousins. Perhaps you have similar taboos?"

"Grek, just tell her I'm curious," Skikkan said impatiently. "I'd like to try sleeping with a Human. Since you two are good friends, I assume you'd rather have me join Davin?"

I couldn't help smiling. "You're welcome to him." I waved at Davin's tent. "If you ask him too."

"He shouldn't mind." Grek took my arm and led me toward the makeshift burrow.

Just as I was thinking I'd have to crawl back out to retrieve it, Skikkan reappeared with my sleeping bag, and told us Davin had okayed the arrangement. "I think he's too tired to care." Skikkan sneeze-chuckled and rushed off again.

The rain began to pound and I worried aloud about flooding, even though Ziehl's sleeping bag was probably good enough to handle it.

"We picked elevated ground, added to it and protected it with trenching it," Grek mumbled as he curled up in his thin blanket.

"What's the big deal, anyway," I said, while I fought my usual battle to settle comfortably in my bag. "If you can't do anything besides sleep at night, why do you care who you're with?"

"It's sometimes a custom with which we demonstrate trust." Grek shifted onto his back.

Distant thunder rumbled through the night while I reacted with silent, pleasantly surprised shock.

"I have heard Humans wake up much more easily during the night," Grek said. "So I guess you wouldn't feel the same way about it. We suspect that before we could make fire, or killed most of our predators, our ancestors may have slept in large huddles together. That way they could hope at least one would wake up at the first sign of danger and arouse the rest."

"And—Skikkan—already feels this trust towards Davin?" I said uncertainly.

The thunder approached closer, sounding louder.

"I'm not sure about that," Grek said. "She just got interested after I told her what it's like to sleep next to a Human."

"What is it like?" I'd grown rather curious myself, and I turned on my side toward him.

"Sort of similar to sleeping near a fire pit. I don't get so slowed down, and I wake up earlier."

"Oh." Turning over on my back, folding my arms under my head, and not feeling very slowed down myself, I wondered whether Grek had grown fond of humans simply for their body heat. I could see he wasn't falling fast asleep either, from a brief glint of lightning on his green eyes. We both lay listening to the rain beating down on our tarp and the leaves nearby.

"I'm glad Skikkan and Davin have figured out where we're supposed to go tomorrow," I said next, as

I considered what the storm must be doing to our trail. Even if I'm not sure why any of you are here, I thought to myself. A loud crack of thunder vibrated the ground under us and lightning briefly made the tarp glow. One of the horses whinnied shrilly, and one of the lizards shrieked back. I doubt whether even the Pios slept soundly that night.

CHAPTER 32

Davin was in a silently fused mood the next morning. None of us knew why, and we carefully tiptoed around him as we ate leftovers while packing up. Fortunately the quelsh-drive trail was so extensive that even last night's furious storm hadn't erased it completely. Apparently we needed to follow the tracks at least a couple hours longer before we could completely trust our next shortcut. Davin and Skikkan conferred for nearly half an hour over his map before we mounted up again, and Skikkan made an announcement.

"You don't need me anymore. The trail has become ridiculously obvious—even Grek can follow it. Let me know how it all turns out, cousin. I've come far enough, and I want to rejoin our quelsh patrols."

"I could have done it all without you, Skikkan," Grek teased her back. "You're just leaving while it's still easy."

I cringed inwardly, hoping he wasn't taunting fate.

The three of us set off in a line, and Davin's anxiety seemed to grow the longer he led us on the trail. Later we reached a more exposed, windy, level area, with only scattered trees and fewer streams. He began to really press our pace, taking advantage of smoother ground to alternate between trotting and galloping. More than once I had to give up on side-saddle altogether, and I rubbed the inside of my knees raw again trying to hang on.

When our lizards began to pant and I could see sweat foaming up on the horses, I coaxed my lizard up alongside Davin. Before I could yell at him for the sake of our animals, he pulled to an abrupt halt. Grek and I had to act fast to keep our mounts from overrunning and attacking his horses.

"What's wrong?" I yelled at Davin.

Davin pointed straight towards the horizon. "Company."

A man and a Pio, both on horseback, galloped along the quelsh trail toward us. It was too late for us to hide, and within minutes they pulled up in front of us.

The Pio was the first native I'd seen wearing a sword, in a curved scabbard strapped across her back. One scar made her unforgettable—an empty, dry left eye socket. Grek hissed softly, and the strange Pio didn't even bother to glance at him. Maybe she had to work too hard at keeping her seat, on a Pio saddle badly adapted to her filthy, sore horse.

I scanned the scruffy man and felt even more immediate repugnance—towards his cocky grin, the heavy hand on his reins, and the foam on his horse's lips and flanks.

"Rakke. What are you doing here?" Davin leaned back in his saddle and smiled, his anxiety seeming to vanish under a look of mild annoyance.

"Mohrogh. Old friend. This time I'm afraid it's you who owes me an explanation." The human grinned back, showing food caught between his teeth. Revolting. Not to mention the odor that wafted from dark slimy outlines around the Pio's scales. I wasn't much in comparison. At least I'd had some sponge baths, and I had kept my hair brushed and my teeth clean. I couldn't even tell for sure the color of the man's hair and beard under all his filth.

"I suspect someone else told you to stay off Riddock's back," Rakke said, after Davin just sat there grinning at him. "Why don't you heed that warning before you're in too deep?"

"Hah! If I'm a parasite on Riddock's back, you're a virus on mine. Don't think you can convince me you've been hired by Riddock. Go back to the piss-puddle you came from, and get off my horse's ass."

"Better think twice about that, Mohrogh," the big scruffy man said. He slid a hand under his dirty faded vest, and pulled out an odd-looking stunner. He didn't seem to care about aiming the weapon, as if mere display suited his purpose. "This time I am hired help. Not by Garth Riddock, and my boss is a much bigger parasite than you."

Davin had eyes only for the stunner, and all his self-confidence seemingly melted away again. His face froze, an inadequate mask for sheer terror.

Puzzled, I glanced between him and Rakke's stunner. Did Davin somehow have good enough eyesight to read a dangerously high setting? Or maybe he was more worried about what Rakke could do to us if he stunned us into helplessness? In some ways that scared me a whole lot less than the Pio's sword, which she hadn't touched so far.

"Well, Mohrogh? Had enough? Ready to stay out of Chothark's way?"

"Chothark is here?" Davin's face unfroze, and his features visibly crumpled.

"Yeah. She's a little upset about the situation Garth left her with, the last time she tagged after him. This time she's out for more than his garbage. Com that? Fortunately she's willing to give smalltime vac-heads like you one last warning to stay out of the way, before you make the action more nova for everyone, especially yourselves. I suggest you take the hint." Rakke slipped the weapon back into his hidden holster as he kept his glare on Davin.

"I'll take it." Davin at last looked disgusted. "Great Galaxy, if I ever catch you again at less of an advantage—"

"You needn't admit your lack of even a pocket knife." Rakke snickered as he shocked all of us with his knowledge. "Blast out of here while you still can, Mohrogh. Otherwise, you'll find yourself in deeper piss than you'll ever be able to wade out of." With that, he yanked his horse around and kicked it into a gallop in the direction he'd come from, his Pio companion wheeling after. Neither bothered to glance back.

Davin swore vehemently under his breath and rubbed the scar on the back of his right hand, clenched on his saddle horn. He turned toward us. "Well, folks, looks like the hunt has ended. Sorry."

"Sorry?" I said. "I don't com it. You've had stunners pointed at you before and that didn't discourage you at all. Why are you letting this big piss-hole scare you off?"

"That was no stunner." Davin stared at me.

"It did look a little strange—"

"He's got his grubby, fused hands on a stinger. Do you have any idea what I'm talking about?"

I gulped and fell silent. FIL banned stunners here because they exceeded native weapons technology. Criminal laws ban stingers everywhere in FIL space.

"I sort of thought—she was just someone people told stories about—to scare small children into not straying," Grek mumbled.

"Who?" I said.

"The swordswoman. She used to be a professional skitsh killer, and she's not one I ever hoped to meet. Rumor says she'll hire out her sword now for more than just skitsh meat."

Pios also had criminals? That was another let-down.

"Well, it's time to rethink how far we've strayed." Davin scanned back the way we'd come. "We can return to the station, and I'll even risk helping you inform whatever authorities you want." He faced me. "That scum-head is right. We're in completely over our heads if Chothark wants revenge that badly."

I discovered I'd had my fill of warnings against doing what I knew I'd have to do, no matter what. "I fought off a bully with a similar name once," I snapped back, only slightly exaggerating. The food riot had come out a draw, only because Orphan Center honor guards had interfered.

"Not this Chothark, you haven't," Davin said coldly. "Obviously you don't know who in FIL I'm talking about. You really should believe me when I say this situation has gotten far too serious for the three of us."

"It'll take us days to ride back. And this means Giem may be in far more danger than she realizes."

"I'm afraid that's her problem. Hopefully she'll receive the same warning and have the sense to heed it. I've had enough." Davin turned his horses around and started back, while Grek kept his lizard standing with mine.

"Quit acting like utter fools." Davin stopped his horses a short way off. "What good can you hope to accomplish out here? Grek! You know that Pio means bad business. Your mother will worry about you. Use some sense, and ride back with me."

I scanned my Pio friend. He remained unmoved. We both sat out the long minutes it took for Davin to finish ranting and ride away.

"Maybe he's right," I admitted. I slapped my reins against my palm. "I hate to be the one to tell you, Grek, about stingers, but I'd better. Tuned correctly, they can make you feel great pain for however long their power lasts, because they stimulate nerve pain receptors without causing any physical injury. They're very illegal, and I don't know how that man smuggled one here, and he may not have the only one. And you know more about his Pio partner than I do. From what you've said about her alone, you probably should go home."

"And you, Taje? I'm not a Guardian for my people. I have no such training. I'm a student farmer. Are FIL student animal doctors taught any more than our agricultural students about how to defend themselves against a sword? Or don't you know what that weapon can do?"

"I know, well enough," I said. "Human history is full of bloody swords. Return home, Grek. This isn't your fight."

"These people are running loose on my world."

"Go report it."

"What are you going to do?" His green eyes caught mine.

I caught myself in a silent agony of indecision. The logical part of my brain tried to launch its argument against any further rash rescue attempts. However, I had no family, and Giem was the only friend I'd made since I'd parted from all my old friends. Besides, I enrolled in vet school because the worst stress for me is not knowing what's wrong.

I had no idea whether Giem was still safe. And with Davin gone, surely people out here would at least quit mistaking me for a rival trader. If someone stopped me again, I could simply report an unelaborated truth—that I was searching for a missing friend. How could anyone consider me important enough to hurt? Yes, I know, coming from a vet student, that was a very nova argument. And there was really no stopping me, regardless of logic.

"I'm going on," I said, with one last fear: "Grek, you'd better ride back to your village. I can't defend you either, and I'd hate to see you get hurt over this."

Grek hissed quietly. "You're going on because Giemsan is your friend. I'm going with you because you're my friend—"

"Why?" I couldn't help bursting out, although I felt like I just drew a sword against my own throat. "You haven't known me that long. What do you see in me, that you could take such a risk?"

"Not a big brain," Grek retorted. "Have you even considered how you're going to find Giem, with no reasonable sense of direction? You act ten times more lost out here than I do, and you'll need to leave this dangerous track immediately. Who else is left to show you the way?"

I might have considered that an insult. Instead, I couldn't help smiling back at Grek—if in bafflement—and feeling some relief. I reined my lizard in behind his, and we set off cross-country.

CHAPTER 33

Ironically, I began to understand Davin better as Grek and I pressed on without him. The quieter it became on our journey, the more nervous and jumpy I felt. I suspected Grek suffered similarly, for I rarely saw the merry fluttering of his eyelids, and he became pensively quiet. When I pulled out my raingear the second day, I could feel our tension hovering like an extra cloud.

"Grek, what do you consider most curious about humans?" I asked, in an attempt to lighten the atmosphere, and hoping I'd get an equal chance to learn more about Pios.

Grek turned to stare at me. A hint of a wink appeared. "Where should I start?" he said, with a small sneeze. "Your many over-skins? I used to think you wear them to carry things. Now I'm beginning to suspect they're more for holding in all the heat you make, right?"

"Mostly." I found myself thinking hard about it. "We must keep our bodies within a narrow temperature range, or we'll die. Human ancestors lost most of their protective pelts a long time ago. Our 'fringe,'" I tugged on a lock of my hair, " is just a remnant. Even when the weather is easy for us, most of us still feel silly or vulnerable when we are naked—without any 'over skins.'" Would the words "naked" or "clothes" translate at all for Pios? "So we wear coverings, adjusted to the weather—"

"So you cannot just be, with whatever is."

"That came out sounding rather profound," I said.

"Perhaps it is. Maybe that's why Humans feel they have to work hard all the time, just to live. We enjoy lounging in the sun, and we have to spend time in it, or we have problems with scale-scum, and other weaknesses—"

"You mean, like between the scales of the swordswoman?"

"Yes."

"Is that why your mother took your vest from you?" I hadn't understood it at the time.

"Yes. I miss carrying stuff in it."

"Humans need sunlight too," I said, "to set our sense of time, to keep our minds healthy, and to make one nutrient. I don't think we need it as much as you, and we've found substitutes. When do we need to stop for you to bask in the sun?"

"Don't worry. I'm okay. I'm mostly getting what I need while I ride along with you. Do Humans lay eggs?"

I laughed. And realized I had to think. "Inside ourselves, we do. They're too small to see—"

"Like parasite eggs?" Grek wheezed with amusement.

"I guess." I grinned. "Human eggs have no shells and they grow directly into babies, inside our mothers.

We give birth to live young, ready to nurse—uh, suck nutrition from their mother's glands." I didn't think "breasts" would translate either. "Do Pios lay eggs?" I had just assumed they did.

"Our females do. Up to several eggs in a clutch, at regular intervals. Our mothers don't have food glands. They regurgitate food until their young grow big enough to eat their own solid food."

"Fathers don't help?"

Grek seemed quite amused. "Why should they? Do Human fathers help? Male quelsh can't help nurse."

"No. Our men don't have milk glands." I patted my raincoat, over my own modest examples. "Most of our fathers try to help in other ways. Can't male Pios—regurgitate?"

Grek tapped his face with his claws. "I guess not. I never thought about it before. We wouldn't even know who to feed."

"What?"

"Do Human fathers know who their children are?"

"Usually." Did mine? Or was he dead? Or had my mother received an anonymous sperm donation, or cloned herself? I would probably never know. "Can Pio females store sperm—uh, lay eggs with more than one father per clutch? That happens with some species I've studied."

"Sure. It's almost impossible to know who fathered any particular egg a female chooses to keep. Don't Humans produce many eggs?"

"Only about one a month, usually. Is that how you keep your population under control? The females don't keep every egg?"

"It's lots of work to properly care for an egg, and raise the infant. Females only do it when they really want a child."

"If they don't know the father, how do they choose which egg to keep?"

"We say it's a woman's mystery!" Grek sighed. "Don't ask me. Except I guess they can tell certain features by the color and size of the shell, like whether it's female or male. Male eggs tend to be much more beautiful—my mother says mine was brilliantly irresistible. If you give birth to hatched babies, I suppose you have no choice about what you get?"

"Well, we do have techniques to help us select traits, before birth. We mostly use them to eliminate diseases, not to choose sex. Some of our species did that for a while, and they ended up with far too many males. Can you imagine the absurdity?" I never could understand that curiously recurrent part of human history—no better than any unfortunate hetero male of those sad generations— much less explain it to aliens.

"Too many males! Why wouldn't your women prefer more of their own kind, like ours?"

"Why have any preference?" I said.

"Why, because women get to have children, if and when they choose. Do you get to choose?"

"Only by using—special treatments." I reflexively rubbed my left thigh, over a subtle subcutaneous Center implant, which freed me—so far totally superfluously—from any risk of pregnancy, as well as some sort of messy monthly discharge. "A long time ago, we didn't know how. What do you do with unwanted eggs?"

"Our females have to eat most of them. Otherwise, their bones grow soft and their muscles weak. On very special occasions, they let us share. Their eggs taste very good."

"We would hardly ever consider eating a newborn baby, and thankfully, we don't need to."

"A hatchling? I can see why not."

Along with my general interest in exobiology, I was raised in a huge multi-species FIL orphanage. I learned open-mindedness about the ways of other people early in life, which has served me well on my travels. I began to feel a bit peculiar until he added that comment. Next I reflected on a few more odd cruelties of human history, and I thought of one last question for Grek that day.

"Do you feel less important, being a Pio male instead of a female?"

Grek turned thoughtful, and took a while to answer. "I guess . . . maybe . . . sometimes I do. But—never when I'm around you."

That almost startled me out of my saddle. He'd just added another piece to the puzzle of our friendship.

CHAPTER 34

I lived more like a native during our journey. I spent warm if often wet days riding Pio-style, and sore, restless nights in makeshift burrows. I gratefully supplemented packaged meals with nuts, hard rolls, dried fruits, and even dried insects from Grek's food bag. I mostly declined his dried meats. However, I was never quite sure what-all he slipped me in his mother's version of pemmican. He kept snickering whenever I ate it, especially when I seemed to enjoy it.

We talked often about nearly anything except what we were doing. I found out that native names for Grek's species and world weren't humanly pronounceable (or wristcom translatable), though I tried to say the correct terms anyway. Pios can't say "P," so "Thio" was as close as I got to the real word, and Grek still laughed at me.

Grek wondered why humans don't look at you properly when you're interacting with them. I guessed my species considered staring a dominating or predatory act. In turn, I asked him whether his mother was eating one of her own eggs the first time I met her—she probably was. Grek hadn't bothered to notice or ask.

A couple hours after our third makeshift breakfast together, we left our lizards tied up in a stand of round-leafed saplings, and hiked up the short remaining distance to the top of an overgrown ridge. From there we could hear the faint, unmistakable sounds of hundreds of quelsh. However, the view was fused. Grek slithered up a towering tree, while I began a long slow skulk down to a better lookout point.

We felt almost certain we'd found the small sheltered valley we suspected was Riddock's destination. As I crawled, crouched, and slid down behind all possible cover, tantalizing glimpses of blue and green quelsh, and hissing complaints from somewhere below, quickened my pulse. Was this what it felt like to be a real FIL undercover observation agent?

I hadn't intended to end up nearly halfway down the rocky dirt slope. Patchy views of the valley floor revealed temporary corrals partly filled with restless quelsh, and a neat cluster of large tents to one side. I unsealed my jacket and caught my breath. If Riddock's minions had captured Giem, they must have her stashed in one of the tents. I still couldn't scan any hint of an illegally landed ship or shuttle, which would command instant action from authorities, if I could find any way to report it. Maybe Grek could see more from his tree. I turned back. I needed to rejoin Grek anyway, to decide on our next intrepid move.

However, I very unintrepidly didn't check the ground under my hiking boots, and I knocked loose some rocks. They rattled down the hillside, startling a pair of karcs squabbling over an unusually large red fuzzy. The karcs launched screaming into the air.

I dropped to the ground and froze. I could only hope my dirty camping clothes would hide me from distant lookouts until the disturbance passed.

I found myself in the next moment staring up at the excited face of a muscular human and into the muzzle of her stunner—I eyed it carefully. I grabbed the woman's ankle and yanked hard, toppling her downhill—I'm stronger than I scan.

I leaped up, heedless of setting off more dirt and rock slides. I found it tough to run back uphill—much harder than slipping down here. Above me I spotted several more armed people who also seemed to know all about my presence.

As I frantically veered off, trying to race across the hillside, I wondered how long the patrols around here had watched me act like a completely oblivious vac-head. Perhaps they had scanners set up all around the valley perimeter, and they might know about Grek too. Somehow I'd have to make a fast loop, to try to lead them away, and return to warn him, if I wasn't too late.

However, the woman I'd tripped managed to recover faster than I could run along the steep, brushy slope. At least I assume she shot me. I felt the stun absorb into my back, and all my voluntary muscles went instantly slack. The next moment I found myself rolling downhill.

I covered several meters of hard ground before a large tree trunk caught me in the middle and I wrapped around it.

I was completely conscious—someone gave stunners a ridiculous name—and I was thoroughly paralyzed, to the point that I gladly felt myself breathing against rough tree bark. My attacker must have had her stunner set at the upper limits of safety. I couldn't even feel a hint of the peripheral tingling that typically precedes rapid recovery.

Later my cursing captors caught up with me, unwrapped me from the tree, and turned me over on my back on the ground. I looked up at several frustrated faces, blinked at the sun between tree tops, and my head rolled to one side.

"Think that could be her?"

"Not nova likely."

"Hey, we haven't got time to waste on anyone else. Search her, tie her up, like the rest—"

"Here?"

"Where else? We'll deal with her later. You do have some rope, don't you? Okay, just use this tree. Hurry up, we haven't got all day."

Someone checked my pockets and my belt pouch. "Just fused food here." My captor frowned at the garish picture on the meal pack and shoved it back in my pouch, obviously recognizing the nova brand. I caught a glimpse of blue synthetic cord while they sat me up against the tree. They pulled my arms around it. It was a wide trunk, and my hands didn't meet, which meant the knots at my wrists were out of my reach. I guessed they'd had some practice. I cursed Davin in my head, which I couldn't lift to watch my captors leave.

CHAPTER 35

When the tingling pain of recovery shot through all my muscles, I choked on nausea that had nothing to do with latent stunner effects. Vomiting is a hazardous act without full muscle control. I just couldn't imagine I'd received the sort of easy warn-off Davin and Grek had suffered, trussed up only long enough to think twice about tagging after Riddock.

Thanks to the Pios, I wasn't wearing any wristcom. I also wasn't sitting within shouting distance of a major trail. Instead I'd gotten tied up much too close to the scene of the crime. I concluded that Riddock's minions had some other pressing errand to run, and next they would indeed return, as promised, for who knows what mischief.

I found this worse than anticipating an impending final exam, even for a class I'd neglected all quarter. Somehow I no longer believed my lost-friend story would satisfy my captors. My vivid imagination took over the confrontation to come, replete with angry questions about my obvious spying, and more than just a rotten grade when my answers didn't satisfy. Maybe they'd kill me.

I commed I'd better just honestly answer any questions put to me. The truth was probably a lot less dangerous, and more laughable, than anything Riddock's people might fear from me.

What I didn't understand was why they hadn't even bothered to wait the few minutes it would have taken me to recover enough for questioning. Trying to reason it out didn't help me much, either. I still felt sick, and risked having to wear it on my shirt or in my lap.

I could lift my head at last and spit out excess saliva I feared swallowing into my roiling stomach. The sun reached my face and side, drenching me in a clammy pool of sweat. A cloud of tiny grey and silver insects formed in front of me, attracted by my weird smells, I suppose. They tickled my face and hands as they brushed past me. I drew my knees up defensively.

I sat facing uphill. I couldn't watch the valley or see the sky, except for small blue patches through the tree branches overhead. No clouds today? The sun filled my nostrils with the smell of hot duff, while my sweat exceeded my shirt's absorptive capacity. I wanted to yank off my coat, wipe sweat from my face, shoo away the bugs, puke into a bush, or shout for help—why hadn't they gagged me? Too vac-headed, or in too big of a hurry?

Maybe they did want me to be found, after sufficient discomfort to deter me from returning, and I'd also warn off any cohorts. That assumed they knew or suspected I had at least one partner trailing me. And maybe this close to their camp, they couldn't afford to let anyone go. If they hadn't caught Grek after spotting us both on a scan, perhaps they'd left me for bait.

I clamped my mouth shut on a half-formed shout. I stretched my legs back out, and twisted my feet and wrists to work out kinks. I'd die of exposure out here before I'd draw my Pio friend into a trap. I shifted my rear end around. I didn't have enough padding to comfortably sit in one position for long. I tried to work my swelling fingers around any of the knots behind my back, and failed again. I yanked angrily and my bonds just tightened, making me rue the day I'd laughed at Davin.

Gangrene of the hands—I was going to die from rope tourniquets on my wrists, bed sores on my butt, dehydration from nervous sweating and puking, and claustrophobic insanity. Just wait until I told Giem about this rare method of murder. We ought to enter it into the Manual, under the heading of Unique Tortures by the Other Side. I amused myself with the stories of heroic stamina I'd tell her when this ended, until I realized Grek and I had made the very same mistake that Giem and me had made. We'd split up.

I slowly learned the intimate details of the rocky slope in front of me. A red fuzzy crept over one of my boots, and at last the other, and a meter later a fat little grey toady-lizard ate it. Maybe an hour after that, something larger than a karc swooped down and snapped up the fuzzy-eater. Was it all supposed to be some lesson presented for my benefit? If so, I didn't like it. Not one bit.

Shade replaced sunlight as the sun soared beyond the branches of my tree, and I spent some time in hard shivering until my sweat gradually dried. All in all, I suffered through an extremely thrilling morning. I could complain more. But I finally realized that being forced to do nothing for a while was a smooth break. I guess I was looking on Giem's Bright Side.

By midday my stomach was growling loudly and I would have groveled for a water bottle. By afternoon my stomach had tied itself into hard knots, while my head began to ache. Don't let me give the impression that all this zapped by with any speed. It's just difficult to describe mind-numbing boredom, interlaced with sheer terror, without becoming mind-numbingly boring.

The contradiction of it did zap me when I found myself longing for access to even the most vacful com programs. In the hectic days before finals, I often suffered a craving for a day when I could simply lounge on my bunk and stare at a blank screen without feeling guilty about it. When I had it, I was fusing. Maybe anticipation, boredom, and being completely ignored were worse than any real physical torture that might lie ahead of me. When one got right down to it, pain could be almost tolerable, with the right amount of distraction. Vet school was an excellent example.

I worked my legs again, and tried to sit sort of sideways to obtain some relief. I caught tears in my throat more than once, and savagely choked them back. I didn't want to make any sound that might possibly attract Grek into this miserable snare.

As the afternoon wore on, my mind spun around in its own trap. I was such a vac-head, letting myself get caught like this. What good was I doing Giem or the wild quelsh? How could I have been so nova careless? Once again I stood a good chance of causing those who cared about me nothing besides grief and worry. Not to mention drawing Grek into terrible danger. I wondered how I could have any friends left, I was such a stubborn jerk.

As if having other people shooting at me wasn't enough. I was old enough to know to loathe my relentless onslaught of self-criticism. It was such an old pattern, I had no idea how to stop my assault. And I had plenty of time now to punish myself.

The breeze overhead barely sifted through the trees, and only a few small reptilian squabbles broke into the silent thrashing in my mind. I just couldn't help thinking whatever happened to me next would probably serve me right.

Where were my attackers? Perhaps I had overestimated my importance, and Riddock's people might simply forget about me. As shadows lengthened, I considered this fresh irony. After all those fanciful adventure scenarios Giem and I had dreamed up, what an unexciting non–adventure to die from. No daring rescues, no hard-fought battles, and no glorious citations—just a decaying human corpse, lost somewhere in the woods of South Maxson—

Footfalls and anxious voices interrupted my morbid thoughts. My captors reappeared with relieved exclamations, and I almost cheered them on. Someone at last went to work on the knots around my wrists behind my tree, while I watched somebody else step back to make a wristcom call.

"Okay, Garth, we found her again."

"Since you had forgotten all about her, I guess that's an accomplishment."

Even I could hear the thick sarcasm in his voice over the wristcom, as my arms fell limply to my sides. I stood up too fast and nearly fell down, dizzy, almost scaring the woman in the trio into shooting me again. Only the tree trunk saved me.

"Can you tell me anything about her?"

"Uh, sure." The man making the call glanced over at me, while another freed my wrists from the rope. "Hmm . . . well, like we said before, she looks like another trader."

Well, there goes that theory. I couldn't suppress some loud curses, as sharp needles of returning circulation stabbed my hands.

"I don't want your assumptions," Garth snapped, "and if you're beating her—"

"We haven't touched her."

"Tell me what her wristcom tells about her, and what answers she gave before you left her."

"We couldn't find a wristcom on her, and, uh, we stunned her, so we couldn't ask her anything."

"You had to shoot her? A simple trader? With no wristcom?"

"Well, we didn't think—"

"Obviously not. Standing right next to her, maybe you can at least describe this alleged trader. What color is her hair? Does she remind you of—"

"No, that's what we've been trying to tell you. She looks a bit too young, and she's tall, skinny. She's unusually pale for a human, but her hair is more red than blond, and she's got green eyes, not blue—"

"What! Are you sure?"

The man blinked, and stared vacfully at me. "Uh, yeah, at least I think, I mean, here, I'll aim my wristcom at her face for you."

"Have you even bothered to ask her for a name yet?"

"Tell him you've caught Tajen Jesmuhr!" I crowed hoarsely. He would recognize me anyway. I badly needed a drink of water. So much that I considered—only briefly, mind you—trying to tackle someone to rip loose a bottle from a belt. However, of many minor details, my hands weren't working well enough, and the man behind me was industriously untangling the rope to tie my arms back behind me, while my legs shook too hard to kick him.

"Get her down here at once. And don't take any chances with her."

Ejected from an exploding ship, only to be dumped into space vac. I almost laughed with hysterical mirth as all three frightened guards made sure their stunner safeties were disengaged, even though my arms were securely bound, and I could barely stumble down toward the valley floor on weak, cramping legs. The forced march took long enough to remind my stomach about its anxiety attack, and I felt cold and sweaty as I met up again with the infamous Garth Riddock, awaiting our arrival in front of the tents.

Riddock was as neatly dressed as ever, with not a blond hair out of place. Not only was he the palest of his crew, he was also cleaner than anyone else present. I wondered distractedly how he managed it out here. Under his thoughtful gaze I couldn't help feeling like a wild, filthy, scared beast.

He folded his arms, and a slow smile crept across his handsome face. Relief? For a micro his reaction startled me out of my fear.

"Well, Tajen Jesmuhr, how funny we should meet again like this," he greeted me. "You're not quite my current concern. Perhaps you should have been. Somehow that doesn't surprise me. Where's your partner, Giemsan Fane?"

I grew bolder, and I was tempted to say, "Hi, Garth, suck it all up your right nostril." I did com that probably wouldn't help matters much. A diversionary tactic seemed much more reasonable.

I raked the ankle of the guard on my left with my boot, stomped her foot, and lashed my other booted foot out at the knee of the guard on my right. At last I had a chance to put my self-defense lessons to work. Fortunately, not having my arms free for balance—let's not discuss my lack of coordination, please—I toppled with the kick. That way, I didn't have too much farther to fall when the third guard shot me.

Once more that day, I could no longer move—or talk—at least until I had a little longer to think about my answers. Occasionally I'm not as vac-brained as I scan.

Riddock interrupted his guards' curses with an impatient retort somewhere over me. I was down on my stomach, staring at trampled, tri-bladed grass, and a tiny yellow creeper hiding in a miniature yellow bud. "Don't you dare kick her back, you idiots. She's a FIL rep! You've caused me enough trouble. Garnen, you and Tullin haul her into a tent and make sure she can't leave us, until I can spare some more time to waste on this fused mess."

Riddock stalked off, and the limping, angry guards dragged me into a tent, and dumped me on my stomach on a wonderful little cot. My smooth reward for stomping my guards and my silence at the end of a long, hard, fused day. Ha, ha. I won!

My captors argued back and forth about who had to babysit me, until they just lazily tied my ankles to one end of the cot and left me alone.

The second stunning took me even longer to recover from. Maybe more than one of Riddock's minions had shot me. The moment I did recover, I went right to work on another escape attempt. With my arms tied behind my back, I knelt on the cot to reach the knots around my ankles. I found the knots too complicated to untie blindly, and toppled off the end of the cot.

Well, there went another chance to break away, or even for the consolation prize of a soft, semi-civilized bed. I didn't have enough remaining strength—or a free arm (both now under my back)—to pull myself back up.

I lay on my back on the tent floor, with my feet still tied up on the cot, and tried to puzzle it all out, with a head throbbing from stress and lack of food and water. I couldn't stop wondering where Giem was—whether Riddock honestly didn't know, or whether he'd been taunting me. I'd have to try to find out when he returned to question me, somehow without also letting him learn anything new. What would he want from me? It might get rather tricky.

When my back-and-forth arguments began chasing their tails, exhaustion called a halt to the whole miserable party. So I smoothly did what any good, stressed-out vet student does with otherwise wasted time—I anesthetized myself with sleep.

CHAPTER 36

"Made yourself at home, I see." Riddock stood over me. "Looking rather more confident than your position would seem to merit."

I jerked back to consciousness, from dreams of hopeless chase scenes across slippery landscapes, only to find my feet still asleep up on the bed, while I lay on the floor.

My heart pounded as I scanned the same amused smile and twinkling blue eyes that Garth Riddock had shown us in town. I didn't feel the slightest bit confident at this point, and I had to remind myself that whatever crime he planned to commit out here was probably worth murdering for. "I haven't heard of you killing anyone yet," I muttered to myself. I turned onto my side toward him, to shift my weight off my arms and back. That set off some ripe bruises, and I winced, while sharp recovery pains ran through my numb arms.

"Nor do I order beatings," Garth said angrily, as he yanked loose the knots at my ankles and freed my arms. I sat on the cot and gaped at him.

"No one beat me," I said hoarsely. I threw in a groan or two for good measure, as I massaged my throbbing, bloated-feeling appendages back to painful life. "I've just suffered a few unfortunate falls. Could you spare me some water?"

Garth's anger faded, as he moved around the tent to find a liter water bottle. I clumsily drained it. My nemesis sat down on the cot, close enough to lean against me, which he did. It startled me more than almost anything else the blond man could have done, which I suppose was his goal. "Tell me, Tajen, what motivated you to find out I'm not a murderer?"

Even as I realized I'd given away too much in one careless phrase, my body was perversely responding to mere contact with him. Hormones have absolutely no sense of honor or timing. I was glad Garth appeared entirely human, rather than a member of a telepathic or empathic species. How was I ever going to answer his question without giving away more? I decided on silence as the best policy.

"Okay, Tajen, how about a question you can answer? Come outside with me."

I still felt weak, and I stumbled a bit following Garth out to the nearest pen. He paid me no heed, however, having eyes only for his other captives. He pointed out quelsh in the herd with obvious problems. Some appeared quite depressed, and some stood splay-legged, breathing with open-mouthed labor. Others moaned, paced, and cried incessantly, as we both waved away irritating glitter-bugs that seemed thicker here than anywhere else on Big Maxson, especially for this time of day.

Even in the dimming light of sunset, I could tell most of the complaining quelsh possessed blue scales. Females. I didn't find it hard to guess they'd been separated from their eggs on the drive here, or needed private nesting areas immediately. A local variety of shipping fever could explain the rest, but what could I possibly do about it?

"How many are affected altogether?" I asked, my scientific curiosity getting the better of me.

"Probably over a quarter of our take."

"Not good." I thought I might have to suppress a malicious smirk. Instead, scanning the sad quelsh took care of that. Especially when one of Riddock's minions used a wristcom code to unlock a gate, and dragged out a dead quelsh.

"I accounted for some losses in my plans." Riddock shook his head. "This is quite wasteful," he added, as if this were a normal, everyday sort of herd health consult. "And I have more quelsh due to arrive from other areas within the next week. Any suggestions?"

"What do you intend to do with them?" I asked next, without hope, although the question was a legitimate part of taking a proper patient history.

"Ship them offworld illegally to avoid rebugging, and I can sell them to people who want to try to make expensive cheeses. What else do you know that you want me to admit?" Riddock grinned. I was shocked by his honesty, and I felt drowned in fear again. My body poured the water I'd just drunk into some intensely wasteful sweat, while I decided I'd better not say anything more. Riddock also remained silent for a while longer as we both pretended to study the quelsh.

"Well, I can't tell you how helpful this has been." He turned at last toward me. "Isn't there something in your veterinary oath about a commitment to the relief of animal suffering?"

"I won't take my oath until graduation."

"Oh, you don't care yet?" Riddock sneered at me.

"You should talk," I said. " Finally anger overcame fear. "I won't take any oath to help criminals! Stick it all up your right nostril! You're willing to risk planetary epidemics for the credits you'll make."

"And how big a risk is that? Everyone knows infections rarely take hold in foreign species, and no one visiting here has gotten sick from quelsh or their cheeses."

"Sure, native microbes rarely adapt immediately to foreign species," I said. "That's why they're devastating when they can infect at all. You ever meet a survivor from one of the outbreaks that occurred before the microfloral replacement programs? There aren't many."

"I take it you have? Where was your friend from?"

"Istrann," I said, sullenly. I hadn't expected Riddock to notice the personal anger in my remarks, and his question seemed irrelevant. Nor did I expect him to recognize the name of the planet, since it was involved in one of the least publicized incidents, over a decade ago.

"That was a deliberate, political, specist act of mass genocide." Riddock looked revolted.

"No one has ever publicly proven that. It doesn't matter. I can give you better examples."

"Like Drexus or Trikan? Or even Beta Two?" Riddock seemed quite well informed. "What no one bothers to point out is that these worlds are so memorable because they make such glaring exceptions. Thousands of colonized planets have done just fine for years before the recent rebugging efforts. Efforts which, by the way, still can't claim perfection, and are too recent to explain the good health of Big Maxson's oldest colonists."

"The earliest colonists here don't represent a properly complete sample of at-risk FIL populations," I said. "And sure, the rebugging program plays the odds, and it should also help improve them significantly."

"It seems to me that you FIL people play the odds a lot more than you're willing to admit."

"What do you mean?" I said, and heard an echo of Giem in my voice. Was it fear that sometimes drove her to attack? I felt like Riddock knew how to expertly back me into the corner of a very small cage.

"You're willing to infect worlds with whole macro-organisms," Riddock countered. "Almost every colony brings along its own livestock and food crops, and what a bonus to leave behind all natural predators. If any of these imports gets loose and flourishes, native species haven't got a chance against them. You've even brought mammals here, to a planet that's never seen them before, not to mention foreign technology, economy, and culture! Can you reasonably predict you won't cause any problems?"

"The worst nonnative species are highly controlled or banned now," I said. "And you have to have an environmental impact study to okay the rest. Most farm produce is designed to be genetically crippled if it gets loose, and pets can't be imported without neuter certificates. As for tech and culture imports, haven't you just about topped that problem off here with your illegal stunners?"

"Hah! A lot safer and more humane than an imported crossbow," Garth shot right back at me. "Who should have the power to decide for everyone else how far we can go? I'm sure the Pios didn't fully understand all the risks of allowing us here. Our adventuresome FIL government decided to move in anyway.

"Admit it, no matter how cautiously you try to slow down the process, sooner or later it simply becomes a matter of survival of the fittest—on a galactic scale, thanks to paraspace travel—and as far as I'm concerned, the surviving might as well happen now, and it might as well include me.

"Anyway, I probably would have caused far less trouble if you and Giemsan hadn't come along and immensely complicated matters here on Big Maxson. My original schedule is a wreck. In our haste we rounded up quelsh we quite likely shouldn't have. Nor do we have enough time left to learn more about quelsh disease prevention and treatment. How can you feel so certain of the morality of not helping these animals?"

And interfere with another round of evolutionary selection? Well, it was what I was training for, and I couldn't defend myself with that obvious retort. Instead I stared back at Riddock, and wondered just what he thought Giem and I could have done to interfere with any of his plans in the slightest manner. Obviously I didn't want to reveal such significant ignorance aloud. Did we also have him running scared, thinking we were FIL spies?

I wanted to laugh hysterically. I looked away from him and back at the penned quelsh, who were no laughing matter. Some looked like they'd die tonight. Even if I correctly guessed what was wrong, I still had neither the ability, equipment, nor a FIL license to treat the sick ones. Nevertheless, what about the complaining females— most likely a simple matter of better husbandry?

Riddock had a terrible talent for completely twisting my arguments around. In stubborn self-defense, I decided I'd better return to my policy of silence, at least until I could get my brain working better.

"Go ahead and think about it—you have a little longer. I've got too much to do to stand around here and wait for you." With that, Riddock strode back to the tents, and just left me there to consider his ominous exit.

I scanned around, startled by my abrupt lack of obvious restraints or guards. With all the patrols around, maybe that was unnecessary. Was Riddock merely carelessly displaying his complete power over me? If he had the technology to carry out illegal interplanetary shipping undetected, surely he had a protective scanning system of some sort, set up to monitor at least the more accessible areas of the valley perimeter.

What did he expect me to do? Dock myself here out of the goodness of my heart, or make the useless gesture of attempting sabotage or escape? Did he know I might still have at least one friend, and possibly several enemies, spying on him? And where in all this confusion were Giem and Grek?

For all I knew, Riddock was playing another game with me. Maybe he'd imprisoned both of my friends right here in this camp. Or they might be riding back to the station for help, and I'd have taken all these risks for nothing. If that was true, when would help arrive, and would it be soon enough? Perhaps Riddock would become anxious enough to leave before gathering up more quelsh. Maybe it was too late for anyone to stop him.

I found the whole situation more than baffling. I slumped to the ground, my back against a fence post. I put my face in my hands. I couldn't hold back a flood of tears any longer. Some future FIL veterinary agent. I had about five minutes to realize just how scared and confused I felt. A sudden blow against the inside of the post, accompanied by a loud crack, threw me forward to the ground and the Dim Side.

When I realized I'd nearly been gored through the fence by an angry young quelsh looking for a convenient target, I felt truly vac-brained. Had I really won? I coughed out dirt, wiped muddy tears off my face, and I forced myself to start thinking. I stood up, and began wandering as casually as I could around the campsite.

The few underlings around ignored me, even when I worked up my courage to start peering into tents. I wasn't bold enough to search any of them thoroughly. And I saved the largest tent, in which I spotted Riddock busily talking into a deskcom, for a last quick scan. I got a good enough look to convince myself that if Giem or Grek was stashed in there, they were well-hidden indeed.

I returned to the quelsh pens. Twilight grew dim as I meandered around the fences and pretended to study the sickest animals, which in turn made me sick. The pen gates were all locked, and I couldn't let any quelsh loose. Instead I heaved inside a portable latrine, even though my stomach was still quite empty. Later I reached the northeast corner of the pens, opposite the path we used to get here.

I trembled and my heart pounded against my chest as I gazed around once more. I didn't scan anyone watching me, and I couldn't afford to lose any more time or light.

I launched into a run across the valley meadow, leaped twice over small streams bordered by glowing skinsh, and feeling victorious, I bounded up the nearest hillside into some woods. I win, I win, I thought, even if Garth's quelsh had lost. That wasn't my fault.

Under cover I slowed to a hard-breathing, long-strided jog as the slope grew steeper, and scanned carefully this time for anybody or anything that might trip me up in the growing darkness.

I reached the top of the ridge without spotting anyone. I thought I could hear some distant shouts. So I plunged on down the other side, letting the slope run me into the nearest and densest woods I could find.

I crashed my way into a thick stand of thorny bushes. I found a small cave-like clearing inside. I dropped to my knees, and tried to recover from my adrenaline shakes and oxygen deficit. I was certain someone would find me from my wheezing alone, and my whole body felt too rubbery to go on. And then I heard a voice—

CHAPTER 37

"Taje? Taje, are you in there?" whispered a low, hissing voice.

A moment later Grek broke into my shrubby sanctuary, and found me in a terrified, puddled heap on the ground. He gripped my arm with his cool dry fingers and asked if I was hurt. I shook my head, and remembered to mutter "No" for his translator. Giem softly cursed her way between tangled clawing branches to join us. She had to shake me to stop my relieved laughter.

"Giem—you're okay!"

"Shhh. Riddock's patrols will hear you."

"I thought you were one of them. Where on Big Maxson have you been?"

"Later. Let's get out of here." She had a light, and used it in a miserly manner. The bushes whipped us all soundly before we fought free of them. My two companions hustled me away from the ridge, where we would be outlined by a starry sky.

"Great Universe, Giem, you've got to tell me what happened," I insisted. I tripped over a moss-slick root, and interrupted myself with a curse as I almost hit the ground. Grek caught me just in time. Was his night vision better than mine? I stood up holding my head, which felt hammered by my pulse.

"Hush," Giem whispered back at me. "Wait at least until we get back to the lizards."

Grek grabbed me barely in time to keep me from walking right into a stream. We leaped across it, and minutes later we reached a small clearing between some trees, and three tethered lizards.

"Grek found me while you were busy getting yourself caught," Giem said, with soft amusement as we unclipped our mounts. Grek had also obviously managed, in some wondrous manner, to save both of our lizards as well as himself.

"You should talk about getting captured." I picked impatiently at a horrendous snarl that had perversely enveloped my lizard's triple reins in my absence. "You've had me nova with worry, Giem. What have you been doing all this time?"

"Spying on Riddock." Giem mounted up beside me and aimed her dimmed light down on my work. "How do you think we've felt, trying to com some way to rescue you from his camp without getting ourselves caught too? Once we scanned you running in this direction, we had a hard race scrambling around the long way to intercept you.

"Anyway, when the Pios took my wristcom, I assumed you would follow after me, and I knew you could straighten out the situation with them. I commed we'd find each other soon enough. I just didn't count on having to save you, too."

"Rather clumsy of me, eh?" I muttered caustically. I stared back up at Giem. "You had rather a lot of confidence in my diplomatic abilities."

"You weren't doing too badly when I left you back at Grek's village," Giem said, with a surprising hint of jealousy in her voice, while Grek silently fought to keep his edgy mount near ours.

"Anyway, hurry up and get on your lizard," Giem urged me. "We need to gain a little more distance from here, and make some plans. If you're hungry, Grek's got a fresh stash of wild krava fruits in his saddlebags. While you're eating and we ride on, you can tell us what you learned from inside Riddock's camp." Giem slapped the ends of her reins against her thigh impatiently.

"I think you can stay right here and tell all of us," a horribly familiar voice shot from behind me, just as I undid a tenacious snag in my reins. A horse snorted explosively, and Grek's lizard hissed and bolted with him. Startled, Giem hauled on her spooked lizard's reins and turned in her saddle, in the direction of Rakke's voice.

"Giem, get out of here!" I yelled at her, and she glanced with some confusion back at me. Choking on an explanation I couldn't articulate fast enough, I desperately swung around and smacked her lizard's butt with a loud whack.

The beast screamed and nearly raked me in the chest before it ran off into the night. I threw myself onto my awkward Pio saddle as my lizard also tried to bolt, and we danced around in a tight circle until I could get my reins roughly sorted out.

A harsh yell and the beam of a powerful light caught me for a micro. I launched my steed into a reckless gallop through the darkness, hoping the ground ahead would prove too difficult for horses.

Unfortunately my tangled delay in the dark kept me from catching up with my friends. It didn't take long for the crashing of various mounts through the woods, haphazard lights intermixed with darting glow-bugs and fluorescing flowers, and random noisy shouts to grow completely confusing. I had to just let my lizard have his head, in the hope that he would seek out his trail-mates over strange pursuers.

About five minutes into the chase, banged up by my saddle, my reins straightened out, I resorted to yelling for my friends. I thought I detected an encouraging reply along with a waving beam of light, not too far ahead, while pursuers roared not far behind.

I veered my lizard towards the light and goaded it into its fastest gait. If any of us got caught, we'd have a better chance of fighting free with all three of us standing together.

That's how I brilliantly rode straight into the wrong camp. Several excited guards immediately stunned me, before Rakke and the one-eyed Pio could catch up with me.

No chance for nauseating anticipation here. I just rolled out of my saddle and slammed into the ground, hard. My lizard quite wisely ran off before anyone else could grab his reins. A huge furry person turned me over on my back as my pursuers rode up.

"There's still two more, at least," I heard a Pio's translated voice off to one side. "We should keep riding—"

"Don't bother," Rakke said, dismounting. A whole ragged-looking group gathered around to peer at me under dim camp lights, hung amongst a cluster of camouflaged tents. "We're in luck. This is the one we want."

"Are you quite sure?" a harsh woman's voice said. "This is the trader you scanned running from Garth's camp?"

"I'm positive. How many other humans look this pale?"

The questioner stepped into view. I didn't find the angry look on her unusually pale human face very amusing. I was too busy going invisibly nova. This was my sixth fall and third stunning in the same day. I was having trouble breathing, and nobody seemed to notice that it might contribute toward my extreme pallor.

A bunch of them began to argue enthusiastically while my eyesight started to sparkle. The blond-haired woman squatted down to take a closer look at me. She had to shove a couple people out of her way to feel my chest. She stood up and yelled at all of them.

"You vac-heads—you set your stunners too high! She's suffocating."

The excited babbling turned to frantic shouts, and someone started clumsy mouth-to-mouth on me. I wanted to kick and fight, and most of all to take in my own gasp of air. I just couldn't even twitch.

"Get a stimulant," the woman ordered, as my lungs filled with someone else's breath. "No, no—a muscle stim from the medkit, you vac-brain!" I felt a horrible sting in my right arm. Just as I gained a little more control over my chest muscles, a tremendous wave of drug-induced nausea hit me, and I began to gag.

"Too fast!" The blond woman swore. "She's going to puke! Hold her head down before she chokes, you dumb lizard scum!"

The furry giant simply picked me up by my ankles, and hung me upside down until I lost a bolus of stomach juice. Throughout all this I struggled to get air in and out of my lungs, while my nose and eyes streamed. They laid me down again, finally thought to slap a medkit respirator on my face, and gave me a more careful injection. Minutes later I totally fused, and nearly everyone in the camp threw themselves into the fray.

CHAPTER 38

When I became too spent for any more mindless yelling and thrashing, they dragged me into a tent and dumped me on a sleeping bag. Thank the Galaxy they left me alone for a while.

I lay there as limp and stinky as the giant saury carcasses we'd had to excavate in anatomy class. I still had to work on every breath and fight more nausea. Despite my jacket, I also shivered convulsively, shaking pain from every bruised part of my body. The throbbing in my skull felt like it might pop my eyeballs out of their sockets and send them rolling across the dirty tent floor. Maybe, if I felt like this much longer, it would be okay to die.

Later voices rose and fell through the tent wall, and in and out of my consciousness.

"I'm certain she's the trader that escaped Riddock's camp—"

"—had it with your blundering. She'll be useless for another couple hours at least—"

"What's he up to, anyway? Our percentage—"

"—Garth must have at least one private shuttle for that."

"—the timing and location for a hijacking—that's the crucial—"

"I'll make sure she tells us what she knows—"

"Unless she's a plant, special delivery from Riddock—"

"So she'll know more. Don't worry about it—"

"—illegal shuttles—how—"

"—lots of credits, that's all. It's like smuggling in stingers and stunners, only bigger and more expensive. If credits are no object—"

"—with the cheap satellite alarm system here, I've heard a good scrambler or screen could—"

I slipped into a fitful, nightmare-ridden sleep, no better than staying awake, a state I was roughly shaken back into, all too soon.

I found myself lying in a cold sweat, desperately thirsty again, tasting rotten bile, and still battered by a ruthless headache. The night didn't seem close to ending. Someone had turned on a blinding light, and tried to ply me with questions. I blinked confusedly and began helplessly dry-heaving.

It was a good delaying tactic. I'd have to add it to the Manual, right before I resigned, which would be ASAP. Whoever was bothering me turned green and rapidly exited the tent.

I shut my eyes against the light, and I gradually drifted off into a more oblivious sleep that carried me almost through dawn. I woke up again, and discovered

I had become too sore to remain in any prone position long enough to escape back into sleep. I was surprised to find someone had thrown a stained blanket over me, and after I recovered from dizzily sitting up, I spotted a water bottle alongside another sleeping bag. My captors found me recklessly guzzling the last of its dubious, cloudy contents.

The blond-haired woman ducked into the tent first. The tall hairy person and a Kralvin followed, all wearing weapons on their belts.

"Sorry about last night," the human said without scanning the least bit sorry. She sat down on a low camp chair next to me. Her two followers stood behind her, hands on stunners, yawning tiredly. "Not much of a reception after your amazing escape from Garth's camp."

I was tempted to return her sarcasm. I felt too tired to think of a suitably brilliant reply, and I had to work too hard at trying to com just where I'd landed myself.

"If it's any consolation, Rakke no longer works for me," she added after I offered no response.

Somehow that didn't improve my pessimism at all. How did she get rid of him?

"My name's Chothark. I'm a competitor of your partner, Mohrogh, and my group will probably get away with a whole lot more than Garth's trash. Perhaps you'd prefer to team up with us."

The Kralvin guard stepped forward, tail lashing. "She could be a—"

"Enough!" Chothark shot back at him. "I'm handling this before someone else fuses it even worse, just shut up and do your job." She gave him a look set on kill and turned back to me. "What's your name?"

"Tajen Jesmuhr," I rasped. A plant? Was that what the Kralvin had almost asked? And what I seemed to remember someone worrying about last night? How ridiculous. I was a Galactic nobody out here, amongst all these black hole criminals—a weak, underfed, bruised-up, filthy FIL vet student—

"Well, Jesmuhr, first we need some information from you," Chothark interrupted my swelling self-pity. She seemed to have the attitude that she was doing me some sort of huge favor. "What were you doing with Mohrogh—anything besides trying to collect Garth's scraps?"

Was I an unwitting setup from Garth Riddock? Was that why he had let me escape, and not out of the goodness of his heart? "Davin and I rode out here to search for a lost friend," I said, uneasily. I massaged my dirty face, trying to relieve the last remnants of my headache. How much could I afford to tell this person? Should I be making up some story?

"Did you find your friend?"

Was someone truly going to credit my original line? "Yeah. I found her after Davin gave up and left." There, that should get Davin off of at least one suspect list, whether or not he deserved it.

"What was your friend doing out here?"

"Same as everyone else—spying on Riddock." I'd give away the smallest truths possible, I foggily decided, until I had more information to go on. Lies were far

too difficult to keep track of at this point. Not that I
had all that much to hide. No doubt I was proving a big
disappointment to everyone who caught me out here.
Too bad. Ha ha.

"Spying—along with your Pio partner? You're not
talking very much."

Evidently Chothark wasn't impressed. She was
threatening me—I could see it in her icy blue eyes,
when I worked hard at focusing on her. I noticed rather
distractedly that like me and Riddock, she didn't have a
hint of an epicanthic fold.

Come on, I told myself sternly, start paying attention
and use your brain, or you'll lose this game for sure. I
shook my head in an effort to concentrate, which was a
mistake. It felt like I'd just ricocheted a bunch of rocks
around inside my skull, churning my brains to mush.
"Rakke scared off both my friends when he chased me
into your camp," I said. "Why did you send him after
us?" I redirected with a question of my own—the Vet
Student Way, when-confronted-with-difficult-questions-
which-we-ought-to-know-the-answers-to. "We were
ready to leave." Maybe. At least I was.

"We know Garth's arranging some illegal exports,
and we expect to benefit from it." Chothark leaned back
in her chair and folded her arms. "Timing and location
are critical, and we must know if you found out any of
the details of Garth's plans. You might as well let us in
on it. I doubt you could gain any serious profit from the
information alone from Garth's plans—even with your
various friends."

Great Galaxy, Taje, you'd better get your own plan commed, fast. I ran my fingers through my sweaty hair, trying to get it out of my eyes. Was this the core of it all? Had Riddock told me the truth about his plans, or just glibly fed me a bunch of misleading lines to pass on to his archrival?

I found it hard to remember Riddock had accused Giem and me of interfering with his plans—what a puzzler. Maybe he had vengefully lied to me. Perhaps he truly planned to take off much faster than one week. If that was the case, maybe I could in turn foul his escape by telling Chothark my suspicions. However, I liked her group even less than Riddock's, and if I wanted to mislead her, my answers would depend on whether Riddock had told me the truth. Great Universe, what a confusing toss-up.

"Did you find out anything about his timetable or his launch sites?" Chothark pressed me, as she stretched her legs out, and crossed them, tying herself in a knot.

"Time—timing?" I stuttered. I remembered how Aerrem and Giem had always tried to impress on me what a poor liar I was. Rather than risk letting this get nasty, I resorted to an abbreviated, uncreative report. "I don't know anything," I said wearily, "except that Riddock told me he plans to stay at least a week longer, for more quelsh his people are rounding up. And I don't know where he's hiding any of his offworld transportation."

"Why did he tell you that much?" Chothark asked me suspiciously.

Why indeed? I refrained from shaking my aching head again. "He seemed to take it for granted that it was obvious what he was doing."

"And what were you doing, spying on him, when you were supposedly looking for a friend?"

"I thought he might have captured her."

"Why would he bother? And why did he bother with you? Even showed off his quelsh herds to you, didn't he? I don't think you're telling me a very good story."

So spies on all sides. I squirmed uncomfortably, and shifted my wandering attention to the guards. I stared harder at the Kralvin, trying to com whether I'd seen him before, at the station. I just couldn't tell. It did make me think. If Davin could make the FIL agent connection with similar evidence, it might be deadly to tell Chothark that I was a FIL vet student. I could no longer respond to any of her questions honestly safely.

"Not so full of answers anymore, huh?" she said. "I guess there must be more behind this business than you care to admit. Well, you'd better reconsider your position—we haven't much more time to waste on you."

Like everyone else, I thought bitterly. "I've told you what I could—"

"Exactly." Chothark glanced at her larger guard. I chose that moment to lunge over the woman while her legs and arms were crossed, in a wild attempt to bowl her over and dive through the tent door behind her. Instead we both collapsed in a tangled mess with the folding camp chair. I got close enough to scan faint traces of repaired scars on Chothark's face, before her guards pulled me off.

"Take her outside," Chothark ordered, breathing harshly.

The tall furry person grabbed my collar and my belt from behind, with a reach too long for me to fight back. I cursed and struggled weakly anyway as I was marched out of the tent to a tree equipped with ties. They promptly had my wrists bound to ropes hanging from a branch overhead, and my ankles knotted to exposed roots below. Spread-eagled like prey caught in a giant spider web. It all happened so fast that I wondered who else they'd done this to. Chothark still stood cautiously out of kicking range as she drew a stinger from her holster.

I wasn't surprised. Squinting against the rising sun, I could tell her weapon hand shook with fury.

"Alright, Jesmuhr, tell me what you're truly doing out here."

"I told you." My head returned to pounding in rhythm with my thundering pulse, as I gripped the thick red cords tied to my wrists. Maybe it was even convenient that my stomach was still empty. I might have guessed this adventure would never end with simple murder. That was too easy.

Chothark steadied her aim at me. "You remind me of a little red-headed snob I trounced once, a long time ago. You'll either tell me the truth today or later, because I'll beat you too. Except I can inflict as much pain as I want without any inconvenient damage—unless, of course, you crash from a heart attack."

"Go ahead and waste your time on it, Chark, just like you did before!" I teased her and laughed, remembering a ridiculous food fight at the Center. "What good did that do you?"

"So you're the little pup-squeak who put me in Rehab!" she spat.

"That clearly didn't do any good."

"Watch your mouth." She made a show of dialing up her stinger. "And don't ever call me Chark again."

"I don't have anything more to tell you, Chark," I crowed as my pulse grew hot. So this was Chothark, and this was The Adventure! I almost made the mistake of laughing again when her first beam hit me—because the faintly burning wave made such a pathetic impression compared to the bounding pain created by my own head and all my previous injuries.

When was I ever going to learn to quit wasting energy fearing the future? It would arrive, whether I worried about it or not, and rarely did it ever quite match its terrifying billing. If Chothark wouldn't physically harm me, how could she possibly cause me any more pain than I'd caused myself?

Obviously, I would also have to reconsider the idea that I wasn't important enough to try to hurt. After all, more than one of my teachers had thought otherwise. I dimly realized this was a very odd way to boost my self-esteem. I still found it a good antidote for repeated bursts from the stinger.

It also helped to know I had a fairly high pain threshold, compared to various partners I'd worked out with in self-defense. My challenge to Chothark wasn't totally empty. If I could hold out long enough—for what? I was fooling myself if I thought I had an easy rescue waiting right around the corner. Giem and Grek still didn't have anything besides Grek's translator bracelet between them, and they would need plenty of time to ride for help—once they managed to com what had happened.

"Are you a spy from Garth?" Chothark demanded.

"If I were, don't you think he would have found someone to do a better job?" I said sarcastically, for a slightly higher dose of pain. Might as well suspect Hako had sent us here to pester Riddock. That was a thought. I infused my reeking, torn shirt with more sweat, and I wriggled and faked a groan, just for good measure.

"He's such a careful person that you could escape from his camp by simply running away on foot? Come on, Jesmuhr, you can do better than that. Why bother to protect Garth? What's he going to do to get you out of this?"

"Nothing. I'm not protecting him." Again I almost laughed. Had I indeed been thrown to the parasites deliberately, to keep the opposition busy? I found it very difficult to think, through the relentlessly stabbing waves, which no longer seemed quite as amusing.

"Tell me all that you know."

"I have."

"Tell it again, without the mistakes."

"I'm not protecting him, I'm not, I'm not! Why should I? He may kill worlds by exporting those quelsh."

"And that bothers you? Who are you? What are you doing out here?"

Silence. Can't say any more. Said too much. Just endure the familiar feeling of pain, everywhere—

"You working for FIL, Jesmuhr? Maybe that's it, huh? Making the atmosphere hot for all of us? Finding it hot enough here—what is it, Karsh? Can't you see I'm busy?"

"Garth's people have brought in another herd from the north."

"Any sign of a shuttle?"

"No—"

"Why are you interrupting me?"

"Quite a few of his first hauls have died off. Just thought you should know."

I heard that, and and tears escaped, for all those pathetic quelsh, caught in this fused trap just like me. I hadn't managed to help any of us.

"Alright, Jesmuhr, isn't it worth it to put an end to this? Just give me the truth." Chothark sounded like she was gloating. I guess she thought my crying was her doing.

When I don't like where I am, I try to go somewhere else. I couldn't sleep or daydream through this. I had only one remaining escape route, and I took it as best I could. As a student, I'd become so good at concentrating that I could sometimes screen out the Universe.

I tried to remember the right neuro lecture. The stinger probably stimulated my group III and IV nerve fiber pain receptors, if I was anything like an Earth dog. A-gamma and C (dorsal root) nociceptors, weren't they? Despite a mostly practical approach, one still had to memorize an amazing amount of comjunk in vet school. I began to review the physiology of various pain receptors, which was really quite complicated—

"Jesmuhr—how long does this have to go on? Stubbornness won't help you."

How many times had I heard that one—and when would I ever believe it?

I continued my grueling neuro review for a number of common domestic FIL species. For the love of FIL, why did being a veterinary student have to involve such pain and suffering? I thought the training was to alleviate a little of that in this galaxy?

"A vet student?" Chothark bent nearly double with laughter, as I sluggishly realized I must have recited at least a part of my litany aloud. "Is that all? It's no wonder Garth considered you valuable. You simply didn't want to get involved in any nasty animal smuggling, did you? The real question is, how can I make this useful for us?"

We learned right at the beginning of freshman year that jumping to a diagnosis, without at least a thorough history and scan, can lead to fatal errors. Chothark shut off her stinger and I relaxed, trying to wear a mask of defeat as my weight pulled on my aching arms. I wondered if my hyperventilating would make me pass out, the way we learned in one of our respiratory physiology lectures. I felt I'd earned the release most story heroes get to indulge in at some point. I'd won this round despite all the pain blasted at me, and Chothark didn't even know it. I had to work at smothering a victorious grin on my aching face.

I didn't pass out. I guess I didn't work hard enough at it. I was left hanging (sorry, bad pun) for a couple hours, while everyone else retreated to the other side of the tents to argue out the situation. I'd gone beyond caring or struggling, and it felt good just to be left alone for a while. When someone snuck up behind me to slap an injector on my arm, it took me quite by surprise. The ground spun up into the sky several times, and then I might as well have died.

CHAPTER 39

I awoke from an utterly dreamless, timeless state of nonexistence, rather like before I was born, and similar to what I commed it might be like when I died. Oblivion—normally my biggest fear—but right now I felt too disoriented to care.

Too weak, I couldn't lift my blood-filled head. I also discovered I was tied down, and salty horse sweat flooded my nostrils, while a saddle gouged my belly. I could hear one of Chothark's underlings talking.

"—and I brought your escaped prisoner, to trade for a position on your crew."

"Garnen, why did you let this scum down here?" Garth Riddock's disgusted voice said.

"He surrendered to me on the ridge, and brought along the escaped vet student. I didn't think—"

"No, you didn't. I don't need any parasite trader joining me, and recruitment ended a long time ago. Escort this man right back out of here, and give him the usual warn-off."

"What about the vet student?"

"Oh, take her off in some other direction and let her go." Garth moved closer and picked up my head in both hands, so we could scan each other in relative comfort. "We have to quit meeting like this, Tajen." He grinned at me, looked closer, and frowned as I tried unsuccessfully to make a snappy reply. I thought at first, with fuzzy panic, that someone had stunned me again. But I could breathe easily, and the scenery kept spinning and flipping over.

"She's been drugged!" Garth put my head down gently. "What have you done to her?"

"She was difficult to persuade—"

"Get him out of here, Garnen! Tullin, come over here and help me get her down."

They untied my wrists and legs, carried me back to one of their tents, and left me on a cot. "Controlled Death," I remembered, right before I drifted off again. That's how our pharmacology prof had introduced the subject of anesthesia, to make us take it seriously.

"I don't know. I have a bad feeling about this."

"You can't seriously think Chothark's back, after the jam you left her in the last time?"

"I would have my doubts, if it weren't for some of the snares we're running into again. This whole project is turning into such a luckless, nova mess, with nearly a week still left to go on our mutilated schedule. Oh, sorry," Garth said. "Tajen, did we wake you up? Are you okay now?"

I'd broken loose from a recurrent, frustrating dream out of my deep past. The Search for the Missing Piñata. Only this time I'd found it, dangling from a rope, well out of reach. Not a surprising outcome, considering my recent ordeal. My dorm parents had surprised me with the piñata on my first birthday at the Center. They'd ordered one in the shape of a yusahmbul, my favorite childhood farm animal. Being an ignorant fringe kid, I'd thought it a wonderful party decoration. I didn't know the game was to take turns beating it with a stick, to get at what it held inside.

What fused timing. I woke up feeling like a vac-head, and I wondered why I'd ever felt victorious anywhere along this whole harrowing adventure, as captors passed me back and forth. And I didn't want to look weak in front of Garth, even though, as I awoke, I couldn't prevent real tears from replacing dreamed ones.

I gazed back at Garth through a fluid blur. He had an oddly concerned look on his face, which upset me more. Why couldn't he just stick to being a bad guy in my story? He made this much more baffling and difficult.

"What happened to you? Who drugged you?" he asked.

"Cho—thark—she—they—you—" I couldn't stop crying long enough to explain. Nor could I think in a straight line anymore. Too much had happened to me on top of too little real rest, and I never liked losing control like that, in front of anyone.

"Never mind—I can imagine. Chothark—I knew it! She's an embarrassment and a hateful vac-headed jerk.

What should I do with you now? I suppose if I tried once more to set you loose on foot, so you can't call the troops in time, Chothark would just nab you again."

I nodded as I swallowed more tears, and waited for him to come to the obvious conclusion. I was of no use to anyone, including myself.

"Garth, if Chothark has truly landed on Big Maxson, she'll want real blood," a young woman seated across from him said emphatically.

"I know," Garth said. "I'll have to alert our patrols. This puts even more pressure on us to launch out of here as soon as possible—"

"I thought we'd have to wait out the health scare back at the station," the green Telmid sitting next to the woman interrupted. "The IPHA ship is still in orbit—"

"I think we'd better hope their ship sensors don't work much better than the Big Maxson satellite alarms," Garth said. "It no longer sounds as if the IPHA team is going to leave any time in the near future. Their whole investigation is getting more involved and troublesome, and I've heard they may even impose a sector-wide quarantine. What I wonder is whether we might improve our odds by cutting our losses and making a run for it as early as tonight."

"Some of our people would have to move very fast," the woman said. "I suppose we could do it. If we ordered a couple extra shuttle stops, and gave up on most of our current roundups, we might make it out of here by midnight."

"I don't think anyone would object too strongly," the Telmid said, twitching his feathery antennae nervously. "The risks of this expedition have escalated far beyond anyone's expectations."

"Good. Go ahead with immediate orders for an emergency evacuation—" a call on his deskcom interrupted Garth. "Yes?"

"Perimeter patrol six here, sir. Some unusual activity a couple kilometers northwest of the valley—"

"Investigate it at once," Garth ordered, while my heart started thumping again out of reflex fear.

"We did, sir. Looks like somebody had a fair-sized camp out here—"

"Had? Where did they go?"

"Scattered, as near as we can tell. The whole area was just trampled by a stampeding skitsh herd. We did find a stinger in one of the flattened tents, so it wasn't FIL—"

"Not faked, was it?"

"Not possible."

"Could it be Chothark's camp?" Garth looked to me for confirmation, and I nodded. He laughed. "Well, something's going right, at last."

Giem and Grek's doing? I hardly dared think it. If anyone could com how to motivate a wild skitsh herd, it might be those two.

"Also, you should have another quelsh herd entering from our direction very soon."

"Excellent." Garth turned back to his associates. "Let's get those orders out and start packing. Tajen, you might as well just get some more rest here. Fortunately for you, you're clearly in no shape to help us—even if you didn't object on moral grounds." And with that, they left the tent.

After sleeping off the rest of the anesthetic, I learned that Garth no longer cared what I did, as long as I stayed out of the way. I was able to wander around the campsite, and watch everyone frantically organizing for a quick exit. They herded in a couple more small groups of quelsh, and called most of the rest of the roundups off. The only other herds Garth okayed were those they could coordinate with shuttle pickups. I heard most of the details of their plans, toyed briefly with various frivolous thoughts of impossible sabotage, and was ignored the rest of the day. I hadn't felt so helpless since the day I'd had to put Ked down, because I knew nothing about how to doctor a badly wounded sann.

I came to rest on a packing crate, and succumbed to a bitter depression. As I watched workers ruthlessly culling sick and dead quelsh from the pens, it did dawn on me that with Chothark's nasty outfit scattered to the four winds of Big Maxson, I could leave without much risk.

I'd have to com how to locate my friends, probably somewhere not too far away and desperately trying to sort out the plot themselves. I definitely didn't feel like trying to walk all the way back to the station by myself, especially with nothing besides the clothes on my back. Maybe I could talk Garth into giving me a mount, now that he was finishing up here. I still couldn't ride anywhere fast enough to stop him.

"Look, I'm not here to cause you any trouble—" came a familiarly troublesome voice from around the tents, shocking me out of my tangled thoughts.

"I can't believe you'd risk riding back here again, Mohrogh," Garth said, disgusted. I slid down off the crate, and trotted stiffly toward their voices. "You never would have made it this far, if I weren't bringing in my patrols and dismantling my scanners."

"He didn't even try to sneak in, Garth. We found him riding down here, and he just surrendered to us."

"Another volunteer? Doesn't anyone who's been spying on us realize we'll be lucky to break even on this whole vacful mess? If we even get away with it—and what will happen if we don't—"

"I'm not seeking any part of your profits. I'm just looking for two foolish young vet students with silly delusions of heroism. If you have either one of them here, you must realize how harmless they are. Release them to me, and I promise none of us will cause you any more trouble."

"Thanks a lot," I told Davin as I walked around a tent, and joined the little group in the orange light of sunset. I almost didn't recognize Davin, in a full beard now.

"You've caused too much trouble taking any of my time." Garth glared. "Tajen can go with you if she wants. I don't know where Giemsan Fane is." I looked at Garth as he returned to his communications tent. Did I want to go?

Davin scanned me with blank surprise. I matched his look and regretted my sarcasm and my hasty judgment of his character. He must have needed a lot of courage to return here for me, presumably still without any weapons. What had changed his mind?

Davin had only one other saddle horse on a lead. He had to help me mount up. I wondered what had happened to the pack horse while we rode back out of the valley. I didn't feel like asking aloud. I had a miserable struggle just keeping my battered body in the saddle, and I was feeling cold and dizzy.

"What in FIL were you doing down there, running around loose in Riddock's camp?" Davin said as our horses began the climb out of the valley. Yet another person who just had to know.

"What does it matter?" I hadn't meant to snap at him. My brain crashed just trying to answer him.

He studied me more closely and frowned, at all the dirt, scratches, and bruises, I supposed. I didn't want to know how I looked—or smelled. I couldn't remember when I'd last bathed. I pulled a serrated leaf out of my tangled hair, and nudged my horse a little farther away from his.

"When was the last time you had a real meal?"

Startled, I looked at him, and discovered I had to think about it. "Well, assuming it's still today, about a day and a half ago—I guess." I began to giggle hysterically, and Davin shook his head.

"As soon as we ride out of here, we'll have to remedy that, with what little I've got left. Do you have any idea where Giem is?"

"Right here waiting in line for your dinner, lizard-brain." Giem laughed as she and Grek rode out from behind a stand of trees growing from an impressive nurse log at the top of the ridge.

"Giem! Where have you been?" Davin slid off his horse, Giem slipped off her lizard, and they hugged excitedly.

"Spying on Riddock. Why did you come back?" Giem said, her voice muffled in their embrace. "Grek told me you gave up and left."

"Fooled everyone, didn't I?"

"Ah, together again at last." I sighed and winked at Grek. He gazed at Giem and Davin, and back at me.

"Are you okay?" he said, as he shifted on his lizard's side-saddle. "Your skin has changed color in spots, and you smell bad."

I scanned him, tried to accept his obvious sympathy, and couldn't help laughing anyway. "You don't know the curious ideas humans have about politeness," I said, when I could manage to answer his puzzled look.

"Come on, let's get farther away, and have that dinner," Davin suggested, swinging back up on his horse.

"Better not make it too far or too elaborate," Giem said, mounting her lizard. "From the look of it, Grek and I suspect Riddock may try to clear out by morning. Once Taje tells us everything she's found out, we'll have to act fast. We've not sure what Riddock's up to. It can't be good. At the very least, he's a thief, and a lot of quelsh are dying under his care—"

"He's got illegal shuttles, and he's going to try to ship off as many untanked quelsh as he can load up by midnight," I said, my sense of humor rapidly fading at the thought of having to do anything more, much less with any speed. Everyone else abruptly halted their mounts in their tracks.

"I can't believe it," Davin exploded. "Here we are, all together, safe, and sound, and you still think we're somehow going to stop Garth Riddock?"

"Help should arrive soon. However, midnight tonight is pushing it," Giem said. "We'll at least need to stall him, until Ziehl can cut through all the comcrap and quarantine madness going on back at the station—"

"They never found their simple answer, huh?" I snorted. "Serves them right for jettisoning us. I suppose they really do think they have a microfloral barrier failure?"

"That's right," Giem suddenly got it. "Smuggled weapons and illegal shuttle landings. I suppose I should call again and try to tell them—"

"You found a wristcom you can use?" Davin managed to get a word in.

"I picked it up along with several stunners, after we scattered a nest of Garth's rivals with a wild skitsh herd. Grek taught me how to catch sort-of-snakes we used to scare the herd into stampeding through their camp. The wristcom doesn't like me much, and I barely got a call through for help."

"Great. At least we won't be totally without weapons, while everyone in the area with a wristcom has probably heard your call."

"I was circumspect." Giem looked insulted. "Come on, Davin, you've made it this far. Why not show a little more fortitude, and help us out? Maybe after this, FIL will clean up your record."

"I don't need my record cleaned up. I need to get out of here before I run up my parking bill so high I can't leave the orbital station, since I'm obviously not going to collect any profits here. It doesn't seem to matter what I want anymore. Have you thought out even a scrap of a reasonable plan of attack?"

They still argued while we ate dinner, a Pio-style stew Davin and Grek dashed together from saddlebag contents. I ate mechanically, barely tasting the meal. My stomach felt very strange and warm food seemed to provide the only remedy, although I felt like I'd somehow left hunger far behind. The more I ate the more sleepy I got, and I remained sitting with great difficulty on my sore butt.

Grek kept giving me concerned looks, and he didn't make any more comments about my condition, for which I felt vaguely grateful.

"You're a pilot," Giem said to Davin. "You ought to know some ways to disable shuttles."

"Sure," Davin admitted, "but how am I supposed to get near them? Unlike Taje, I'm not free to walk in and out of Riddock's camp."

"Riddock let Taje wander in and out of his camp? Come on, don't make fun of her for getting caught." It was only okay for Giem to tease me?

"I'm not." Davin unfortunately defended himself. "Ask Taje, if you don't believe me."

Giem frowned as she scanned me more closely. "Taje, is it true? Would Riddock let you back into his camp— hey, what's the matter?"

"Nothing. I'm just tired." I looked down, and felt Grek's claws lightly brush my shoulder.

"You've hardly said a word tonight, and you look like someone has beat you." Giem wrinkled her nose. "You also need to bathe, even worse than me."

"I'm okay," I insisted. "I won every fight. Just some unfortunate falls." I set my bowl down on a rock. I'd eaten about half my dinner. Maybe Davin would let me heat up some water on one of his stoves, for a quick sponge bath—tomorrow morning. I hoped someone had a sleeping bag to spare. I supposed I could just lie down right here and fall asleep without too much trouble.

"What happened with those nasty characters who tried to nab us last night?" Giem said. "Grek told me how they threatened all of you. We feared they'd caught you. When we felt sure we'd lost them, we turned around and searched for their camp. We still had to wait for daylight to catch some sunning snakes, and it took us half the day to set it up scaring the skitsh herd into running in the right direction. After that, we couldn't find you, and we didn't know whether we'd scared you off too, or if you'd escaped by yourself."

"They'd returned me to Garth."

"Why?"

"They tried to use my veterinary knowledge in trade, to slip a cohort into his outfit, or to at least get another close look at his operation."

"Is that all they wanted with you?"

"No."

"What else then?"

"Information. About Garth's plans. They'd scanned me down in his camp."

"Is that why they beat you up?"

"They didn't beat me," I repeated, feeling my face flush. "I won! I beat them." I insisted to my sympathetic audience. How could I explain feeling victorious over such torture? Too embarrassed, I guess. That I'd let myself fall into the hands of evil more than once, and barely managed to escape. I didn't want to talk about it or even think about it.

"Could you really return to Riddock's camp?" Giem tried another vector.

"I suppose it's possible, although I don't understand why they'd let me back in. I refused to give Garth any help with his sick quelsh. I'm no closer to understanding that man."

"Well, I guess it doesn't matter why, as long as you can do it. I still want to know what happened to you."

I shook my head. "I'm just thoroughly stressed from three vac-brained visits to criminal camps, and I don't know if I said too much to anyone."

Grek said, "They didn't need to hurt her. Taje injures herself all too easily."

"And I can't remember when I last had a peaceful night of real sleep," I said. "Can't we just leave Garth to the proper authorities? If they don't catch him here, chances are they'll nab him in orbit. He's very worried about the sensors on the IPHA ship up there."

"I should think he'd worry much more about the whole planetary satellite alarm system."

"Apparently it's not all that impressive," I had to admit. "If you can afford it, an illegal scrambler or screen might outwit the entire system."

"You're willing to gamble that one small orbiting FIL ship will catch him in time?" Giem said, outraged. "I would have thought you'd be especially motivated to fight the potential spread of interplanetary disease. The way you go on about your old friend Shandy—"

"You leave him out of this!"

"Fine. Just don't ever complain to me again about what happened to him, his family, and most of his planet's population—"

"Alright, Giem, alright. I'm just so exhausted I can barely sit up."

We'd settled down in a small clearing not too far from Garth's valley. We all suddenly scanned the sky as a patch of darkness passed briefly overhead, blotting out the stars. A sonic boom followed it, and next we heard the unmistakable sounds of a shuttle landing in the valley.

"Okay, Taje, suggest a way we can all get into Riddock's camp, before it's too late."

CHAPTER 40

"What's the matter? It doesn't hurt. I thought you'd experienced this before."

"Just turn the setting very low, please."

"I set it on 'light stun.'"

"Make it lighter."

"Are you sure? If this doesn't look just right—"

"If you don't make it lighter, I'll look very dead. Just do it. It'll work. You'll see."

"Okay—you're the expert, I guess."

"You'd better believe it."

"Well, this should be a pleasure."

Davin and Giem carried me down into the utter confusion of Garth's camp. Tents lay collapsed, three shuttles had parked with lights on and all ramps down, and underlings herded quelsh and equipment aboard in a frantic rush.

I lay limp in my friends' arms, after an artistic soaking with all the cooked-down, pulpy red juice we managed to squeeze from the last of Grek's bruised collection of wild kravas. We'd taken almost an agonizing hour just to pick out all the little black seeds. I hadn't found the color, smell, or consistency of our concoction very convincing.

"Human blood isn't magenta, and it doesn't resemble a fruity syrup."

Giem had insisted it was good enough to pass, especially at night. "After all, we're not trying to fool an MD."

Not wanting to confuse the issue with the presence of a Pio, we'd left Grek stationed at the top of the ridge. He took charge of our mounts and remaining equipment, including Davin's field glasses and Giem's wristcom. Grek would continue calling for help, and become even more urgent about it if it looked like we were getting into trouble. Or, more realistically, if we launched into even worse trouble than we were headed for.

"Goodbye, Taje," Grek had said, right before Giem had stunned me. He swept his claws lightly down my arms, sending a shiver through me. "Don't get too damaged. I still have more I want to try doing with you." I puzzled over that wish on our way back down into Garth's camp.

"What in the FIL Galaxy are you doing here?" Garth scanned us out of the corner of his eye, as he directed anxious herders and beasts. "You made me a promise, Mohrogh. Get out of here."

"She's hurt!" Giem and Davin cried out together.

"Chothark's gang attacked again," Davin added.

"Look at her. We need help to keep her from dying, and you're the closest help we've got," Giem pleaded.

They hauled me right on up to him, close enough that I worried about my disguise. Garth scanned me a little more carefully, turned more pale than normal, and rapidly looked away. Maybe it was the eye glued shut with clotted red pulp. "If you can find my medic, you're welcome to her services until we lift, which won't be long. Then you're on your own. Hey, where do you think you're going?"

"We've got to get her somewhere warmer," Davin said, as he and Giem paused halfway up the nearest shuttle ramp. As if the inside of the shuttle was warmer with all hatches open, and FIL forbid the medic should get one look at me. My heart tried to pound its way up into my throat.

"She's in shock. We don't want it to become irreversible," Giem said, and Garth simply turned away and ignored us. Yes, I peeked.

"I can't believe how vac-brained he's acting," Davin whispered as we jostled inside. He and Giem had to squeeze past Garth's minions and circle around pens filling almost the entire shuttle interior.

"Shhh. It doesn't make sense. Just feel thankful for it," Giem whispered back. She and Davin found a quieter corner near the rear engine room. There they carefully lowered my tingling body to the deck. "Now go find the medic while I watch over her," Giem said more loudly.

Davin left to do whatever shuttle damage he could manage. Neither of us, as biologists, not engineers, understood any of his ideas, and no doubt we had all begun to feel more than a bit nova after getting this far. Giem couldn't pretend to do much for me without a medkit, and the light stunner effect was definitely wearing off.

"How are you really doing?" she whispered.

"I'm returning to normal," I mumbled through semi-functional lips.

"Want another dose?"

"No thanks. I'll just fake it."

"Sure? Oh well, no one's paying us much attention, anyway." Giem sat back, and quit bothered to put on a show. "I sure wish Davin would hurry up." He was supposed to rejoin us when he finished sabotaging the shuttles.

Personally I thought Davin would be lucky to get anything worthwhile done in this madness, before the shuttles lifted. I couldn't do anything about it except lie here looking deathly wounded, and watch the pens fill up.

Maybe we should have waited outside. We had each acquired stunners from Chothark's ruined camp. If Davin got caught and couldn't shoot his way out, we'd planned to split up and cause as much trouble as we could. Staying here theoretically gave one of us a head start on this shuttle. We'd based our planning on the assumption that we couldn't count on official help arriving in time, the only reasonable calculation I commed we'd made in the whole precarious strategy.

Well, maybe I was wrong about that. Giem and I heard the distinctive rushing sound of multiple aircars arriving outside. Either Garth had a whole fleet illegally flying in, or station authorities had finally arrived. Giem turned her head, and I sat up. Both of us saw Garth dash inside.

"You two better get out of here pronto, and go join your friends," he shouted at us, as he ran forward to the pilot room.

I got up, stumbling over a pile of tangled blue rope, and made it to the large hatchway he'd entered. There I stood and looked out on a huge ruckus: Garth's shocked crew, Davin and Grek, milling quelsh, angry lizards, panicked horses, and aircar loads of security personnel, everyone yelling and threatening each other, and most of the humans waving stunners around.

I began to grin so hard my face hurt. Giem hauled me back from the awesome view by one sore shoulder, just as the deck beneath my boots began to vibrate.

"He's trying to escape!" She turned us toward the pilot room.

"Hey—"

"Come on, we have no time to lose."

"Yeah, in getting help!" I made a last desperate lunge for the open hatchway, only to find a starlit view of dark treetops careening beneath us. I gulped as Giem rescued me with a strong grip on the back of my jacket.

"Come on—we've got to stop him!" The ramps slid home. Giem slapped an emergency hatch lock, while penned quelsh scrambled and fell against each other. I grabbed onto the nearest pen rail and hauled myself against the pitching deck, to follow Giem forward to the other open port hatch.

"Go close the starboard hatches!" Giem waved me off.

"If we close all four, he'll be able to leave the atmosphere," I shouted over the roar of engines and the hissing of frightened quelsh.

"He can anyway." Giem closed the front port hatch. "He could just seal off the front compartment."

"That would mean two murders, and the death of any remaining profits."

Giem impatiently led our way back between pens to the starboard hull. "He may think we've left, and he must have remote hatch controls. He probably just hasn't bothered with them. I don't want him to forget about them, either."

She broke off as the sounds of an angry argument made it back to us from the pilot room. For a micro I entertained the impossible. I had to convince myself that Davin couldn't possibly have slipped onboard.

"Hurry up." Giem rushed to the forward starboard hatch control, and I dashed aft to shut the rear. I fought the lurching deck again to follow Giem. She headed forward towards the pilot room with her stunner drawn.

I fought more than poor grav-control, as I drew my stolen stunner from under my shirt and released the safety. The voices ahead had my whole body prickling with dread.

Giem plunged through the open hatchway of the pilot room, and a micro later she came reeling back into me. She moaned and doubled over in shocked pain, and my hair tried to crawl right off my scalp as I dodged on around her.

"Don't go in there!" Giem shouted at me. "It's too dangerous."

Now I knew whom Garth had argued with, and I'd rather ditch and run. I had no way to escape, nowhere to hide, and precious little time to think. What was it Giem had said, way back at the beginning of our externship? "One of us has to be strong," I said. I commed it was my turn, and I had learned that pain couldn't stop me from doing anything I wanted.

I sucked in a breath, set my stunner for short-range high-strength, took a deeper breath, fingered the trigger, and gripped the stunner in both hands. I lunged into the small pilot compartment and fired at the woman first.

I hit the right target immediately, and caught only the edge of her weapon's beam in the process. I also hit Garth, sitting closest to me, with the edge of my beam, in the surprisingly cramped quarters. Through a haze of rapidly fading pain, I realized we had no pilot. Garth scanned me with obvious horror, and tried to say something that came out as an indistinct mumble from his slumped position over the controls. Chothark had collapsed over the console to his left. I froze in panic as red lights began to flash all over the board.

"What happened?" Giem gasped from behind me, as the shuttle shuddered hideously.

"I shot them both—we have no pilot!"

"Well, don't just stand there—take over the controls." Giem pushed past me, and struggled to pull Chothark's limp body off the console and strap her into her seat. I started to follow suit with Garth. "Leave him to me," Giem yelled in a harsh panic. "Get to work on the controls, before we crash into that ocean in front of us!"

"I don't know how to fly this thing." I pocketed my stunner and stared helplessly at starlit waves dimly growing on the large main screen. Below it the whole dizzying array of little control screens on the console flashed crazily, in rhythm with a loudly insistent alarm.

"I thought you told me you learned how to pilot in your pre-ecology class."

"I just learned basic com controls for a little private yacht."

"Well, find the com, and control it." Giem crammed around Chothark to work on Garth. "We don't have any other choice."

I braced myself between the two pilot seats and frantically scanned flashing instruments. When Giem finished heaving and strapping Garth out of the way, she squeezed between his seat and the rear bulkhead, and pointed over him at a small comscreen. "Look."

"That's it!" I said.

"Guess we can't get any worse off. What will you try first?"

"Nothing. Look at the warning on it!" I said. "The com has taken over emergency control, automatically."

"Then why does it still feel like we're about to crash?"

"I don't know." Giem had a point—we both leaned on or grabbed onto anything stable—bulkhead, console edge, seats—and spread our feet apart to stand on the pitching deck. "Look—we've leveled out—we're no longer losing altitude." I pointed at the main screen, which showed us skimming above the night surface of the ocean. We had very little altitude left to lose. At least the waves had stopped growing large enough to engulf us. "Phew! That was close." I wiped sticky sweat from my face.

"Almost too close," Giem agreed, letting out her own sigh of relief. "I wonder, where are we going? Anywhere in particular? Or can we take control of our destination?"

"I don't know. We should be able to find out." I reached for the controls.

Giem focused again on the main screen. "Taje," she screamed, "hurry!"

I had only enough time to look up, and share a brief view of the dark land mass we were about to smash into.

CHAPTER 41

Garth's shuttle com apparently worked well enough to make a controlled crash—just about six or seven dozen trees died for our cause. Giem and I were thrown onto the deck in the process, and my poor body got battered again. As I groaned, cursed, and slowly picked myself off the deck, I discovered Chothark slowly moving, and somehow she'd gotten her hands on her stinger.

She trained it rather unsteadily on me. I pulled my stunner out of my coat pocket, and saw the red recharge warning light flashing on it.

"Go ahead and shoot me." I dropped the useless stunner on the deck. My ears began to buzz.

"Taje—" Giem scrambled to her feet.

Chothark stared at me and pulled the trigger. I ground my teeth as I took a wobbly step closer to her, and grabbed her wrist. I bent one of her weapon fingers backwards until she released the weapon with a shriek and the blast of pain enclosing me stopped.

Giem drew her stunner and I pocketed the stinger. I left the pilot room and staggered along the tilted deck to the forward port hatch. I found it badly jammed. I moved on to the aft hatch, hit the release, the ramp lowered, and thank the Galaxy some floodlights turned on. An exhausting clamber over and under broken trees brought me to a beach with noisy breakers. I stumbled behind a receding wave, down hard-packed wet sand, and almost fell over. I hurled Chothark's weapon over the spray into the dark water, as far as I could throw. It disappeared a long way out. I don't throw like a girl. I whirled around and tried to race the next wave back up. Instead I got soaked.

Shivering, I found Giem backed into the starboard hatchway of the pilot room, covering both of our fully revived captives. I expected her to be angry with me for leaving her alone with them. Instead she had an odd expression on her golden face.

"Look at them," she said, with a note of wonder in her quiet voice. I squeezed in beside her.

I scraped krava pulp off my face and swiped my hands on my wet pants, so I could look at them with both eyes wide open. I looked, mystified for a few micros, until the resemblance between the two zapped me.

I also again scanned the faint scars on Chothark's pale face, and I remembered a brief nemesis from my Center days. Chark's name didn't match exactly, I suppose it could have been her nickname, and it had gotten a rise out of her while she tortured me. It didn't really matter, except that it made me feel like the Universe had collapsed on me.

"Yes, what are you two going to do with me and my little sister?" Garth relaxed in his seat harness and grinned at us with a tired and dirty face, drawing my attention away from Chothark's vicious glare.

"Spies—filthy FIL agents." She hissed like an angry lizard.

"Yes, Giem, what are we going to do?" I had to work at ignoring Chothark. Just scanning her made me remember the big fight we'd had at the Center. Had she suffered from that as much as I had? "Where are we, anyhow?" I wondered. "Not on a desert island, I hope." Not docked with these two!

"I don't know," Giem said crossly, still straining to cover both with her stunner. Too bad we hadn't thought to bring a spare stunner. "Ask the com," she said.

I gazed at all the controls, and felt overwhelmed by the enormous task at hand. My vision began to sparkle. I stumbled back against the rear bulkhead of the pilot compartment. I tried to launch from it, and slid down it instead, leaving a wet smear. I dropped my head to my knees, and I had to cling to the idea of breathing.

"*Taje!*" Giem roared, "*what are you doing?*"

"I'm totally drained." I even felt more pale than usual. "I can't do anything more." Giem's outrage seemed justified, but she made me feel like I was whining. I just couldn't stand up any longer.

"Nonsense. You made it through final exams better than this. Here—" in frustration, she forcibly handed me her stunner. She stood between the seats to study the controls. I stared dully at her weapon, until my vision cleared enough to see she still had her safety on, and the power level indicator had fallen extremely low.

I had to take some minutes to remember Giem hadn't had any stunner lessons. We'd lived together closely enough that I sometimes forgot she hadn't always gone to school with me. When I heard Chothark trying to work her straps loose, I released the safety and aimed the stunner straight at her. She saw it and froze, and I stunned her anyway. I gave Garth the last dose.

"What did you do that for?" Giem spun around.

I struggled to my feet, and tossed her the stunner. "Look at the power reading." I drew a couple of deep breaths as I glanced at both our captives to make sure they could still breathe. I staggered out of the pilot room again, and probably took about five horribly long, sweaty minutes to return.

"*Where have you been?*" Giem raged while somehow, in her marvelously coordinated manner, she monitored both Garth and Chothark, and queried the com.

"Rope." I held up blue coils in shaking hands in the port hatchway. "I thought I scanned some back there. It was just all tangled up and knotted." Like everything else on Big Maxson.

"Well, hurry up and put it to good use. I think they're coming around, especially Riddock's sister."

"Okay, okay." I kneeled to tie Chothark's thankfully still limp wrists behind her seat. "Com where we are?"

"Yeah." Giem chuckled nervously. "We made a loop over the ocean. We're back on the eastern coast of South Maxson, almost where we left it."

"Well, that's nice. Just how far are we from civilization?" I carefully coiled the cord around Chothark's chest, her seat, and her waist, and moved on to her ankles.

"About seventy-five kilometers from the station—as an aircar would fly it."

"Tried calling anyone?" I reached into my belt pouch for my knife to cut the rope. I found only a nearly inedible emergency food ration and remembered I didn't have a knife anymore. I just snaked the rope on across to Garth's ankles.

"Yeah, I tried calling for help," Giem said. "It doesn't work."

"Broken transmitter? From the crash? We didn't land that hard—"

"Of course my knowledge of this sort of thing is very limited. However, I would guess the ship com has been tampered with." Giem eyed Chothark and Garth suspiciously.

"Well, what about your wristcom?" I reached the waist-wrapping part of Garth none too soon. He was starting to twitch a bit.

"You don't remember I left it with Grek?" Giem grimaced.

"Oh, yeah." I felt vac-headed, and it commed. Why should any of this prove easy? "Well, how about flying this crate back?" I offered bravely, as I tied off Garth's wrists and stood up dizzily behind his seat, clutching it. "Give me a couple hours to study it, and I might do a reasonable job—"

"I wouldn't—try it," Garth gasped out.

"Why not?" Giem said. "Afraid of sitting there helpless, while we bungle our way back? Would you care to offer to pilot us instead?"

"You'd trust me to do it?" Garth looked honestly surprised.

"Leave the atmosphere and we'd shoot you again." Giem raised her stunner.

"With that low power level? Whoever supplied your weapons was awfully careless, wouldn't you agree?"

Giem scanned the stunner with dismay. It too flashed a small red light. "Senility is setting in, and I haven't even graduated."

"Doesn't matter anyway." Garth sighed, leaned his head back, and closed his blue eyes. "I meant it literally when I said I wouldn't try it. I could tell this shuttle wasn't flying right from the moment I launched it. Our combination stowaway-hijacker here must have been willing to go down with the ship, just to ruin me."

"Vac-head. I wanted this shipment as much as you did," Garth's sister managed to choke out. "You must have enemies you don't even know about."

"Davin." Giem and I matched looks as we both spoke his name aloud. "He must have started tampering from the outside," I finished the thought. He really had come through—too bad it had worked out like this.

"We'll have to walk back right away," Giem said with weary resolution. "Are you done?"

"Yeah. Why not wait until morning?" I said. "Somehow, I just don't feel up to cross-country hiking in the dark tonight."

"We have no time to spare, Taje." Giem glanced meaningfully at our captives, and gave me a stern look. "We have over seventy-five kilometers to cover on foot, and even if we had a water bottle to leave with them, they'd have no way to use it. Nor can we force them to come along." She dropped her useless stunner on the console.

"Oh, yeah." I said vacfully, shuddered, and offered Garth one last chance. "Sure you don't want to fix the board for outgoing calls?"

"Knowing the source of that damage," Garth eyed Chothark's nasty grin, "I rather suspect it's permanent."

"We couldn't trust him untied, anyway," Giem said. "Come on, Taje, let's get going."

I picked up both stunners.

"Why are you bothering with those?" Giem said.

"If they get loose, they could probably use the shuttle to recharge them," I said. Of course Giem didn't know that either.

As we turned to leave, Garth spoke to our backs, stopping us in our tracks. "I knew you two were trouble the moment I scanned you. FIL usually sends someone to monitor me. What would look more innocent than a pair of diligent young FIL veterinary students? How else could this little mudball be worth your attention? Now I have to wish you good luck. I don't care to sit here next to my evil sister, and starve to death."

"You won't—you'll dehydrate first," we corrected him simultaneously, from nutrition lecture material. We put up a good cover to the end, because we really were just students.

I had more time to think about what we were doing as we opened the hatches that still funtioned, lowered the ramps, and released the last of Garth's captives. While Giem began to herd them out, I struggled down to the shore to dispose of the stunners in the same manner as the stinger.

As I worked to return to the shuttle, the aborted ecologist in me wanted to object to the release of quelsh here. They might disrupt the local ecosystem. The vet student in me shut her up, a heartening if perhaps vac-headed confirmation of the direction I'd chosen for my life.

I joined Giem, and our shouts and arm-wavings sent most of the rest of the quelsh rushing out to freedom. A few remained, dead or dying or too sick to move. Except for one still strong and wild enough to fight us off. We carried the rest outside. I let Giem carry most of the weight, but she doesn't have to know that. We put the sick quelsh where they could at least graze on some lush ground before them. If not, their bodies wouldn't stink up the shuttle interior. We left the hatches open for fresh air.

I gazed back reluctantly at the shuttle nose, as Giem and I walked away into the woods. "We could just set them loose, too."

"We could," Giem said, clapping a hand on my shoulder, hard enough that I had to work at not flinching. "Do you want them trailing us? If we make at least twenty-five kilometers a day, which we should do easily without packs, we'll return to the station within three days. We'll get a message in even faster if we meet up with someone with a wristcom along our way. And I still have Ziehl's map memorized."

"Great Universe—thank your brain, Giem."

We laughed, and I stumbled and staggered after her into the night.

CHAPTER 42

No moon rose that night, and several hours and many more bruises and scrapes later, Giem relented and let us rest. We huddled down together in a nest of decaying leaves, under the low branches of a gnarled tree. I shivered through a sick night. Too bad we didn't have Grek here to make us a proper burrow.

"Wake up, Taje, wake up."

"Huh?" I almost lashed out as I jerked half-awake, from precarious, precious sleep I'd at last drifted into. The light of early dawn forced its way between my eyelids to my retinas, and shot through my optic nerves to my brain. I groaned.

"Time to start hiking again." Giem stood over me. "I can't sleep any longer, and we need to use all the daylight hours we can get."

I sat up, rubbing my eyes. "Ugh. I think I remember what we're doing. You didn't sleep very well, either, did you?"

"No, why?" she said, impatiently.

"Where do you get all your energy?" I got up, swaying a bit, and brushed moldy leaves from my filthy, dew-damp clothes. We'd awakened in a small grassy hollow, surrounded by bluish-green triangular-leaved trees. The sun peeked between knobby grey tree trunks, and an amphibian morning chorus began to wail from among hard, forked tree roots. One of the latter had left a dent in my neck.

"I don't know," Giem said. "I'm just ready to get going. Maybe it's lust driving me on again. I wonder how Davin managed last night?"

"He probably enjoyed a soft, comfortable bed, in a cell."

"Nice, Taje. Very nice. Come on—"

"Hey, at least they give you a real bed." I shivered, not because the morning was still chilly—it wasn't, particularly—only because that's how I wake up. Cold. It's very unpleasant. "I wonder how Grek fared?"

"Probably about the same. Let's go. The sooner we get back, the sooner we can straighten it all out—"

"Oh, I com it. I'm going to have to chase after you again, while you chase after some man—"

"What's the matter? Can't remember the way back by yourself?" Giem taunted me in return.

"Hah, we're headed southwest . . . a bit more west than south?"

"Not bad." She seemed genuinely surprised. "If we get split up again, you've got to have some idea where to go."

"Never again, Giem," I said, rather more grimly than I had intended. "I'm never splitting up from you again."

"Shhh. Never say never—are you trying to tempt fate? Come on."

"Or maybe I'll have to climb down an unforeseen cliff, say good-bye to your broken body, and carry on in the name of duty," I perversely continued. If I had put a curse on us, I might as well do it thoroughly.

"One of us has to be strong." Giem laughed. "In the midst of a Grand Adventure, we're off to save more lives."

"Oh, yes, and such valuable ones too. I'd say we're more than a little off! Hey." I patted my belt pouch. "Want half of a breakfast?" I grinned at Giem. I pulled out my emergency food, proving its worth, and emptying my belt pouch. I pulled the meal pack heat tab and I held the pack to warm my hands. My stomach growled. I didn't even think about needing that food later.

"Sure! Hand it over," Giem said.

We each gulped down half of a miserly bland meal, while I remembered my half-finished dinner last night with regret.

After that, we set out on the day's hike. We traveled mostly lizard style, not bothering to go around anything we could climb over or under, and ever mindful of the distance it added every time an obstacle forced us off our straight-line course. We met rocky outcrops, ravines, marshes, and dense thickets with impatience and disgust. We had our mission to accomplish, and woe to anything or anybody who tried to stop us.

Luckily, the only living creatures we encountered that day were small sunning reptiles, chirping amphibians, squalling karcs, and flickering glimpses of fish in the streams crossing our path. Annoying insects seemed particularly attracted to the dried krava syrup on my clothes.

I was tempted, whenever we stopped for cautious drinks, to sharpen a stick on a rock and try spearing a gelssk. The risk of getting bitten kept me from trying to murder a gelssk. That, and Giem's impatience.

She truly missed Davin and she kept saying so, loudly, until I quit trying to act nice about it and told her she was making me nova. That earned me a reprimand for worrying aloud too much over Grek, who probably wasn't beat up or in a cell back at the station, and who wasn't even a potential Romantic Interest.

Annoyed by Giem's narrow-mindedness, I said "I could fall in love with Ziehl," not lying because Ziehl had such a wonderful personality, wrapped up in such gorgeous pigment. "However, she's taken," I had to honestly add.

"How fair-minded of you," Giem spat.

I guess we both got on each other's nerves that morning, until we collected some small tart kravas along our way, and had something else to do with our mouths.

Around noon we came to a bigger creek. It wasn't flowing dangerously hard or obviously swarming with underwater denizens. We moved on to waste nearly half an hour trying to find a section narrow enough to jump, shallow enough to wade, or naturally bridged with a downed tree.

"We'll have to swim." I shivered, as the coiling green surface and the white noise of rushing water mesmerized my beyond-tired brain. "Maybe we could tie our clothes on our heads to keep them dry."

"And risk losing them? No thanks," Giem said. "I'd rather have wet clothes than none at all, and a little extra shielding. Besides, maybe they'll get cleaner."

"I'm not sure anything could do that."

We heaved a shower of rocks in ahead of us, to scare off any aquatic attackers.

I waded into the surprisingly cold water. I howled and turned around. Giem stood right behind me, blocking my way back.

"Keep moving," she said, obviously pained herself at having to pause in the frigid rush. "We can't assume it's safe here. Just make that nice sunning rock on the other side your goal." Deviously clever person. That's the trouble with friends—they com you too well.

The current in the middle was stronger than it looked, and we ended up downstream from our objective. A short dripping hike along the other bank brought us back to the rock. We stripped, to dry our clothes and ourselves. We lounged back on the sun-warmed large flat stone, and told overdue stories.

I described all the interesting details I'd learned about Pios. Giem caught me up on her spying adventures. We both wondered again how Grek and Davin had fared, trapped between the criminals and the cops. I fell silent, realizing just how much Grek's companionship meant to me when I didn't have it, and feeling as wistful as Giem scanned.

The sky chose that moment to cloud up. We moaned. We'd tarried as long as we dared. We pulled our damp, stiff clothing and soggy boots back on, and set off again. The krava syrup had at least washed out of my clothes except for some big red stains.

We came next to a rocky ravine, with a stream trickling along the bottom of it. Clambering and boulder-hopping down inside it made us warm and almost dry again.

Giem paused abruptly, after striding across the little stream, so I had to work at not colliding with her or stepping back into the water.

"Hey, what—"

"Shhh—I think I hear an aircar."

"Out here? It would have to be—"

"Illegal—or an emergency vehicle. I know. Come on!"

We raced recklessly up the other side of the ravine, and saw nothing by the time we made it out.

"Probably just the wind and some wishful thinking," Giem said, disappointed. I didn't feel any wind, until we made it to the top of a ridge, about an hour later.

"There it is."

"What?" Giem said.

"The aircar. Look! No, it's gone—just behind those low clouds—"

"Those clouds look rather ominous."

"I've seen worse." I turned again to the way ahead of us.

Giem rolled her eyes, and gave an exaggerated sigh. "How many times do I have to keep telling you not to tempt fate?"

Sure enough, it began to sprinkle. By the time we reached the rolling green meadow below, dark blue-grey clouds pelted us full force.

I limped a short distance behind Giem, who followed her own sense of direction. As water seeped back into my clothes, an unusual chill for Big Maxson invaded my bones. My partly artificial right knee hurt, a haunting reminder of old exploits. It made each slogging stride along the wet ground a nasty effort. My only distraction became a fantasy of receiving a second chance at Dr. Bioh's banquet, inside his cozy home.

Soaked, I wanted to turn back, but we'd come too far, and we had nowhere to return to.

The downpour quit, and we began making regular stops. However, they never lasted long enough for any real rest, since attacks of convulsive shivering drove us on. Nevertheless, I found them quite necessary for some maintenance of morale.

My wet, tired feet painfully sloughed some vital skin.

I began to dream about the luxuries of civilization awaiting us. Purified tap water. Real toilets. Hot prepared meals. Warm baths and showers. Fresh dry clothes. Clean soft beds in solid, dirt-free shelters. Not to mention all sorts of wonderful transportation much faster than pathetic little human legs.

As I looked up at lifting clouds, I saw early tinges of sunset peach and pink, and an artistic swirl of karcs in the foreground. I glanced at Giem, determinedly striding on ahead, down a long gradual green slope.

"Hey, you're limping," I said.

"You are too," she said, without looking back at me.

"I have an excuse."

"I fell on my right knee years ago, when a horse threw me," she said. "It hasn't bothered me in a long time."

I trotted painfully to catch up with her. "This is totally nova. How will we make it through this night? You realize we'll probably have to keep moving, just to avoid hypothermia? Why are we doing this?" A river wound along below us.

"Because we're such noble FIL vet students," Giem said, with a tired smile on her mud-streaked face.

"Because we're such vac-head suckers," I said. "I've been thinking, once station police took control back at Garth's camp, they could track his shuttle easily enough. We should have just stayed put. Basic Common Sense, for lost-persons-wanting-to-be-found-again."

"With those two creepy Riddock siblings, just waiting for any opportunity to jump us? I thought about it. Not for very long. I couldn't com risking any more time around them than we had to."

"I suppose you're right," I said, reluctantly.

"Besides, you spoke of a ship-sized scan screen—there's no telling whether the shuttle has one operating as we speak."

"True," I said.

"Plus I assume you disposed of our only working weapon."

"Yes." I sighed. Like I'd ever use a *stinger* on anybody.

"What was that terrible thing, anyway?" Giem said. "I thought it burned me, and my skin didn't even turn red."

"A pain nerve stimulator."

"You're kidding. I've only heard of those in spy stories and holo thrillers. I wasn't even sure stingers were real."

"Well, now you know," I said, eager to change the subject.

Giem's almond eyes stared hard into my odd green eyes. I glanced away, studying shifting patterns of forest green and sunset orange and red, swirled together on the surface of the river ahead of us, like the face of a Pio.

"Great Galaxy, Taje, what is it you're not telling me? Don't you trust me? I know most of your friendships developed over a nova number of years in the Center. As Ziehl might point out, we've spent more time cooped up together in the last school year than most married couples. Doesn't that count for anything?"

Why didn't I want to tell her? Every vac-headed move I'd made, that got me into all those dangerous situations? Maybe I didn't want her to think I was a pervert for enjoying each of my victories after every torture. And then there was that weirdly cozy scene with Garth on the cot after he'd untied me, and his outrage whenever he thought his minions and Chothark had mistreated me. What would Giem think of all that?

I reminded myself that Giem had managed over the last school year to tell me all about her gruesome marriage—a tale of abuse I would have never wanted to admit to anyone—and she was still waiting for an answer from me. I'd have to give her something.

I gulped as I turned to face her again. "Well," I thought frantically, "did I ever tell you about my first birthday at the Center?"

"Huh?"

I launched into my vac-headed story. After all, Giem had admired my diversions. "I collected all the pieces of the yusahmbul piñata while the other kids in my dorm family grabbed all the candy and prizes. Later my dorm mother found me crying on my bunk, and repairing the piñata with a sealer. She wanted me to return to the party and blow my cake lights out for everyone. I ignored her. She told me I'd ruined my whole birthday party."

Giem stopped, stunned. "I can't believe anyone would say that. Once when I was quite young, I reprogrammed a story holo to make the donkey feel less sad and friendless, and my parents thought me quite clever. No wonder we're both vet students. What has this got to do with—"

"Anyway, I kept the piñata right by my bed, named him, and talked to him in the dark. One day he just wasn't there anymore. I looked everywhere, and no one knew anything about it. Except my dorm sister, Aerrem, of course. She admitted she'd spied our dorm mother dumping it in the cycler, the way they did whenever they thought any of our toys had grown too worn out to keep."

"Without your permission? That's fused, Taje—"

"I think they were just overworked. Two dorm parents were assigned to over forty kids. I suspect our dorm parents had almost no time for their own lives. It's no wonder the turnover was so high. I was just lucky Aerrem insisted on becoming my friend. Anyway, I had another nightmare about it in Garth's camp, and woke up weeping in front of him—"

"Is that all?" Giem laughed. "A public display of emotion. Oh my, Taje is fully human after all—"

"I cried in front of his sister too," I blurted out defensively, and choked.

"And which nightmare caused that?" Giem said, unknowingly coming to my rescue. "You have so many of them, it's hard to keep track."

Scanning anywhere to escape Giem's gaze, I spotted two specks against the sunset sky just beyond the river. "What's that?"

Giem spun around. "Aircars—I can hear them."

With an amazing burst of energy, we ran the rest of the way down to the bank of the river.

"What are they doing?" I watched the cars zigzagging across the landscape on the other side of the river. "Why haven't they flown closer or farther away by now?"

"Looks like a search pattern."

"They're scanning for us?"

"Maybe," Giem said hopefully. "Making themselves this obvious, they must be special patrols from the station. It looks like we have a chance for a fast ride, if we can get across this river rapidly enough. Ready for another swim? We're already wet."

"Anything to keep from staying out here without shelter for another night. Let's go."

We pelted the river with another hasty rock shower. Giem slapped me on the back and we plunged on in, wading into water up to our armpits. I was so chilled the water seemed warm. Not good.

The current was powerful and scary. As we attempted our first strokes against it, a flash of panic struck us both at almost the same micro. Seconds and centimeters from being swept irrevocably apart, we managed to grab onto each others' coats. We struggled with weakening limbs to stay afloat as the current sucked us downriver, and we grazed boulders. The roaring water drowned our shouts and curses as we fought to reach the other bank.

CHAPTER 43

I couldn't feel my hands or feet by the time we somehow reached the painfully pebbly ground of the opposite beach. We crawled up to the grassy bank in the rapidly fading light.

We collapsed, gasping, coughing, and shivering on the rain-soaked grass. A terrible adrenaline surge faded before I realized Giem scanned even worse than I felt. I rolled over and investigated the rent in her pants below her right knee. My stiff hands came away dark and slick from her calf.

"Giem, you're bleeding!" I scanned frantically for the aircars. They'd headed upstream, and I couldn't see them against the dying sunset.

"What? I don't feel anything." Giem attempted to sit up. Instead she laid down again on her back. "Why am I . . . so weak?"

"You're wounded." I knelt closer, and carefully felt what I couldn't see. "It seems like—something huge bit you. When did this happen?"

"I told you, I can't even feel it."

"How am I supposed to tell how much blood you've lost!" The pallor in Giem's normally golden face made it glow like a skinsh leaf in the dimming light. I tried to tear loose her pants from the knee, and but the soaked fabric had become too tough and heavy.

"What are you doing?" Giem mumbled, feebly trying to brush me away.

"One of us has to be strong," I tried to joke, fighting tears of frustration and rage. I tried to remind myself of the time Dr. Korax had nonchalantly informed me, in the middle of a very messy surgery aboard *Onnarius*, how much blood most animals could lose without any problem.

I knew getting frantic about this wouldn't help either of us. Giem's blood rapidly spilled out of her leg. Without a knife, I couldn't even bind her leg with material from her torn pants. What creature, lurking under the water, could have bitten her like this? And why had we assumed we'd never become prey to anything bigger than a gelssk?

Abruptly I cursed my soggy brain. I yanked my jacket off, pulled off my shirt, wrung it out, and wound it above Giem's ripped pant leg. I tied it off to make a pressure wrap. Shaking and dripping, I pulled my soaked coat back on, and grabbed Giem's shoulders. Her eyes were closed.

"Giem, talk to me! Have you got anything in your pockets—anything I might use to help you?" I patted her down.

"What? Don't yell, Taje. You're hurting my ears. Go flag one of the aircars to pick us up."

"They're too far away. And I'll yell all I want to!" I said, turning hysterical as dark liquid continued to well from her wound. How could I lose her now? If the whole Universe was trying to punish me for not telling my latest roomie everything, it was sure doing a great job of it. "Blast, my tourniquet isn't tight enough!"

I proceeded to untie and rebind her leg with hands so freezing and trembling I didn't know whether I'd be able to wrench my shirt any tighter. How much of a vet would I make in a crisis? I slapped my hands on my thighs, forcing circulation back into my fingers. I had to make this bandage work. I had nothing else. Wrong! I pulled my belt off, pocketed my empty belt pouch, and yanked and cinched the belt around my shirt. Still a challenge with frozen hands.

"This isn't fair!" I cried out, into the rising wind, as I lifted Giem's ankles to my shoulders and struggled to stand up, to send what little blood she had left in her legs back into more vital areas, and away from the bite wound. "I couldn't ever help Shandy much, all those years we roomed together, and I can't help him at all now. And even though I know what to do for you, Giem, I still can't do it for you out here. Giem, answer me!"

"You'll answer to the law," replied a dark figure, melodramatically backlit by a harsh set of lights. I blinked my eyes and they teared as I stared back over my shoulder. There was no wind. One aircar had arrived, and another whooshed down next to it, and coughed out more people and lights. Two white uniformed Telmids boldly ran straight to us, sensitive antennae quivering at the scent of alien blood. They bent over Giem with a medkit, while a blue uniformed human pair approached us more cautiously. I hung onto Giem's ankles as I straightened up, in a dizzy haze of exhausted relief.

"I told you I picked up a warmer reading on our scanner over here," the uniformed woman, walking cautiously toward me, said to her male partner. "Let me see your wristcom for your ID," she demanded of me, aiming her stunner at me.

I peered at both humans—Giem and I had met most of the station police in the course of our swine seizure and slaughtering duties—unfortunately I didn't recognize anyone here. Maybe I just felt too tired. I certainly didn't feel like a warmer reading. And asking for my wristcom seemed incredibly trivial. Just thinking about it greatly taxed my few remaining on-duty brain cells.

"Present your wristcom ID right now," the uniformed man ordered, also aiming his stunner at me.

"The Pios have my wristcom," I finally remembered.

"You're under arrest," both said coldly.

"You can let go of her now," one of Giem's attendants said more gently. They had a real bandage inflated around Giem's wound, and an injector on her arm. I slowly lowered her legs to the ground.

"Fine. Just do whatever it takes to help my friend," I said, and sniffled, while one of the cops cuffed my wrists behind my back with spider stick. "She's lost a lot of blood."

"No thanks to you, I'm sure," the man said. He searched me. "Nothing in her pockets except this empty belt pouch." He dropped it on the ground. My old ecology class pouch.

"Hey, put that back!" I sat down, ready to refuse to move. Maybe I could pick it up with my teeth. The female officer guessed my next move, picked up my belt pouch, stuffed it back into my pocket, and helped me back up.

The two officers each grabbed one of my jacketed but bruised arms, ouch, and almost carried me to the nearest car. I glanced back frantically, and found another appeal unnecessary. I could see the Telmids had started fluids and shock meds, and they'd efficiently slid and strapped Giem onto a stretcher.

"We'd better fly her straight back to Dr. Devlin's clinic," they told my guards.

"Weapon or wristcom?" the man said.

One Telmid rapidly searched Giem. "Nothing. We must leave immediately."

"Okay. Send a report to the police station," the woman said. The cops promptly dumped me, soaked and dripping, on the plush backseat of their thankfully sealed and heated aircar.

I leaned back against my arms and cuffed wrists, shut my eyes, and realized the irony—Giem and I had just split up again. Never is such a foolish word. I fervently hoped for Giem's sake that they'd found us in time.

"Fork River Patrol to Big Maxson Police Station," the man spoke softly into his wristcom, while the woman launched the car.

"Big Maxson Police Station. Go ahead, Fork River Patrol."

"We believe we have escaped crew from the crashed shuttle. They've tossed any weapons or wristcoms. They gave up without a struggle, after interception en route to the Station. One badly wounded—put the station doctor on alert. We're on our way with them."

"Good work. See you soon."

"We left Garth and Chothark Riddock back on the coast, tied up in Garth's shuttle," I mentioned rather incoherently, remembering to discharge my duty, as I lounged in a foggy warm haze. I began to wiggle my thawing fingers, and my toes in my soggy boots.

The man looked back at me and wrinkled his nose with disgust. "Save your confession for later. We're just vacationing FIL Patrol personnel, stranded by quarantine and drafted into Big Maxson emergency service, but we can still make very good witnesses."

"Well, we thought we were vacationing," the woman grumbled, keeping her eyes on the controls, as she punched in directions for her autopilot.

"We were supposed to find a little time for a vacation too," I said.

CHAPTER 44

Before I remembered to tell anyone else about Garth and Chothark, a guard summarily escorted me painfully through the noisy, crowded police station to a small hallway for holding cells. I looked for Grek. Instead I scanned Garth as a guard hustled me into a closet-sized cage right next to his. My dorm parents used to say "Life isn't fair." This was just too much.

"We must quit meeting like this," Garth said, watching with his usual merry amusement, while my guard applied an enzyme patch to release my cuffs.

"They found you already," I said, stunned, as my escort exited and locked my cell. I dropped onto the little cot that filled most of the cell, shook off my melting cuffs, and swiped my disgusting, dripping hair out of my face.

"They tracked us down several hours after you and Giemsan left," Garth said, after the guard rushed off. "Someone camping down the beach reported our crash."

"We needn't have taken off cross-country after all." I groaned, feeling ridiculously vac-brained, as I yanked off my soggy boots. I grimaced at huge ruptured blisters on my poor feet. It occurred to me to ask, "What did you tell them about us?"

"Nothing." Garth snickered. "They drew their own conclusions. And maybe my sister put in a good word for you."

I snorted, wondering what sort of story she had fed the authorities, and how much of it they believed. "They didn't even bother trying to ID me before they threw me in here. Isn't that illegal?" I must have felt truly tired—vacfully asking a criminal about the law.

Garth laughed. "There's too many of us for this little station to sort out right away. I suppose they can call it an emergency. You should have looked out more for yourself."

"Yeah, well, that attitude sure did you a lot of good. Survival of the fittest is a law of nature, not of civilized people," I roughly quoted a nova teacher. I sighed.

"Hey, everyone has runs of bad luck, even with the best of intentions."

I didn't bother to answer that.

"Tajen, I think I owe you an apology."

"For what?" I looked at him with shock.

"Look at your feet. Why did you do that?"

"To rescue your miserable hide!"

"Exactly." Garth laughed.

I looked again at my miserable, shredded bare feet, stood up, flung myself onto the mesh separating our cells, taking some of the weight off of my feet, and asked Garth what I never understood. "Why did you let me go out there in your little valley? *Twice?*"

"I could tell from the look on your face that it was useless to ask you to help me."

"Oh." I collapsed on my cot and wrapped myself up in a blanket.

Around noon the next day, an exasperated guard vigorously shook me into consciousness.

"Ow! Stop it." I refused to open my eyes. I thought I had a desperately important job to finish.

"Great Galaxy, if I hadn't scanned you breathing, I'd have thought you dead! Come on, get up. Ziehl Ruck has bailed you out."

By rudely awakening me, she saved me from a sickening nightmare, in which Giem, Grek, Ziehl, Krome, Davin, Garth, and Dr. Bioh all bled copiously, simultaneously. I had to run between all of them, unable to help any of them fast enough. Thank the Universe it wasn't true. I forced my eyelids open, sat up enough to pull my damp boots back on, and almost screamed, but I am not a screamer. When I stood up at last, Garth Riddock saw the grimace on my face, and he gave me such a look of sympathy that I almost wept.

I leaned forward and hung onto the mesh separating my cell from Garth's, again. Then I actually said "Goodbye" to Garth Riddock, and he said "Goodbye, Tajen. Good luck," with a wink.

My leg muscles screamed at me as I hobbled, followed the guard out of the cells, and through the hall into the mobbed front office. Ziehl somehow scanned me there, pushed her way to me, and steered me to the exit doors.

"Did you really bail me out? Ziehl, I love you!" I could only gently hug her, and I blinked vacfully against raw sunlight flashing from puddles decorating the muddy street, and again almost wept. We hadn't escaped any of the ruckus by coming out here. Noisy crowds surrounded the police station.

Ziehl gave me a funny look. "No, silly, I just got you ID'd faster, with the help of several police who remembered your IPHA work. Great Galaxy, you're not even wearing a shirt." She sealed up my jacket, while my face flushed, thinking about who saw me this way. How long had I left my jacket open? I couldn't remember, and I didn't want to know.

"Great Universe," she said, "is this dried blood all over your coat? And what are these big red stains on your pants? Are you in any shape to ride? I couldn't get an airtruck through—"

"That's krava stains on my pants, and it's Giem's blood on my jacket. Is she okay? What did they do with her? She was hurt—"

"Relax. She's in good hands. You're both going to survive, despite all your vac-headed exploits. I brought two lizards. Just get on one, and I'll lead yours from mine. I don't want to dock here long enough for anyone to realize what an important witness you are—you look like you could use a thorough cleanup and a good rest first."

"You're not full of vac."

Ziehl gave me a leg up into a saddle with real stirrups, and expertly wove us through the throngs, while

I marveled distractedly at the speed at which our lizards covered the ground. My heart thudded. I'd helped to save Giem. For once in my life, I'd rescued someone, instead of just needing rescue myself.

Somehow I kept from sliding out of my saddle until we finally made it back to Ziehl's ranch. She took care of her lizards while I slumped on a bench on her porch. At last she took me inside her home, into a neat little guest room, and pointedly opened my duffle bag full of clean clothes on the bed.

"Hand me your clothes," she said, "and I'll let my cleanser work on them while you shower."

I thought about my whole-body bruise and escaped into the adjoining bathroom.

Ziehl hooted over the com. "Are you really that shy?"

I stripped in the shiny bathroom and ordered the door to open, just far enough to allow one bruised arm to hand over my disgusting clothes.

"Who beat you up?" Ziehl said angrily.

I groaned as I ordered the door to shut fast. "No one." I was a little tired of that question.

I used the marvelous toilet, and stepped into the shower. I took a long time scrubbing carefully, and occasionally winced or cursed. None the less, it felt exquisitely wonderful getting clean, and at last, completely dry. Not to mention having someone to take care of me, I thought, as I dressed in night clothes and drifted off in the fluffy bed. Was this what it was like to have a real mother?

CHAPTER 45

Vague dinner-time sounds and smells partly woke me up later. I struggled to rise, just pulled a pillow over my head, and promptly fell back into unconsciousness. When dawn peeked through the window curtains, I passed through a brief and stunning disorientation— trying to unscramble our dorm room, our hotel room, our tent, Grek's home, Davin's tent, Grek's tarped burrows, Garth and Chothark's tents, and the station cell from where I lay. I sat up with a jerk, my heart pounding, until I remembered Ziehl picking me up at the police station.

I groaned, tenderly pulled on clean pants, a fresh long-sleeved shirt, and some soft socks, and limped out to the dining room.

Ziehl, Krome, and Giem sat around the table, noisily finishing a lavish breakfast. I stared at Giem as I sank into a chair. I pushed some of the wreckage out of the way, to make room for my elbows on the table to cradle my head in my hands.

"Well, you've decided to join the land of the living." Ziehl stood up. "Let me get you some breakfast."

"You're not looking at a ghost." Giem grinned at me as Ziehl left the room. Giem answered my still anxious expression. "I did fine after treatment for shock, including a generous infusion of synthblood, and surgery on my leg—"

Krome scooched her chair back from the table. "If you're discussing gory details, I'll help Ziehl in the kitchen."

Giem and I grinned at her retreating back, and our eyes met again.

"Well, anyway," Giem coughed, "I barely had time to feel grateful for all I'd done in my short life, before I realized I would live another day. I have no serious long-term damage, and it's in the poor doctor's lonely best interest to heal people fast here. Dr. Devlin said hypothermia probably kept me from bleeding to death— along with your cobbled-out-of-vac first aid."

My face burned as I shrugged, slowly, to keep it from turning into a wince. "I couldn't let you die."

"Really?" Giem's dark eyebrows raised. "Truly? I've gained access to the in-group on your list?"

"Sure, and as usual, you proved right," I said, to distract her. It worked.

"Smooth. About what?"

"Worrying about the future is a useless preoccupation."

Giem laughed, and asked me how I felt. "We thought you'd never wake up."

Ziehl returned with a platter stacked with pancakes with quelsh butter and krava jam, a scrambled quelsh egg, and a skitsh sausage. Krome parked a tall glass of krava juice next to my plate as she returned to her chair.

Compared to Giem's ordeal, I couldn't complain. I hadn't suffered any life-threatening wounds. "I'm fine," I answered, and flinched and cried out when Ziehl made an attempt to massage my shoulders from behind me. She stopped at once, startled, while Giem rolled her eyes.

"You need a visit to Dr. Devlin too?" Ziehl said. "She's keeping busy. I could probably get you in to see her today anyway."

By bribing her with skitsh steaks or a riding lizard? I shivered. "No, please, I'm okay." I stared down at my plate, and wondered why I didn't feel ravenous anymore. "I just turned out—a bit more important than I thought, and ended up with a total body bruise. Nothing a doctor could do much for."

"Well, some break from station work you gave yourselves." Ziehl returned to her place at the table. "I guess you two are simply hopeless trouble-magnets. Or the most foolish FIL agents-in-training that I've ever heard rumor of."

Did we appear that obvious? Fortunately, I could tell she was fishing—thank the Universe. I had to look away from her to keep from cringing, which is what I caught sympathetic Krome doing. Giem barely broke her stride over her breakfast.

"Hey." She stabbed her fork into her sausage. I turned my gaze away from that too, uncomfortably reminded of the trader's analogy about commitment. "Here we just saved the Galaxy from Garth's devious plot, and all you can manage to say is that we're hopeless."

"You promised me you'd stay away from Garth Riddock."

"No. We just said we'd try not to attract his attention if we ended up on the same trail," I corrected Ziehl. I slipped my sausage to her dog, positioned strategically under the table at my place. He proceeded to enjoy it rather too loudly.

"Taje is very literal," Giem commented as Ziehl frowned, "and she has a very good memory. You should know that by now."

"Taje, don't feed my dog, or he will become your friend for life," Ziehl said.

"Taje, you shouldn't feed Ziehl's dog without her permission," Giem scolded.

I glanced up at Giem, and gazed back at Ziehl. "Besides, Grek would tell you we're not hopeless," I said, as I surreptitiously wiped slimy dog saliva from my hand onto my formerly clean pants. "Maybe we did get in over our heads, and it didn't turn out terribly bad after all. We just didn't meet certain specific expectations—"

"All I know is that I sent you two out on a routine expedition—with good equipment, incidentally, that you managed to scatter all over the continent. Next I know, I have to call out the station troops, retrieve Giem from the clinic, rescue you from jail, not to mention bailing out Davin Mohrogh, of all people, and his sidekick Skorrelsk Tak Grekkan, if I got that right. How could I refuse Giem as she begged from her clinic bed?"

"Giem mentioned Grek along with Davin? And you bailed them both out?" I said. "How can we repay you for everything?" My heart started pounding again. "Where are they?"

"In various spare bedrooms—I insisted—Ziehl's got enough of them for multiple orgies," Krome said.

"Orgies? Where?" Davin asked, as he staggered in with his usual timing, and sat down shirtless, just to be cruel. "They can't be on this planet. How anyone can claim this is an R&R station is beyond me."

"How can you say that?" Giem said, stung, while I quoted, "Ah, 'Beautiful, Relaxing, Big Maxson's Planet,'" and laughed along with Ziehl and Krome.

Grek sauntered in next and pulled up a stool next to me. He scratched a peeling scale off his arm, and yawned widely enough to display his surprisingly thick, purplish, triangular tongue. He of course wore nothing except a translator.

"I don't think I can even make shuttle fare back into orbit," Davin continued to complain, as Krome served him and Grek platters similar to the one Ziehl had set before me.

"You'll get your saddle horses back from station authorities, and you can always find some temporary work around here," Ziehl said. "Once people realize you're a hero this time, you ought to find some way to capitalize on it."

"What do you mean, this time?" Davin scowled briefly, and promptly dived into his breakfast with relish.

"Hey, what happened to your pack horse?" I asked him, after sipping my juice. My food had begun to cool. I pushed my plate out from under my nose, and stared instead at the lovely rich magenta of my half-full glass, in a beam of sunlight from the nearest window.

Davin acted like he didn't hear me as he munched away.

"Yeah, Davin," Giem said, taken aback, "what did happen to Stormy?"

Davin glanced up. "Hey, Taje, there you go again, passing up good food."

"She doesn't usually eat much breakfast," Giem said. "Answer our question."

"What does it matter?"

"You're asking that of two vet students?" Krome laughed.

"Alright, alright. He, uh, got left behind."

"When?" Giem said.

"Where?" I said.

"I, well, when I gave up and started back. The quelsh valley villagers still weren't very happy—"

"Skikkan's village, all up in arms—I'd forgotten about that—why didn't you just ride around their territory?" I said, baffled.

"Well, I had at least hoped to recover my wristcom, before returning to the station. They—well, everyone still acted rather angry, and, uh, in the excitement, Stormy broke loose. I imagine he made himself at home in the village," Davin added, with a hint of gloom.

I could imagine a few more answers, like less heroic reasons for Davin's return to Garth's camp. Perhaps a wristcom reconstruction wouldn't quite match his original? Or he didn't want the original found by FIL with his crossbow? And maybe he had commed one of us could bargain with FIL or the Pios for him? I decided to be generous anyway.

"Cheer up, Davin," I said. "All is not lost. If you really need funds to leave, hunt up a bunch of karc eggs."

"Karc eggs?" He gave me a satisfyingly puzzled look.

"Yeah, only call them Dwarf Dragons when you sell them as pets to humans. Grek can tell you all about them."

With a little more explanation, Davin began to get excited about the idea. Grek described the various nesting sites he knew about along the streams on the way back to his village. Giem suggested we all go hiking back there, so the two of us could get a real little vacation near the end of our stay here after all—

"Hold it, everyone!" Ziehl shouted, and we all, gradually, shut up.

"That's better," Ziehl said, more quietly, and just as firmly. "I guess all of you need to know that the IPHAs have put the whole station under quarantine, and they've said it will remain indefinitely. No one here can leave station boundaries until the IPHAs determine how the local swine roundworm infection started. It's endangering Pio relations, and the continuing existence of this station—not to mention travel throughout FIL, with the whole microfloral replacement program starting to come under serious question—"

"That's ridiculous," I said. "Are they still that far behind on the story? Giem—"

"I didn't tell them either." Giem shook her head. "I haven't had a chance."

"Tell them what?" Ziehl threatened to stun us both with her stare.

"Garth must have illegally landed some of his people here months ago, in preparation," Giem said. "At least one of them must have come from an older human colony with an established infection. I would guess they hauled the eggs along by accident, didn't go through any rebugging or baggage sterilization before they arrived, and hid right away. And that's also why the infection hasn't had much time to spread."

"Or maybe the carrier was even one of his competitors," I added. "Ziehl, remember that Kralvin you caught?"

"How do you know they brought the parasite infection by accident?" Krome said.

"Oh, it draws far too much attention from the very authorities they wanted to evade, for Garth or any of his rivals to ever consider it a good diversionary tactic," I said. "It was purely bad luck for him."

"Bad luck?" Ziehl frowned. "It never gave him away—and the quarantine made it much harder to call anyone out to stop him."

"Yeah, although it was the arrival of the Interplanetary Public Health Authorities that panicked Garth into the hasty, sloppy exit that got him caught. And introducing a swine-human parasite infection will lead to even greater charges of planetary endangerment, whether intentional or not," I said.

"Only if you report it," Ziehl said, sadly. "I was going to hide the bunch of you for a while longer, and get you all rested before the Big Inquiry. However, I think we'd better not wait."

Ziehl got up from the table. "Come on, we're wasting everyone's time. Let's go straighten out this fused mess with the FIL IPHAs. We don't want them deciding to shut down FIL interplanetary travel."

Giem and I piled into Ziehl's truck, to return to the police station and courthouse. There we spent a long day on talking and comcrap. Of course it dragged out into a couple weeks of meetings, reports, and hearings which I thought would never end, topped off by nights of cramming to finish up our comparative parasitology report for Dr. Bioh.

Although we wanted to, Giem and I couldn't forget about our homework. We still had to pass our summer externship, and even if we hadn't collected as much data as originally planned, we could hope our most notorious conclusion would adequately pad our final write-up.

CHAPTER 46

"There's always backpacking," we kept telling Ziehl, whenever station IPHA and court hassles felt never-ending. However, I don't think she believed our insanity until we proved it. First we had to convince authorities that we'd reported all we could, in triplicate, and that they couldn't legally eat into our measly mandatory FIL two-week vacation allotment. We headed straight back out into the wilderness—as soon as we could reassemble enough equipment.

Fortunately we didn't have to pay hefty litter fines, replace most of Ziehl and Krome's valuable gear, or buy some of Ziehl's prime stock for Grek's grandmother or Skil. A clean-up crew had found Giem's lizard, with most of her camping equipment, wandering around Garth's campground, the day after they caught his troops. My mount with my gear showed up many anxious days later, tagging a skitsh herd in for its weekly feeding at Grek's village. And the quelsh valley villagers at last returned the rest of our confiscated belongings, including my precious old pocket knife.

Four of us hiked out of town on vacation together—
Grek showing Davin how to find karc eggs, while Giem
and I had time to enjoy the scenery. We set a leisurely
pace, stopping to camp often, though we'd loaded our
packs on Davin's horses. (We hadn't the courage to
borrow more lizards from anyone.) By our last trail camp
Davin almost had his portable stasis units filled with
eggs, and he and Grek set off at dawn to finish the job.

I quietly followed Giem along a stream as it burbled
and chuckled down its rocky bed, every bend a different
music under the wind that flowed through fluttering
tree leaves overhead like warm ocean waves. We found
it difficult to tear ourselves away from our peaceful
creek side breakfast, and we started back late, so I led
us straight back to camp. We had both worn T-shirts and
shorts, and Giem noticed the rainbow of bruises on my
legs and arms.

"Why didn't you tell me who beat you up, Taje?"

"That's because no one did!" I said. "Why doesn't
anyone believe me?"

"You don't have to shout at me!"

"It looks like your calf scar is almost gone," I said,
embarrassed, and trying to mollify her. I found myself
basking in warm thoughts of friendship as I fell back to
following her again. It felt good to be together, sharing
our enjoyment of the wilderness without any worries.
Well, except for how we were going to get through our
next looming, long planetary year of vet school. I tried to
remember not to worry about my future.

We returned to find Grek packing up equipment, and Davin muttering over one of his finicky stoves. His budget had reduced him to grilling countless gelssk, which Grek skewered for us with endless ease. I felt hungry enough these days I forced myself to not care about the killing and meal monotony. I could hardly blame Pios for lacking meat and fish cell vats.

"We finished the egg hunt today—perfect timing," Davin said, after he and Giem set their nibbled lunch fillets aside. "And we found the last nest in a smooth little meadow not far from here. Some red, orange, and yellow frog-things are singing up a storm out there. Want to go hear them before we leave?"

"Sounds beautiful," Giem said.

"They're remarkably disgusting," Grek said, strapping a saddlebag firmly shut. "We call them slime-skins."

Davin laughed, and Giem joined in. They left for the meadow, hand-in-hand, without asking whether I wanted to hear the local fauna. I could guess why, and I still felt hungry.

"They hardly ate any of my catch today," Grek said.

"I know. I'll finish the rest of the gelssk." I refused to waste their deaths. "You ought to eat at least one of them yourself."

"Ugh, do I have to?"

"Have you eaten anything else today?"

Grek managed to choke down the two smallest gelssk, and he waited patiently for me to finish off the four largest. He suggested we carefully wash the gelssk-goo from our hands in a small pond off the stream, so the

327

glitterbugs would leave us alone. Afterwards we lay on our backs in the sun, on the smooth mossy bank.

I tucked my arms under my head and gazed over at my sprawled-out friend. The fingers of his right hand lay near my cheek, and he used his long black nails to lightly caress my rather shaggy and sun-bleached hair.

"You'll leave soon," he murmured. "Has my world satisfied all your hopes for your visit?" Pios can't grin, instead he winked, and I heard the tease in his translated voice. I rolled over toward him, and found myself entwined in his arms as I studied his emerald green eyes with their tiny racing stripes of yellow, orange, and red. I wondered if my green eyes looked small and dull in comparison.

"I didn't even expect all the good friends I'd find here," I said, smiling. "I'll miss you a lot," I added, as I boldly traced an orange stripe across his smooth cheek, and my heart began to race.

"I'll miss you very much too."

I couldn't help laughing. "After all the trouble I've dragged you through?"

"It was—interesting." Grek's eyes closed as he touched the end of my nose with the tip of his plump, wedge-shaped tongue. A shiver ran down my spine.

"Giem would call it an Adventure," he gently added. "And I like you very much, Taje. I would like to mate with you in our Homeriver." He embraced me, and he snickered. "You would probably get too cold and shake too hard!"

"Hah! I've figured you male Pios out," I said, with nervous happiness. I tried not to feel awkward as I returned his embrace. "To ensure you pass on any of your genes—uh, father any children—you must have to mate constantly, all over the place! Yet you had to abstain through our entire journey. How long has it been for you?"

"You should consider it an honor." He tickled my cheeks with the tips of his claws.

"Anyway, I'd probably drown in your homeriver." I gave him a shy, human-style kiss, in his intermandibular space. Where his skin paled yellow, and felt incredibly soft. He smelled oddly good to me. Some say the pheromone clash should make this sort of interaction impossible. Maybe it helps that most humans don't have a great sense of smell, and I'm no exception. "I can't hold my breath nearly as long as you," I said. "What keeps you from slowing down too much, underwater? I know it's cold!"

"We start out as hot as possible." He ran a claw lightly down my side. "And we move fast—for us."

"Okay, I also doubt I'd be coordinated enough."

"You must have some coordination." Grek fingered my shirt. "How do you Humans manage to do anything, with your bodies all packaged up like this?"

"Oh, we have our ways." I stretched to remove my boots with shaking hands, hit my belt release, and opened my shirt and pants, while my crotch pulsed hotly. "You'll have to tell me what feels good," I said, frantically reviewing social memories from the sunning rock. Somehow I'd just have to relax and ride with this, which seemed to be one of my big lessons this summer—along with appreciating what I had, instead of longing for what I couldn't have.

"You'll do fine." Grek was kind. "You're wonderfully warm, and it's you that has to tell me what to do. You Humans are so secretive about it."

Oh, no, I couldn't help thinking. In over my head all over again, on Big Maxson's Planet!

CHAPTER 47

Giem threw her long shadow over us, to wake us up from sound naps in each other's arms, late that afternoon.

"Better get up. We want to make it to dinner at Grek's mom's restaurant by sunset, and we'll arrive late if we don't hurry."

Grek sat up, rubbed his face, yawned hugely, and left to help Davin finish loading his horses. Giem just stood there, hands on hips, and waited for me to wake up, dress, and pull my boots back on.

"Well?" Giem frowned as I slowly stood up.

"Well what?"

"You didn't do it, did you?" Giem spat.

I gaped at her. It wasn't her question as much as the accusation in her voice. "It's anatomically impossible," I said, "even if I could hold my breath long enough under water. He has two barbed hemipenes tucked inside his crotch slit!" I revealed more than I meant to. "How was it for you?" I asked, intending the redirection, not the jealousy in my voice.

Giem looked down, and I could see a certain suspicious smile growing on her face. She sighed happily as she looked up at me again. "Grand! Just grand! I'm sorry, Taje. Someday you'll find a *real mate* too."

A *real mate*? That irked me too. So I didn't even bother to inform her that I didn't have to go all the way to derive pleasure from someone else's touch. It just required an open mind, and a willingness to experiment. What was unreal about that? Was my current roommate a bigot? Or had I just assumed she was my friend because my last roomie was one of my best friends?

As we hiked the final kilometers to Grek's village, that last conversation continued to haunt me. I'd almost missed all the clues, but Giem's attitude upset me. After all, my dear friends Aerrem and Shandy were the engineered progeny of interspecies marriages. At last I brought the subject up again, indirectly, when Davin and Grek got ahead of us with the horses.

"What do you think of Ziehl and her girlfriend?" I challenged Giem.

"I don't know what they do together, and I don't want to know. They've never asked me for my opinion of it, either."

I hadn't asked for her opinion of my affair either. I shut up, before I said too much. I was still so angry.

We both grew silent, and after a bit, Giem lengthened her stride to catch up with Davin and Grek. I let my pace drag farther and farther behind, while a lonely dread gnawed at my guts. I'd given up so much for vet school.

I was trying to not let anything bother me. I commed I just couldn't endure one more loss.

CHAPTER 48

"Hey, you started without me." I sat down at the last empty stool at our table, and discovered they'd left plenty of salad. I picked up my freeform utensil and served myself a generous portion. The salad tasted sharp and tangy and contained pieces of marinated gelssk, which maybe explained why no one had completely demolished it.

I'd found Davin in the middle of a conversation with Grek's mother, and everybody ignored me. "I'm not really broke," he admitted. "The karc eggs will probably help me a lot, but the longer I stay here, the narrower my margin gets. I'll ride on back to the station tomorrow."

"Tomorrow?" Giem looked startled and dismayed. "Can't you stay even one more day? Taje and I have half a week left before our departure flight."

"I know." Davin sighed, and gave up on his salad. "I still have some loose ends to take care of back at the station. I've got to sell back the horses, for one."

"They're not rentals?" Grek's mother asked.

"No. I got them cheaper this way."

I had naively assumed they had a permanent part in his outfit, and that he would shuttle them back up to his ship.

"We might be able to get someone to loan us a couple lizards, to see you at the station until you leave," I seemed unable to stop myself from offering, for Giem's sake, even though I wanted to curse myself for the suggestion. To manage it, we'd have to spend all the rest of our short time here rushing back and forth, returning borrowed lizards and their equipment before we left.

Thank the Galaxy, Davin shook his head. "Enjoy the rest of your time out here. I hate spaceport goodbyes—they always depress me. Unless—" and he visibly gulped "—you want to go partners, and ship out with me?" He smiled forlornly at Giem, obviously trying not to hope.

You jerk. I had to grit my teeth to keep from saying it aloud. *You conceited vac-headed scale-scum!* There it was, the question I'd feared from Davin all the way here, and it shouldn't have surprised me to learn he had the ego and thoughtlessness to ask.

Davin versus vet school—it wasn't fair to have to decide between them. What putrid timing! I knew what I wanted Giem to decide, despite our difficult friendship. I didn't want to be the one she left behind. The friends I'd made in the Center had saved my life on Shielvelle, and departing from all of them still felt like a raw wound. Now I had a whole new set of friends, all made during one amazing summer break. Soon I'd have to leave them all behind, and getting through vet school was a tough enough challenge without some support from Giem.

I had to forcefully remind myself that I had a selfishly personal stake in the matter, and I quietly resigned myself to honorable noninterference. Every friend has flaws, and you either accept them, or go friendless. Shielvelle had taught me that too.

Giem chuckled. "Thanks for asking, Davin." She looked pleased, and my heart sank. "I am sorely tempted, although you'd think I'd had enough adventures this summer to last me a lifetime."

"My life isn't usually this exciting."

"It doesn't matter, Davin. Your life still seems more interesting than school! I just can't quit in the middle of my education. It's too important to me, and to my parents back on Ballophon. I don't expect you to understand, which is part of the reason I'm saying no to you."

Davin gave up, without anger or further argument, which earned some grudging respect from me. I felt even more admiration for Giem, who had evidently gained something more than a little extra knowledge of parasitology this summer. Like more respect for herself, and what she deserved. I guess maybe I could say the same for myself. A surprising number of people on Big Maxson's Planet couldn't ignore me!

The rest of our dinner seemed rather subdued. Davin and Giem left for one last night together in a hostel room, while Grek and I snuggled in his mother's sleeping pit.

In the grey morning both Giem and I discovered ourselves abandoned again by our partners. We hardly spoke a word as we ate breakfast together at one of the outdoor tables, and proceeded to pack up for our own slow hike back down to town. Just before we felt ready to leave, Grek appeared, with a small quelsh-hide pouch he placed in my hands.

"For me?" I said in a small voice, while Giem impatiently strapped into her pack.

"A farewell present," he said, holding my hands gently around it. "Open it and look."

I pulled the lace loose and peeked into the pouch. "A karc egg?" I asked, puzzled and a little embarrassed. "I'm afraid I'd find it rather difficult to keep a karc happy in the small room we live in at school." Dried grass cushioned the egg in the pouch.

"No, not a karc egg," Grek said. "I didn't think you'd want one, or you would have found one for yourself. This is something else—a small pet many young Pio children start with—not difficult to keep, especially by a student animal-doctor."

I closed the precious pouch back up and tucked it carefully into a protected part of my pack. "You won't tell me what it is?" I gave him a quick kiss and a long hug.

"No. I want it to be a surprise." He touched the tip of my nose with his tongue, and gently tickled my cheek with a claw. "All you need to know is that it's mostly carnivorous and has to eat under water, and it needs dry land and sun too, of course."

"Sounds complicated." Just like a Pio, to assume we had sunshine on Olecranon!

"Not really. Don't worry about it. If you have any questions, you're always welcome to return for a visit with us!" he said slyly.

"I hope I will," I said emphatically. "Thank you, Grek. This is a special world!"

"We're no better than any other." Grek sighed.

"How do you know that? You should come visit us too, sometime." My smile quivered as I swallowed saltwater in the back of my throat. Giem watched us, with an odd mixture of emotions on her silent face.

Grek looked surprised by my idea. "Maybe I will, someday!"

I wished I'd thought of a farewell gift for him. I suddenly remembered his fondness for his vest with all its pockets, and removed my pouch from my belt. I took out a new emergency meal packet, nothing near Pio food, and slipped my precious pocket knife into a pocket, since he had a sheath knife. I gave him my pouch for his belt.

"Are you sure, Taje?"

"This belt pouch has come with me everywhere. Maybe it will remind you to visit me."

Grek winked, and put the pouch on his belt. "Thank you, Taje. This is very special. Safe travels."

"Safe travels for you too, Grek. Don't forget to also visit Dr. Bioh, if you want another friend."

"I will never forget you, Taje."

We hugged again, and tears spilled down my face as I heaved on my pack and followed Giem down the road.

CHAPTER 49

We didn't find the rest of our farewells any easier, four days later, in front of the spaceport. Dr. Bioh's agouti fur soaked up our tears when we took turns bending over to hug him goodbye. And we found it impossible to find the right words for Krome and Ziehl. Instead we made the usual inane promises about keeping in touch, and trying to visit again when we could get enough time off. Giem and I grabbed our bags, waved, and passed back through the clear doors that locked us in.

I discovered some green incoming tourist had one of the comscreens going. "BEAUTIFUL, RELAXING, BIG MAXSON'S PLANET," I repeated after it, trying to sound amused and disdainful. I choked up instead.

"Hey," Giem said, with a sniffle, "I bet you'll end up missing this planet even more than me."

I wiped goodbye tears on my sleeve and another flood took their place. "Now I care about a bunch more people I may never get to see again!"

"Would you rather not have met them at all?" Giem said, bringing us to a halt in the middle of the busy port building.

If I could somehow choose my history, I might have chosen to never meet Shandy. Was that what I really wanted? And would I still be alive, and standing here today? As the person I wanted to be? The pain of loss measured the size of what I had gained. "No," I answered Giem, "and humans supposedly possess an amazing ability to forget pain."

"Oh, why don't you just admit it, Taje! You didn't hate this assignment—you enjoyed every last fused bit of it. Pain just makes the good parts even better!" Giem managed a smile, as I gave her a startled and guilty look.

"I'm supposed to learn how to relieve pain and suffering. Not how to enjoy it."

"Neither of us will ever tolerate the suffering of the innocent, and animals are the most innocent bystanders of all," Giem said. "How did you feel about all those quelsh, distressed and dying in Riddock's pens?"

"Terrible—Giem—"

"So the rest of it makes a great story. You said it yourself at the beginning. You can't have a real adventure without pain. Just let's ask Dr. Hako wait until you see the jealousy oozing out of our classmate's pores when we tell them about our exploits here. I bet we'll beat all of their stories, without even trying." Giem began to move forward again.

"After all, we stopped an interplanetary crime, and averted a FIL quarantine crisis, when Dr. Hako thought he was just making us review parasitology." My mind flooded with memories from Big Maxson's Planet. I tried to stop my partner-in-adventure at the back doors. "Hey, Giem, it's our last chance to look up who Big Maxson was—"

"Absolutely not." Giem showed her wristcom ID to the doorcom. "You'll just have to live with one last mystery. Our shuttle awaits us, and I can't wait to sit down in it."

"A chance to sit and do nothing for a while does sound amazingly good now," I said, struggling to offer my wristcom next, before the exiting crowd split us up. "I'm exhausted."

"When we return to school, let's ask Dr. Hako for a vacation from our vacation," Giem said.

We spilled out onto the landing field and strode toward the shuttle parked in the middle of it. I glanced back at the lush greenery one last time.

Davin was right about spaceport goodbyes. It hit me like a crashing shuttle. To go to vet school, I'd had to say goodbye to all my best friends on FIL SEAR Ship *Onnarius*. Now I'd just had to just say goodbye to another set of great friends, just to return to vet school. I was paying big time for my new profession. I hoped it was worth it. Perhaps it was, having just saved quelsh herds from theft, and perhaps whole planetary populations from infection.

It also helped a little to remember that once one becomes addicted to travel, it's worse being left behind to watch the shuttle take off. So I tried to look on the

Bright Side, even if we were just shipping back to school, and headed for another nauseating Dim Side bout in the microfloral exchange tanks along the way.

"Come on, Taje, you'll miss our flight!" Giem called, from the top of the shuttle ramp, and I ran to join her.

CHAPTER 50

I used nontank ship time to frantically finish up my "vacation" journal, and we arrived at school just a couple days before sophomore classes would start. Returning to our brown, barren, slightly higher-grav campus almost felt like a homecoming. Sickening. We spent our first day back unpacking, and frantically dealing with my cracking gift from Grek. A summons from Dr. Hako's office curtailed our last day of freedom.

Dr. Hako had reviewed our final crammed-together parasitology report for Dr. Bioh, which included my Pio village comparison, and our hastily written, vast footnote covering the suspected origin of the foreign nematode infection. In some ways it quite surpassed any expectations, in our lowly opinion.

However, our Dean of Student Welfare insisted on hearing more, in person. In fact he wouldn't let us gloss over any of our escapades on Big Maxson. He had an unfair advantage over us. Ship's mail from other rather talkative sources must have arrived with us. No need for this professor to beg a look at my journal. At the end of his relentlessly on-target questions, he shook two of his pale blue fingers at us.

"Of course I received an outstanding evaluation from Dr. Bioh. He's quite diplomatic, as usual. It's simply amazing how much trouble you two managed to churn up on poor little Big Maxson's Planet. Not to mention the tussle I'll have with vet school authorities here, to explain all the time you didn't spend on your assigned summer externship project."

"Most of our work ended up related," Giem said.

"And a lot of it wasn't our fault," I said. "Talk to the IPHAs. They wouldn't let us."

"And it's a galactic wonder," Hako ruthlessly continued, "how you two managed to evade any FIL charges against yourselves—use of force and smuggled weapons, littering, piloting an illegal shuttle, and spying without a license or warrant."

I sat up straighter, and tried to appear mortally offended. This was not the sort of glowing reception Giem and I had eagerly anticipated. Yet I had to stifle an urge to laugh at how much Hako sounded like Riddock, complaining about all the trouble we'd caused him.

"Us two?" Giem gave Hako her best tone of insulted outrage. I sat back, folded my arms, and didn't try too hard to suppress a smirk, as I let the expert go to work. "What about Garth Riddock?"

"In a way, I almost pity him having the misfortune of running up against both of you," Hako said.

"Aren't you proud of us?" Giem said. "Here we bring law, justice, and a little veterinary medicine to Big

Maxson's Planet, and all you can do is pity the archvillain? How about a little praise once in a while around here?"

"Giem, this is vet school," I reminded her, a smile twitching at my lips.

"Sorry!" Giem clapped her hand to her brow. "I forgot myself."

"From the sound of it, Tajen," Dr. Hako turned his beady electric blue gaze on me, erasing the grin on my face instantly, "you should get a 'C' in Tracking, Skulking, and Evasion."

"I wasn't even aware that was in our curriculum."

"They ought to be, in your case. Instead, your sophomore schedule includes weaponry and martial arts. That's what really scares me."

"Why? Running out of even marginally safe externships, on supposedly quiet planets, with convenient family members to keep an eye on us? How closely is Krome Meki related to you, anyway?"

"She told you?" Dr. Hako was taken aback, and even Giem quit laughing and looked surprised.

"No. I guessed, from the family resemblance. You confirmed it." I grinned triumphantly, while Dr. Hako groaned. "Not that I'm at all surprised," I couldn't help adding, bitterly. Academia seemed to attract manipulators. I wondered if Hako also had a hidden motive for setting up extra protection for us. Just the act of putting any unusual FIL personnel on Big Maxson would have worried Riddock. Leaving us uninformed meant that if we got caught trying to do anything more than our vet work, and Riddock proved just an innocent vacationer, he couldn't charge FIL with deliberate harassment.

Hako caught the look on my face and glared back at me. "So. You didn't like my cousin?"

Startled, I clenched my sweaty hands, and had a moment to notice Giem just let me squirm on my own. "No. Of course not. I mean, Krome was quite nice."

"And her partner?"

"Ziehl? A perfect friend. I'll never forget her!"

"Perhaps you didn't enjoy working with Dr. Bioh? He can be rather demanding."

"No, no, he was wonderful." I was almost in tears, Hako sounded so angry.

"Then maybe, like a good doctor, who doesn't make snap diagnoses before a thorough history and exam, you shouldn't be so quick to judge, Taje," Hako said, in a gentler tone. Yet I found it more painful than ever to listen to his words. "Krome reported that Ziehl said you fell on your behind doing that, your very first day on Big Maxson's Planet."

Giem and Hako shared a chuckle over that, while I shifted my behind uncomfortably in my chair. I had to remind myself forcefully that I wasn't a kid back at the Center, under a teacher or my dorm parents' willful power.

Despite myself, I began to smile again, along with Hako and Giem, despite myself. The friends I'd made on Big Maxson were quite irreplaceable, whether I'd ever see them again or not. And Hako was probably even more correct in his diagnosis than he could ever know.

Anytime I had made a hasty assumption on Big Maxson, I had fallen flat on my face—or on my butt. At least I always got back up again. And whenever I had kept an open mind, I'd had a lot of fun.

Dr. Hako sat back, and his pale blue face grew impassively smooth again. I tried to tell myself, in this moment, to never again attempt to outguess this person's motives.

Hako caught me scanning him, and he met my eyes once more. "I hear you also brought back a small present from Big Maxson. Did it survive decontamination?"

"It not only survived," I happily allowed him to change to a less serious subject, "it hatched yesterday."

"Truly? And what is it?"

"It's ugly!" Giem said. "It's a mud-colored, tiny shelled reptile with a ridiculously long tail. It knows how to walk and swim, and keeps trying even when it bumps into something, until a different reflex takes over. It must have a brain about the size of a pinhead."

"What's a pin?" Dr. Hako asked.

"It looks a bit like those cute baby Earth turtle clones you can buy in some interplanetary pet stores," I said.

"A superficial resemblance only. It's much uglier," Giem insisted

"And it's already eating!"

"That's great. It?"

"You haven't taught us how to use bioscanners," Giem and I chimed in together, accusingly.

"Patience. That comes in your junior year."

"Grek's gift is an absolute glutton," Giem said. "A micro black hole. It must have come from that last stream Grek fished from."

Dr. Hako gave her a suitably puzzled look. "What does it eat?"

"The hatchling eats meat-flavored, soggy geeper chow just fine," I said, "and it seems really partial to cheese we filched—fetched from the cafeteria."

"Which is just fine by me," Giem said. "I'm sick of cheese."

"And it hatched just yesterday?" Dr. Hako's brilliant blue eyes widened. "That's amazing. Taje, your Pio friend has given you a heavy responsibility. You must thoroughly research proper nutrition and care."

"I know. I didn't intend to take on another pet right now. I just couldn't refuse it. I'm stuck with the little beast, and it's kind of cute in its own weird way. I cheated, and had a talk with Dr. Bioh about it before we left. He said the Pios would call it a skildkret, and he gave me his report on the species, and on the spectrum for the solar lamp I'll have to buy and tune for it."

"If I know Dr. Bioh, you haven't much more to learn. Have you named it?"

"Because of the way it sticks out its tail as it zips across a pan of water, I was vacillating between Jet and Rocket."

Giem and I scanned each other and burst out laughing. Dr. Hako looked like he thought we both had brain parasites. We hadn't told him every detail—we didn't want to spend our entire last day of summer vacation in his office.

"Inside joke," Giem said at last, when she could talk again.

"I decided on Jet," I added.

"Hmm . . . yes, I suppose you'll need to get back to your room promptly, to feed it again." Dr. Hako coughed, and appeared almost embarrassed, if that was possible for him. Giem and I exchanged puzzled looks. "I do have a few last bits of news for you two," he said.

"First of all, for discovering the imported ascarid infestation, and its cause—which, incidentally, saved the Big Maxson Planet R&R station from complete economic disruption, and the reputation of the whole FIL microfloral replacement program—FIL would like to award both of you Interplanetary Public Health Commendations—"

"Smooth!"

"That's more like it!"

"However, since you are both undergoing some rather sensitive training, our administration decided it would be in the best interest of everyone concerned not to take any action on it."

"Oh," we both said.

"And . . . there's one other item you should know about, in the remote chance that it may someday affect your safety. Garth Riddock escaped."

"What?" we roared.

"Somehow his transfer to FIL authorities on the Big Maxson orbital station ran afoul, and he managed to escape on his own ship. He slipped into paraspace and vanished, of course."

"After all that work," Giem said.

"He wasn't the only one with vac-heads for hired help," I said, snorted, and grinned. And wondered about Chothark, and whether The Adventure ever truly ended. I might get into a whole lot more trouble if I ever ran across her again.

"I'm sorry," Dr. Hako said. "What can I say?"

How about admitting you sent us to Big Maxson to put a scare into Garth Riddock, I barely kept myself from saying. No more rash judgments here, at least not aloud, and not today.

"How about wishing us good luck on our next standard year and a quarter of classes?" Giem suggested, as we both stood up.

"Good luck." Dr. Hako nodded at us human-style, and just as we stepped out of his office, we thought we heard, "You'll need it." We spun around, but the door had slid shut.

Outside we fought the wind, and tried not to trample the few ground-hugging weeds.

"Let's go to the cemetery, before we return to our dorm," Giem suggested.

"Why? I want to get back to see Jet." Jet had this funny trick of climbing nearly straight up the steep part of a water ramp, turning around, and diving back into water. I loved watching Jet. I smiled.

"Because it's the only so-called Olecranon park within walking distance, and because I want to give thanks for my survival, after Dr. Devlin's IV injector finally found a vein and she was able to pump a bunch of synthblood into me," Giem said.

"Why do you want to give thanks for your life in a cemetery? That seems rather contrary," I said.

"Did you know there are a few vet students buried there?"

"Why? What happened?" Death from some gruesome disease, and a family unwilling to pay for shipment of remains, even ashes? My brain crashed. "I thought only a few last military fatalities were buried there."

"It's considered an honor to be buried there if you die in school. And Very Large Animal Medicine can be quite dangerous," Giem said. We both shuddered at the thought of rotating through VLAM our senior year. Rumors of a senior stomped flat by a saury—as big as a skitsh—persist.

I supposed they could call this cemetery a park because trees grew only here, the only place on this war-torn world. Black tree branches clattered coldly overhead. Oh how I missed greenery! I still grinned.

Giem gazed at the open arched gateway, encircled by dying vines. She stopped us before the first sad row of infantry markers. She turned and smiled up at the arch holding out against the wind and overcast sky, and then looked at me. "Why do you look so happy?" she said. "You haven't looked this good since we finally went backpacking on Big Maxson's Planet."

"I don't know." I shook my head. I was lying. I was kind of glad Garth had gotten away. Giem took almost an hour to wheedle that out of me.

Of course it shocked Giem. "Why on Olecranon, or should I say on Big Maxson, Taje? He hurt animals!"

"He didn't mean to!"

"Oh, that's okay," Giem said sarcastically, rolling her eyes.

A few tears escaped my eyes.

"Taje, are you actually crying in front of me?"

I swiped my eyes and sniffled. "Giem, you haven't grown up with me. So you don't know how few adults have treated me with respect and kindness."

"Garth Riddock?

"Yeah, he's literally a riddle. I have a few stories. What else can I say?"

"Not much more," Giem said, shaking her head. I guess she didn't want to hear anything good about The Big Criminal.

I followed her back to our dorm room, never expecting her to understand. But Big Maxson had left my heart completely full, and that was good enough.

ACKNOWLEDGMENTS

I confess I first devised this book on a cold, food-deprived backpack. (We'd taken too much on our last trip, as we hadn't worked out exactly how much to bring. We'd also just eaten before we went food shopping, a huge mistake.) During this bitterly cold, underfed fall trip in the South Sierra, along the North Fork Kings River, two of us spent midday lying outspread in the sun in wide, beautiful Big Maxson meadow, at 8,480', soaking up what warmth we could get from the sun. We had endured a hard hike to get there, and we had to strictly ration our food to stay as long as we wanted.

Lying in the meadow, I explained my desire to write a sequel to my first book. I had taken epidemiology and wanted to include a way to control the spread of diseases between planets. My partner-in-crime, one year behind me in vet school, helped me devise a method, and she helped invent some of the characters I needed for this book, as well as the veterinary crime that would occur. (And if you know a lot about veterinary medicine, you can find a tiny clue in this story that will seriously date the first draft of this novel.)

Later, Megan Armstrong, a friend and botany major, gave me some important advice about the setting, after I explained the native fauna I wanted. She was concerned about their caloric needs. Hence all the lush greenery on Big Maxson's Planet!

As a vet student immersed in anatomy classes, reconstructed fossil dinosaur skeletons fascinated me, and I could easily imagine their attached anatomy. I recognized the giant holes in their bones, for nerves and blood vessels. As a SF writer, I couldn't help wondering how a veterinarian might work on similar animals.

Giemsan Fane in particular is basically my backpacking partner's invention. (I believe Giem is named at least partly after a cytology stain.) And although I encouraged this person to help, she left me to write the entire story. So I take full responsibility for Giem's actions.

I must admit Garth Riddock is extremely loosely based, in total disguise, on an evil small animal reproductive physiology medicine professor, who unforgivably, unreasonably, loudly, shockingly, rudely belittled one of my classmates in lecture in front of my whole class. My heart sank when I found out he was my senior year small animal medicine clinician. He gave each member of my small group a rude nickname, except me, because I stayed too quiet in rounds to label easily.

At last in morning rounds I had reason to give him the finger as we exited, for ignoring a decent question of mine (maybe he didn't want to admit he didn't know the answer), and my group thought me very courageous. Yet he did surprise me that evening by sitting next to "my quietest student, who has at last grown brave." We sat in the hallway outside the ward for our patients during evening rounds, and he leaned against me. He will also show up in very heavy disguise in future books. A less than bright art teacher became his minions in this story.

I used a photo of Orland, a very hilarious packer, for Davin Mohrogh on the back cover. Below him Taje rides lizard-style on one of Davin's horses. To the left and below TJ lies dreaming in Big Maxson Meadow, alongside North Fork Kings River, as humans call it; she has just completed a journal hard copy brief outline of her summer travails.

Curiously, as with my first book, I've found some important lessons for myself in this novel. I hope I can take them to heart, especially with the losses I have endured.

I must also again thank my editors for an awesome job well done: Erika Milo, Brian J. Boudler, and especially Jackie Melvin. Any errors in the text are entirely my fault.

And I owe a big shout out to Cricket Harper for the glorious cover of this novel, also using scenery painted by my Danish great uncle Anders Andersen.

.

ABOUT THE AUTHOR

Liz J. Andersen earned a B.S. with Highest Honors in Animal Physiology and a D.V.M. degree from U.C. Davis. She is a retired Veterinarian who also worked for many years for the Eugene Public Library. She told Tajen Jesmuhr's early story in her first novel, <u>Some of My Best Friends Are Human</u>, and several stories featuring Dr. Jesmuhr in <u>Analog Science Fiction and Science Fact</u>. She has also edited and published her grandfather Hans Holst Andersen's semi-autobiographical novel, <u>Along The Margins, South Dakota Immigrant Homesteaders</u>. Writing seems to run in the family.

Liz lives in Eugene, Oregon, with her husband, Brian J. Boudler, a Musician and retired Veterinary Technician.

You can find Liz at LizJAndersen.com and GoodReads.com, and Brian at: labbwerk.bandcamp.com, and on Facebook and YouTube.